THE HOUND OF THE BORDERS

THE HOUND
OF THE BORDERS

Peter Tonkin

This first world edition published in Great Britain 2003 by
SEVERN HOUSE PUBLISHERS LTD of
9–15 High Street, Sutton, Surrey SM1 1DF.
This first world edition published in the USA 2003 by
SEVERN HOUSE PUBLISHERS INC of
595 Madison Avenue, New York, N.Y. 10022.

British Library Cataloguing in Publication Data

Tonkin, Peter
    The hound of the Borders. - (The master of defence ; 3)
    1. Musgrave, Tom (Fictitious character) - Fiction
    2. Great Britain - History - Elizabeth, 1558-1603 - Fiction
    3. Detective and mystery stories
    I.   Title
    823. 9'14 [F]

    ISBN 0-7278-5935-8

Typeset by Hewer Text Ltd.,
Edinburgh, Scotland.
Printed and bound in Great Britain by
MPG Books Ltd., Bodmin, Cornwall.

For Cham, Guy and Mark,
as always

Black Dog monsters have been reported all over Europe, North and South America, but their origins seem to be in the British Isles. One is reported as early as 1127 in the *Anglo-Saxon Chronicle* . . .

In the North of England, the (phantom) Black Dog is known as Trash, Skryker or The Barguest . . .

True Monster Stories

CHAPTER ONE

Eve

London, 24 December 1594

A s soon as he heard the screams, Tom Musgrave started to run towards them. At his second step his sword hissed out, its blade glimmering like quicksilver. By his fourth step he knew it was the Queen herself who must be screaming. As he ran towards the shocking sound, his mind leaped onward, questing like a well-trained hound along the thorny, twisting paths of logic. But if quick Logic bounded ahead, cool Reason nipped at his heels like a cur, always a step behind.

Tom tore across the backstage area of the temporary stage that the Lord Chamberlain's personal company of actors had erected at the end of the Great Hall in White Hall Palace at the direction of Henry Carey, Lord Hunsdon and Lord Chamberlain, whose Men they were, against the celebration of Christmas on the morrow with the first performance of Will Shakespeare's new play. The hall was closed by Lord Henry's direct order to let them rehearse. In all the kingdom, few enough would dare disobey Lord Henry – and of those few, only one was a woman.

The Queen herself, then, reasoned Tom, the Master of Logic, as he ran; but what devil had tempted Her Majesty to peek into the forbidden hall, and what in God's name had she seen to affright her so?

At the very point of the question, Tom tore past the heavy curtains that decorated the stage front and hurled himself down on to the floor of the hall; and there indeed, just inside the great door, with her hand to her mouth, her face utterly white and her eyes wide, stood Queen Elizabeth – Gloriana herself. Blade in the variable ward, lowest of the basic defensive positions, he skidded towards her, watching her eyes widen still further.

With Tom's great logical mind too far ahead and his good sense too far behind to see what a mire of danger he was sinking into here, his Good Angel took a hand. Before he could take another step towards the startled Queen he lost his footing and crashed to his knees, sliding to a stop before her even as the door behind her was torn open and a tall, slim courtier hurled himself to her aid, also reacting to her screaming; also drawn and *en garde*. But whereas Tom was supported only by the Chamberlain's Men – and most of them dressed as fairies – the newcomer was backed up by several familiar, unfriendly faces. And by Her Majesty's personal guards.

Tom recognized the newcomer, in spite of the fact that, like the Queen's, his face was masked in the thick white powder so fashionable at court, and his heart sank. Then, as his wild slide slowed, so he turned a little and became able to see what Her Majesty could see. On the stage past which Tom had just run, in the midst of an enchanted forest, sat young Sly, dressed as the Queen of the Fairies. Behind Sly stood Will himself, costumed as the Fairy King, agape with horror; and, saw Tom, the Master of Logic, all too late to moderate his dangerous reaction, the cause of Her Majesty's affright knelt between them. It was Will Kempe, the Clown, the greatest and most famous of the players – Kempe in the revealing rags of Bottom the Weaver, bearing on his shoulders the great ass's head so carefully and realistically fashioned for the magical translation scene.

The icy point of the familiar courtier's rapier resting on the pit of his throat turned Tom's head back, and he tore his gaze away from the stage to look up along the gleaming length of finest Ferrara steel into the steady dark eyes of his greatest enemy.

'Drawn in the Queen's presence,' said Robert Devereux, the Earl of Essex, quietly.

'That means death. Even for a Master of Defence,' added his nearest, sneering companion, as white-faced as Essex, whom Tom recognized as one de Vaux. Like his master, de Vaux was clearly enjoying the situation hugely.

But Her Majesty was recovered now. 'Tush, My Lord,' she said briskly to Essex. 'The man was running to our aid. These latter years we are not so well supplied with gallants that we can afford to despatch such valiant protectors in such a cavalier fashion. And this is the famous Master of Defence you say?' she demanded more generally.

'Thomas Musgrave, Your Majesty.' Tom was well placed to make his own introduction, needing to do and say almost nothing more, bowing on his knees as he was.

It was then that the door swung wider still and friends joined foes around the person of the Queen. 'What, My Lord of Essex!' came the blessedly familiar voice of Lord Henry, the Lord Chamberlain. 'Drawn in the royal presence. Do you put so little value on your head, sir?'

'Robin was protecting our royal person, My Lord. We give him leave. And Master Musgrave, come to that. They may stand drawn in the royal presence if occasion demands it. There cannot be two such game cocks in all our kingdom as swift with their steel or as loyal with their hearts.'

'Protecting you against what, Your Majesty?' asked Lord Henry softly.

'Against an actor in an ass's head, Henry – and good Will Kempe at that, if we are any judge in the matter. We have not been so frighted since we were a girl. By a monster jumping out of the woods! Yourself, like as not, or one of Master Shelton our guardian's children.' Her Majesty recalled that long-lost girl in a peal of laughter that might have graced the throat of any child. 'By an ass's head forsooth! *Walsingham!*'

'Your Majesty?' came the distant voice of Thomas Walsingham, Tom Musgrave's closest friend at court.

'Are the Shelton girls at court within your train?'

'They are, Your Majesty.'

Tom could have told the Queen the truth of that matter, for Kate, the younger of the Shelton sisters, younger daughter to one of the children who might have played with the youthful Queen, was his mistress; as Audrey, the elder, was Walsingham's.

'Good,' said the Queen, sweeping out of the hall again, with all of the court in tow, 'then we can expect much amusingly lewd speculation as to whether the ass's head might be matched by other, more private, parts – and of equal proportion.' Laughter began to recede – laughter no longer so innocently girlish in its nature.

'Course they are,' said Will Kempe, rising as the door closed. 'What else d'ye think gave Will the idea in the first place? "Give me the head of an ass, Will," said I, "for you know I am hung like a donkey in truth . . ."'

As the Chamberlain's Men joined Kempe in their own peal of laughter, Tom pulled himself erect. He stood a little shakily, and it required two attempts, separated by a deep breath, to slide the long Solingen blade of his sword home again, feeling the sensitive side of his thumb rub against the reassuring roughness of the running-wolf trademark etched into the steel. He would never know whether it was the proximity of majesty, disaster or death that affected him so.

Yet, he thought, grimly turning back towards the rudely interrupted rehearsal of *A Midsummer Night's Dream*, given his intimate acquaintance with death and disaster of all sorts, it was the closeness of Her Majesty that seemed most likely to have shaken him so badly.

Or, he came to suspect later, perhaps it was a premonition of what was coming next.

Although Will's new play was set in a magical forest beside ancient Athens, the actors wore the cast-off finery handed down to them from great houses – not least that of the Lord Chamberlain himself. Their costumes were contemporary, therefore, if slightly old-fashioned; and the swordplay between the lovers Demetrius and Lysander was a dangerously comic exhibition match in the new Italian style of which Tom was the undisputed master.

Tom was putting a final polish to this dazzling piece of comic byplay when Thomas Walsingham returned and called up the length of the great Hall, 'Tom. There's a messenger newly arrived from the North. He's with Lord Henry now.'

'Indeed, sir,' answered Tom. He stepped back and sheathed his sword once more. 'Why do you condescend to bring this news to my notice?'

'Because,' said Thomas Walsingham shortly, 'the message is for you.'

The little reception room was on the east side of the palace and its window looked along the river towards the distant span of the bridge where Tom's last adventure had come to its bloody end six months since. Lord Henry stood beside the casement, the glorious colour of his court costume sucking life even from the thin grey light of a midwinter's afternoon – he alone of all the men and women Tom had seen at court this afternoon disdained the rage for powdering his face with arsenic powder – but Tom had eyes for neither the emotive view nor for his dazzling patron. The familiar figure of the messenger turned towards him and he, like the screaming Queen, was put in mind of the most frightful moments of his childhood.

'Hobbie?' he said, uncertainly, striding forward. Then the wrinkled, leathery face creased into the ghost of a grin and uncertainty fell away. 'Hobbie,' he said with simple certainty and enfolded the wiry old frame to his bosom. Halbert Noble, called 'Hobbie' through all the wild Borders, had taught him everything he had known of weaponry and survival until he had entered the Master's School of Maestro Capo Fero at Siena some half dozen years since. Save for the matter of fighting with foil and rapier in the Italian style, even Capo Fero had been hard put to better Hobbie's tutelage; and, as his common name implied, he knew the border country as well as one of the sure-footed tireless ponies of the place. Hobbie horses, they were called; creatures that could go, with a rider, into places a man on foot hardly dared venture. There was no track on moss, moor or fell he could not follow, no mark of bird or beast in all the North that Hobbie could not recognize.

'I've come with hard news,' said Hobbie forthrightly as soon as Tom released him. 'Heavy tidings.'

'Are they for me?'

'Aye.'

'Then if they are mine, give them to me. Straight, man.'

Hobbie Noble's eyes met Tom's, seemingly level for all that one man was wiry and bowed with age while the other stood youthfully tall. 'It's your brother, the Blacksmith of Bewcastle,' he said, adding the unnecessary phrase of his title as a measure of great respect; for Tom had only one brother, John, two years his elder, and Hobbie Noble wasted nothing – certainly not words. 'He's dead.'

Tom licked his lips. The news had shocked him though he had been half-expecting some such words since Thomas Walsingham had called him out of the hall. 'Was it an accident?' he asked. Smithing was by no means a safe trade, even for men as massive and expert as his brother and father had been.

Hobbie's head shook in that atom of communication which characterized that man.

'A raid?' – which was how his own mother had died, cut down by the red McGregors come reiving across the debatable land when Tom himself was scarce weaned; not killed but crippled then, doomed to linger for sixteen more years before winning her blessed relief. But Hobbie shook his head again.

'Then what?' demanded Tom.

Hobbie's eyes slid away. Tom looked, frowning across at the resplendent Lord Henry, who was, amongst other things, the Lord of the North, Her Majesty's eyes on the Northern English Borders as they marched by southernmost Scotland.

'Your uncle, who still signs himself the Lord of the Waste, I note, has written of the inquest he has held into the circumstances,' said Lord Henry. 'He reports that your brother's body was found in the lower branches of the Great Oak that stands at

6

the head of the Black Lyne. It is a dangerous river in a wild place, as I recall. You know it?'

'And the tree, My Lord. It has stood there hard by Arthur's Seat since the beginning of time. It must reach nigh on two hundred feet to the crown. The lowest branches must stand twelve feet above ground.'

'Nigh on fifteen feet,' agreed Hobbie.

'Even so. Your brother was discovered dead on the lower branches, kneeling, looking downwards, frozen like marble.'

'Frozen?' echoed Tom. 'He died of the cold?'

'No. The Lord of the Waste reports that there is no doubt that he died of fear – of sheer, stark terror.'

Tom laughed out loud at that. 'There's nothing in all the world would frighten John to death!' he said. 'What makes them think such a ridiculous thing?'

A fifth figure leaned forward at that, a slight, dark-clad, gold-haired stripling lost in the shadows behind Lord Henry until this moment.

'Something beyond the world,' said a steady, cool voice. 'Something came from another, hotter place altogether. Tell him, Hobbie.'

'All around the trunk, the Great Oak was clawed,' said Hobbie reluctantly. 'From the grass, to near the branches themselves. The bark torn off and the live wood splintered, bleeding. Clawed like a great bear can claw a dog at the baiting. But clawed, as you said, for two full fathoms. For twelve sheer feet. And clawed clear to the heartwood beneath the black-smith's body.'

'By a bear?' said Tom, simply dazed. 'Did you say a bear?'

'No, lad. This was never the work of a bear.'

'Then what? Hobbie, what was it?'

'It was a hound, Tom. They were the marks of a monstrous hound.'

The stripling youth stood up and closed with Tom then, and with another huge jolt of surprise he recognized her. No youth come south at Hobbie's heels, but his own sister-in-law Eve – Eve Graham as was, when they had dallied on the heather fifteen summers since, before she had fallen in love with the slow, shy charm of his big brother, and begun the relationship that had driven Tom himself so far away from home. Eve Musgrave now, his brother John's new-made widow.

Eve's still grey eyes held his gaze as fathomless as the Kielder water. 'Don't you see, Tom?' she whispered. 'It was a hound, but a hound such as no man can look on and survive. It was the Barguest, Tom. We know it now for certain, and rumour says he wasn't the first to die. But he was the first we have found. And so it is certain now. The Barguest is out on the Borders and it has taken your brother's soul.'

CHAPTER TWO

The Lord of the North

Ten minutes later Eve and Hobbie had gone about some undisclosed business, taking Thomas Walsingham as their guide and leaving Tom beard to beard with Lord Henry. Tom was still stunned by the awful news, but the effect of the shock on his unusual mind was to make his faculties even sharper, his logical acuity even greater. Around the awful void at the heart of his mind where his understanding of the world grappled with monster dogs the size of horses capable of reaching twelve feet up a tree and stealing away the soul of his brother, there was packed a glittering vortex of dazzling, blessedly distracting detail.

Even in the absence of the other three the little chamber still felt crowded to Tom. Lord Henry was a big, powerful, virile man, the echo of his father – the limb of his half-sister, begotten by King Henry on Anne Boleyn's sister, so they said, while his unfortunate queen was awaiting execution. He had lately mounted a mistress nearly forty years his junior, the lovely and multi-talented Amelia Lanyer.

However, it was not Henry Carey's personal power that seemed to fill the room so much as his political power as Lord Chamberlain, Lord Hunsdon and Lord of the North. The North had been his stamping ground since before the lovely mistress Amelia had been born. Tom's first childhood experience of war had been the carnage Lord Henry had left all too near his home, keeping the northern Marches safe for his queen as Howard and Drake and the others had been hardily guarding the South.

The shock of Hobbie's news, and Eve's dreadful suspicions, set the Master of Logic to working busily in Tom's head, and his amazing power of reason was focused upon Lord Henry while the wise old courtier thought the matter through and framed his plans for Tom. Clearly there had been more in his uncle's letter than the simple report of the blacksmith's death, though that would have been enough to worry both men on several levels.

This had been a bitter winter, alternately sodden and frozen in London; but snowless as yet. Such news as had come south in the approach to Yuletide had told of similar – if infinitely icier – conditions to the north. The Borders were frozen solid, but open still. The dangerous pathways so popular with reivers and invaders had been layered with ice but none of them blocked with drifts yet this year. For a country still surrounded by enemies to the south, with King Philip by all accounts busy about another armada to replace the last and finish its work, it was nevertheless well to keep an eye on the dangers to the north. King James in Edinburgh had troubles enough of his own, with his marriage to Anne of Denmark scarce five years old, and the witch trials arising from his near-fatal courtship still distracting him, so that the Borders over which he had little control at the best of times remained a potent source of worry to the Queen and her Council.

In such a situation, the mysterious death of the blacksmith responsible for arming one of the most important garrisons in the western Marches must assume a terrible political significance; and if, as Eve had said, this was but the first proof of a rumoured plague of such deaths, then the overall effect was hard to calculate.

Even taking John's death alone and discounting rumour altogether, things might well look bad. In such a situation, at such a time of year, the death of such a man in such a terrible manner must have an impact of almost incalculable weight. For who along the icy wastes by Hadrian's Wall stood to gain most from letting loose the Barguest in the Borders and keeping all the Yuletide revellers from Carlisle, east to Berwick and south to New Castle all locked up fast at home, too fearful to venture out into the hound-haunted dark?

The apparently personal little tragedy that had struck at the Musgraves might well be the signal for anything from a border raid designed to steal a few head of winter cattle to a full invasion designed to set flame to the Catholic tinder from Berwick to Nottingham, Scotland to Sherwood.

'You will want me to go north, My Lord,' said Tom.

'With all speed. To the Lord of the Waste, *self-styled.*'

'To the Captain of Bewcastle, at least,' soothed Tom, giving the uncle after whom he was named the title to which he was due. 'And with all haste, as you say – and as has been arranged, I have no doubt, by Hobbie Noble and my newly widowed sister – to discover the true fate of my brother, beyond the first report of my uncle's inquest. That is knowledge which will set many a heart at ease. Not least your own. And Her Majesty's.'

There came a little silence. Rain blew upriver like a fistful of gravel cast against the glass of the casement. 'If you can prove there was no hellish work in it – that it was never the Barguest . . .' said Lord Henry. 'Such a creature cannot exist,' he added after a moment.

'It is a creature I have feared since childhood, for I learned of it at my mother's knee.'

'But such a thing cannot be real, can it?'

'King James in Scotland is still at work to track down all the witches who held magical black masses to christen cats in graveyards then sailed out on the wild sea in sieves and summoned the devil to drown him when he went a'courting in Denmark – and, indeed, the political enemies at his court, and some others, who employed the witch women to do these things to him. If witches can be employed to summon devils to such work, perhaps they can be employed to call up hell-hounds too – or do it just for evil's sake. Or perhaps, once in a while Satan's gates stand wide and things slip out we wot not of.'

'You believe in this thing – this Barguest?'

'I believe I have seen it – or something like it – when I was a child. But that is not the same as saying I believe it is out on the Borders now. Nor that it was the Barguest that killed my brother.'

Tom leaned forward over the table, frowning with concentration, suddenly burning with urgency and energy. 'That is a tale for another time, My Lord. Now tell me exactly what you want me to do in the North.'

Thomas Walsingham interrupted the very last of this conference when he returned with Eve and Hobbie. The three of them waited for a moment as Lord Henry gave his final instructions to Tom. Then he put his seal – and that of the Queen's Council – on the last of the documents the Lord Chamberlain's secretary had prepared so rapidly in the interim, which the Master of Defence was to carry up to the Bewcastle Waste.

So that when Tom stood at last and turned, he spoke with the voice of the Lord of the North. 'Is everything ready?' he demanded.

'Ready,' affirmed Hobbie.

'We go back the way you came, along the Great North Road,' said Tom, all decisiveness, as though the spirit of the preoccupied Lord Henry had truly inhabited his youthful body. 'Meet me at Bishopsgate within the hour, with horses and passes as arranged. A hard ride will get us to Ware by darkfall; and then our journey will truly begin, I think.'

He turned, bowed to Lord Henry and was gone.

A wherry dropped Tom at Blackfriars steps some quarter-hour later and he hurried briskly up towards his lodgings and School of Fencing above Master Robert Aske the Haberdasher's shop. Here his two closest friends awaited him, all unaware of his dreadful news and the urgent business it had engendered.

Close friends they might be, but both of them had proposed to leave him alone during the next twelve days. Kate Shelton was to be at court, in Sir Thomas Walsingham's train, dancing attendance on the Queen, hoping to follow in a family tradition and become a lady-in-waiting. What with the hot bloods like de Vaux painting their faces with arsenic to go ruffling and swashbuckling in the trains of the wilder courtiers, like Essex, Southampton and their circles, the Queen got through ladies-in-waiting at an alarming rate – even when Sir Walter Raleigh was away. Kate would have no liberty to continue her passionate affair with Tom until after Twelfth Night.

No more would Ugo Stell, invited for the festivities to Bleeke House, residence of the Van Der Leydens, father and two daughters, hoping to get through their first Yuletide in a foreign country – they were, like Ugo, Dutch – and their first Christmas without Frau Van Der Leyden so tragically murdered six months since during the terrible affair of the heads upon London Bridge itself.

Now a swift leave-taking of sweet Kate was all the shocked and grieving Tom could afford; and Kate, like her sister Audrey, knew well enough what the demands of the political and secret worlds could be, for both of them had worked as spies for Audrey's affianced lover Thomas Walsingham and his adoptive father the late Sir Francis, unrivalled director of the Queen's Secret Service for more than twenty years.

Kate, womanlike, went straight to the heart of the matter. 'This woman, this Eve that has run, in her grief and loss, straight into your manly arms – what is she to you?'

'An ex-lover of my callowest years. Not even that, for she was her own woman even then and would never yield to me. She came to me fresh from setting another pair of brothers the one against the other, as I recall, and came near to doing the same with John and me. She is my sister and nothing more, therefore, except, perhaps, a bitter memory come with hard news of a terrible tragedy.'

'Of a hell-hound the size of a stallion that tears oak trees into shreds.'

'A monster that I must go and face, Kate, though it break my heart.'

' 'Tis likely there will be more than the monster to face,' she said, 'and more hearts broken than your own. However, let us see what Ugo can supply in the matter of facing monsters . . .'

Ugo himself, his panniers packed long since and wanting nothing but a convenient moment to ride down to Bleeke House, was happy to take his impatient friend into his workroom. There, as he sorted through his weaponry, he could talk things through at careful length, balancing with his phlegmatic Dutch thoroughness the fiery impatience of Mistress Kate and her all-too-vivid concerns, in the face of Tom's stunned quiet.

'A hound as big as a horse, you say? With claws to rip the heartwood of an oak? Wood as hard as copper, if not bronze. Only a weapon as big as a dunderbus would kill such a creature – always supposing the beast were made of flesh and blood and liable to death in the first place. Do you believe in such a creature, Tom?'

He took Tom's silence as assent and continued with hardly a pause, laying out upon his workbench a range of dags, pistols and handguns as he spoke. 'Even the most powerful of hand weapons would hardly hurt a creature of that size, unless you could direct the shot straight into some vital part or organ. As with your rapiers, Tom, it is not the size of the wound but the precision of its placing that does the damage.'

'On the other hand,' insisted Kate, 'there are times when size matters. A monstrous creature such as this must take monstrous killing. Have you nothing here that can make a huge wound though the gun itself be small?'

'A dunderbus fit for milady's purse?' mused Ugo. 'No. Such a weapon will tax future generations. It is beyond my own talent at present.'

'What is this?' asked Tom, picking up a strange-looking device that lay half-hidden at the back of the workbench.

'A failure. A kind of bastard, ill-born. You see that it has four barrels? Although they are short, they are strong. Each will carry a full load and a shot such as the other pistols. I had hoped that I would be able to rotate the whole so that each barrel would click into place up here by the pan and fire individually of the others; but no matter what I do, all the barrels discharge at once. I have even tried a new type of pan and lock – you see the flint here and the striker here so that a spark may fall on the powder instead of a match? All to no avail. It has near broke my wrist more times than I can tell!'

'But,' said Tom, cradling the bastard pistol in his long, strong fingers, 'were a man wishing to fire four shots at once, then this might indeed do some damage. Four shots delivered at the same time near enough to the same spot, vital or not – this would be like to blast a hole the size of my fist, even in something almost as big as a horse.'

'Are you mad? Only someone fit for Bedlam would trust his life to an engine whose one recommendation is that it refuses to work to its creator's original design. Here, take this matched pair instead.'

Tom had little time for argument and so he took them – and a goodly supply of the powder, shot and accoutrements that went with them. Then, as Ugo went down to arrange the loan of Master Aske's horse from here to Bishopsgate, he went through into his own quarters. Unwilling to waste time on changing into better clothes for the travelling, he simply added more layers – mostly of wool and leather – until his girth had swollen like the belly of an old tavern knight. His waist remained lean, however, and, disdaining the new fashion for swashes across his shoulders, he had no difficulty in strapping at each hip one of the matched pair of Solingen swords that were the richest source of his living and the surest protectors of his life.

As he dressed, at his direction, in the face of his unwonted sorrow and depression, Kate lowered herself to the station of the merest housemaid. She packed his panniers, and slid in amongst the lawn and linen the pistols Ugo had given him. That done, she lovingly crossed, across the base of his spine, the two daggers that matched the swords, and settled the weighty leather sack of his purse beside the Ferrara silver basket of his right-hand blade. Over his shoulder at last went the heavy leather satchel in which the orders and observations of the Lord of the North were packed. As he settled this against his short ribs, Tom felt an extra shape, and extra weight within it.

Frowning, he pulled the flap back a little, and glanced up, to catch the eyes of his loving but frightened mistress. For there, poking out of the parchments and the seals stood the familiar, ugly butt of the four-barrelled bastard pistol. He caught her to him and kissed her, moved more than he could express.

'Take care,' she admonished him, her voice breaking.

'I will,' he promised – lying though he did not know it – 'though I go to chase a tale of froth and fairies. A winter's tale indeed, told me by my dam and grandam.'

'Even so,' she said, prophetically enough. 'Those can be the most dangerous tales of all.'

He clapped Ugo on the shoulder, again in silence. He swung the heaviest of his cloaks around his shoulders and pulled the widest and most waterproof of his hats on to his head, swung up on to Master Aske's strong mare and was gone into the steely, sleety afternoon.

CHAPTER THREE

The Bishops' Gate

B ishopsgate was nearly deserted. In the mid-part of the afternoon of Christmas Eve there were few people making their way into London – and fewer still making their way out. Those coming from any distance to visit the city at this particular season were mostly here and within doors. Those simply coming from nearby to stock up at the markets against the festivities were still at Billingsgate, Smith's Field or on the Cheap; and those still at work were working – for the short days brought fewer hours, not fewer demands.

On the other hand, thought Tom grimly, no one in their right mind was likely to be venturing far away from the city if they could help it – quite the reverse, given the terrible state of the last harvest. Half the country was seemingly on the edge of starvation. The desperate poor were thronging to the city rather than watch each other being famished to death. Going north, particularly, where things were said to be hardest all round, would obviously fit a man for the first big building along the road they were due to travel: Bedlam.

Hobbie and Eve were easy to find in the near-deserted tavern beside St Botolph's Church immediately without the great stone gate. In the little square made by the inn front and the opening of the Hound's Ditch, which ran eastward along the outside of the Wall, Tom made swift arrangements to return Master Aske's mare, then entered the low building to join his travelling companions. He did this quietly, guardedly, made careful in both senses of the word by his sorrow and his suspicions that Eve at least – as ever – was by no means dealing plainly with him here.

Eve's good sense in travelling dressed as a boy was borne upon Tom at once. It was very much in the character he remembered. Like many another border woman, she was quick and able to take the initiative – the equal of any man in many matters, in fact, if not yet in the eyes of Church or Court; but still, he hardly needed to remind himself, although Eve was his sister, she was still a stranger – had never been anything else, in fact, even when she lay laughing in his arms upon Kielder Heights. He had not looked into those sad, still, disturbingly familiar eyes since he had taken the wits of which he was so proud northward from Carlisle Grammar School to the University at Glasgow, leaving his smitten brother wrapped happily in her toils; and that was more than twelve years since.

Now Eve sat at ease beside Hobbie, the pair of them fortifying themselves against the long hard journey with strong bread and weak ale. The last morsels of the bread still steamed with the hot breath of the pottage in which it had been soaked, and Tom was tempted by his wiser spirit to invest like them in something warm and substantial to cling to the inside of his ribs as his good cloak clung on the outside.

Swift as ever to take the initiative, therefore, Tom called over to the innkeeper, 'Another brewis here and small beer.'

Then he settled himself across the table from the pair of them and his cool gaze wandered from Eve's steady regard to Hobbie's guarded visage.

'She made me bring her,' said Hobbie with only half a laugh. 'Or rather, she made the Lord of the Waste to order me.'

'She has good reason, no doubt,' replied Tom. 'Have you not, my lady?'

Her mouth twisted at that. 'More than you know, you turncoat scapegrace. More than you can guess at, I'll be bound.' Her voice was dismissive, bitter. Had there been even more bad blood between them than he remembered?

18

'I doubt that,' he answered angrily, surprised by the anger, shocked that his grief should come out so. 'For though I have been absent in body this long while, I have been there in mind and spirit; and it cannot be that things are so different now that I cannot fathom out your dangers and your desperations.'

'Well then?' she challenged, again with more anger than he had expected. Her rage and grief struck him deeply, for he felt that they were in part directed at him. Had he been in the Borders instead of at Court, her anger seemed to say, then his brother would have been alive today. This outraged woman would not have been a widow. The Barguest might have been kennelled still in whatever cavern of hell normally housed it.

Her rage compounded his still further, for he felt the truth of what he supposed she thought; and that rage spurred on the Master of Logic, so that the Master added to his own fine wits some of the information Lord Henry had shared in his fears for the North and he made of the whole a mirror to hold up against her memories, thoughts and motivations that reflected the whole as though he had been some faery creature sitting in her secretest heart the while.

'The whole of the Borders will have been wild with specula-tion throughout this bitter, bitter Advent if what you said is true. It is the Barguest's season, and if there was talk of dead men stark with fear . . .' He paused and looked at the pair of them. 'But you'll likely have paid less mind to it than John did. For John had seen the thing – with me, when he was a lad; and God knows, he was still scared of it when I left. A fear, I trust, he left behind at last.'

Eve's head nodded, once. 'Until it caught up with him,' she whispered.

Tom proceeded from the general to the particular. 'They'll have carried him home on a wicket – Hobbie, like as not, and the rest that found him. None will have dared to tell you of the Barguest at first and you'll have been shaken and stunned with grief. But the look on his face will have led you to question and your questions will have gotten an answer – from Hobbie himself, like as not.'

19

The pair of them exchanged glances, Eve's wind-reddened cheek beginning to pale still further. Tom's brewis arrived, rough bread sopping in a wooden bowl of thin pottage with a horn spoon to eat it with. His small beer was flat and thin – little more than water, save that it was not like to poison him.

'He died in the night so they brought him home in the morning and you'll have had the story by nightfall. Black night and stormy and the Barguest out and terribly close to home. But you'll have gone in the darkness – alone, if I'm any judge – up to Bewcastle fort, to the Lord of the Waste. Not to ask his advice – not that – but to demand his protection mayhap. But he could not offer it or you would never have left your husband cold to run south.'

'I buried him before I left him,' said Eve, as though she was angry with both the brothers.

Tom savoured his brewis, and chewed on a string of mutton, deep in thought, seeming not to hear her. 'Protection not even Thomas Musgrave, Captain of Bewcastle, Her Majesty's right hand on the Marches, can give. But he has Hobbie here, ready to ride south, for these are matters to be reported to the Chamberlain and the Council. It is the reiving season and the Blacksmith of Bewcastle dead. Could even Carlisle be at risk? With the Barguest out on the Borders, anything must seem possible. So – my uncle cannot protect you but he sends you south to Lord Henry instead. What can the Lord of the North offer that the Captain of Bewcastle cannot? Something more subtle than the protection of twenty men-at-arms on horse and foot that he has at his immediate command; or than the two hundred he can summon within the hour could offer. Something that neither the Musgraves nor the Grahams, nor both combined, can guarantee; and they, combined, could protect you even against the Armstrongs and the MacGregors, like as not.

'Not protection from the violence of war, then,' pursued Tom almost in a whisper. 'Therefore it must be protection from some violence of love.'

Eve was white now, save for the black rings under her grey

eyes and the red wound of her mouth – as white as a lady, powdered for court.

'Perhaps,' continued Tom ruthlessly, recklessly, 'there is a lover close at hand who you fear will overcome you at once, someone who has been battering at your peace already, while yet my brother lived. But that seems less than likely, for my brother was a loving, proud and short-tempered man with the hardest fist in the Border. No man could have loved Eve Musgrave while the Blacksmith of Bewcastle lived and 'scaped with his brains safely between his ears. Therefore this is like to be a more general fear.

'But, beautiful and sought-after though you are, once were, and will be again, Eve, you are not a proud woman concerned with her looks and her conquests. If you fear that you are set to become the hind amongst a pack of hounds on a love hunt, then there is something more than your own fair person at stake; and that can only mean property or land.

'I know our family's worth to the nearest groat. So it is not property. Therefore it is land.

'What land do you own, in your own title now as a childless widow, that puts your peace of mind to such terrible test that you must throw yourself under the protection of the Council for it?'

She stared at him, her eyes wide, as though stunned – as though he had punched her.

'The Black Lyne,' she said, dully. Her voice echoed with wonder, almost with horror, at how clearly the Master of Logic could strip her reasoning bare, like a woodsman stripping the bark of a willow wand.

'The Black Lyne?' he echoed, stunned himself. The three words opened new vistas of darkness and danger. 'The river or its valley?'

'Water and valley both; east side and west, from Arthur's Seat to Brackenhill. It came to my mother from her mother. It came from my mother to me. John kept our ownership of it secret between himself and the Lord of the Waste. Or we thought it was secret. But now . . .'

21

Tom looked over to Hobbie. ' 'Tis the back door to the west march,' he said, simply awed. 'After Liddesdale it is the surest way from Scotland over the border. Whoever holds the Black Lyne can skirt the Bewcastle Waste, bite his thumb at the Captain of Bewcastle, and fall on Carlisle at his leisure.'

'And whoever holds Carlisle,' rumbled Hobbie, 'holds the key to the north, mayhap to the kingdom. You could anchor an armada safely on the Solway under its protection and land an army there.'

'Whoever wins my hand,' said Eve, 'owns the Black Lyne; and should he not wish to use it himself, why he can rent it out, exact the blackmail, let the Armstrongs and the Kerrs come riding south – and bigger men with larger armies than even they, perhaps.'

Just the way she said it made it impossible for Tom to tell whether the word was 'riding' or 'raiding'. Then he remembered that in the Borders, they meant the same thing in any case.

The three of them sat silently for a moment, studying distant vistas of terrible possibility, all of which turned upon what the terrible spectre of a monstrous black dog seemed to have done to his brother.

Hobbie stirred again. 'Ye reet?' and, on Tom's nod, went to pay the reckoning.

The stables were low and dark, but surprisingly solid and secure – not at all what one might have expected behind such a dilapidated inn; but then, looking around, Tom was struck by the quality of the horseflesh they contained. This was where Lord Henry's messengers set out hot-foot to take his orders to the North; and Lord Henry's messengers did not ride broken-down nags.

The creature that the tavern's ostler brought to replace Master Aske's mare could hardly have been more different from the strong but stately family horse used to carry the haberdasher and his wife together. It was a long-legged, fiery black gelding, all thew and temper, one of three near identical, set aside for the use of the Chamberlain's messengers riding the long road north.

'This is something like,' enthused Hobbie, and Tom caught the ghost of a smile crinkling the edge of his sister's eye – a girl who had been taught to ride astride with her brothers almost as soon as she could walk. They bred no fine ladies with precious, courtly airs amongst the Grahams, thought Tom, with an indulgence left over from wilder times, and some relief that his disquisition seemed to have lightened her burdens a little.

As Lord Henry's man and a northener, nephew to the Captain of Bewcastle, Lord of the Waste, Tom had some general knowledge of the system that sent messages flying from the Borders to the Council on a weekly – sometimes twice-weekly – basis; but this was the first time that he had found himself caught up in the overpowering mechanics of it, for all that he had discussed with Lord Henry the details of his proposed journey northward. He was quick of study, however, and soon learned the ropes that seemed so familiar to Hobbie and even Eve. With no further thought, he tightened his saddlebags and panniers, settled the gloves of Spanish leather that matched his thigh boots and leaped lithely into the saddle once more.

CHAPTER FOUR

Ware Riot

S o, as the inclement afternoon began to gather lingeringly towards dusk, three black figures, almost indistinguishable from each other astride three black horses, thundered up the Roman road past the opening to Hog Lane, past Finsbury Fields where the flag on the theatre, for once, was not hoist, and away towards the distant village of Islington.

The road was well maintained this close to the city and the horses seemed to know every flinty stone within its hard-earth, ice-bound surface. Silent, each deep-wrapped in their own thoughts – and with much, God knew, to think about – the riders gave their horses their heads and galloped flat out. Talk would have been impossible, even had any of them been foolish enough to break their concentration. For the horse hooves drummed on the icy ground, the great sides heaved and breath bellowed out and in. The wind, stirring from the north, beat at their faces, eyes and ears like thunder, only slightly diminished by the swathes of cloak gathered up around shoulders up to noses and cheekbones. As they galloped, so every steely piece of tack, every leathery belt, flap, bag and rein made a wild, discordant music, all creaking, banging, jingling and jarring to the rhythmic drumming of the hooves.

An hour's hard riding brought them to Enfield, where they showed their passes at the next waiting inn and, hardly stopping for breath, exchanged their horses for two chestnuts and a rangy roan that heaved smoothly under Tom and that seemed to know the road as well as the black had done, even though the light was fading faster now. As they rode through villages and hamlets, the bells for evensong began to chime. Away to their right, a freezing mist began to gather over the valley of the Lea and the wind that whipped at their faces armed itself with sharper barbs of frost. Lights began to flicker in the gathering dark, bright gleams issuing star-like from the distance, for the most part from the same direction as the echoing bells: Bull's Cross on their left, on the rise beneath the charcoal sky; Waltham Cross on their right, glittering through the gathering mist as though the warmth of gold could freeze. Then the great straight thrust of the roadway through silence and darkness up past Hoddes Town towards Puck's Ridge.

The horses had never been meant to carry them that far. As they crossed the outer reach of Hertford Heath, so the grey-smoking river swung round across their way and the road beneath the galloping hooves began to fall towards the bridge at Ware. They crossed the river as the town clock struck six and night seemed to fall on the stroke of it. Up the High Street they came, the sound of their urgent horses desecrating the sound of a choir at worship, until Hobbie, half a length in the lead, swung his chestnut beneath an arch under the thrust of an overhanging upper chamber, and the other two, following, found themselves crowding into what little was left of an old inn yard beside a big black travelling coach with four great horses harnessed in its traces, blanketed against the cold and waiting quietly to go.

Stiffly now, they all swung down and Hobbie crossed to the inn door and hammered upon it.

'There's like to be little answer from the innkeeper,' said Tom, 'with evensong not yet done.' Even so, he kept glancing over his shoulder at the coach, with its sconces at each corner holding four big torches ready to take fire, its heavy leather blinds tied tight down over the gaping windows, and the dried mud clinging to its solid, businesslike sides – a little more than a day or so old, that mud, he thought.

'You're half in the right at least,' said Eve. 'We are expected and will be answered shortly – though not by the innkeeper, to be sure.'

The door opened as she spoke and two tall men surveyed them. One was cloaked and booted, ready for travelling – ready, like as not, thought Tom, looking at the great padded gauntlets on his ham-like fists, to take the reins of the waiting coach and guide it back whence it had come, to the North; and, like Hobbie Noble, he had one of those still, fierce faces that spoke most eloquently of the hard lands between York and Berwick.

He and Hobbie exchanged a nod that bespoke acquaintance and Tom realized at once that the coach was waiting for them. All they had to do was get their passes checked and they could proceed; but there lay the rub.

Beside the coachman stood a stout country bumpkin, all soft southern roundness in cheek and belly, clutching a constable's staff. 'Papers!' snapped the constable officiously.

From the frown with which the papers were taken, it was clear that the good Parish Constable of Ware by no means approved of folks that travelled on the eve of one of the holiest of days, keeping him from worship as they did so – especially as he saw all too clearly that the journey was not likely to be completed before the holy day itself began in six hours' time, or began to dawn in twelve. Not all the passes and warrants from the Chamberlain, the Council nor the Queen herself – for all she could style herself, like her father, Defender of the Faith – could convince him there was an urgency here that surpassed even the importance of evensong on this most holy festival; but it was his duty to check the identity of every traveller who moved through his parish, and to check their passes and permits. Upon his order, common vagrants could be jailed, pilloried or whipped. At his reference the local justice could brand, lop or chop. It was his duty and his responsibility, though it was clear that he could hardly read.

He took the whole bundle of passes and permits and sat at the nearest table, straining under the meagre light. Tom caught

Hobbie and the saturnine driver exchanging a look, rolling their eyes to heaven at the slow tracing of his diligent finger from line to line and the laboured fish-like gasping of lip as he silently spelt out the words. Then the driver glanced back to another, shadowed portion of the dim, half-lit unwelcoming parlour and Tom saw another man there – a second driver, with his padded gloves; another settled, northern countenance.

Tom crossed towards Eve, thinking that if they were to be cooped up in a coach for the next few hours, then now might be the time to mend some fences with her. ' 'Tis as well I'm not here to be counted at the command of Caesar Augustus and you're not heavy with child,' he observed with dry blasphemy, 'or this would be a sorely familiar situation.'

'Indeed,' she said shortly and, disappointed that the sally had not extended the good work that his description of her true plight seemed to have begun, he wondered for an instant whether she had picked up a Puritan streak she had never shown in her wild youth. Not from brother John, he thought; and the gloom of sadness and loss descended upon him, compounded by the sudden delay, the faltering in the momentum of his quest. As it did so, she walked away from him, past the second driver and out through a side door into the yard.

'Eve,' he called quietly after her, fearing to raise his voice in case the constable have something else to add to his slow outrage; but there came no answer as she disappeared into the freezing shadows. How she must be suffering, he thought. His own memories of John were sunny and warm.

Except for the time they had seen the Barguest, of course.

In the silence after her departure, Tom suddenly became aware that the service in the nearby church must be over. The choral sounds of regimented worship had ceased and the more general shuffling of a departing congregation was suddenly lost beneath a valedictory peal of bells. A moment later the first of the parishioners arrived. A glance at the broad face, as red and meaty as a boiled pig's head, told him this was the innkeeper returned. Behind the tun-sized girth of his belly there crowded a scrawny wife and a brood of brats all like plucked chickens wrapped in sad cypress – not an ounce of flesh amongst them, except for that which padded their well-lined father; but, fat or thin, they all shared the same pinched and disapproving look and, observed Tom wryly, they all bore suspicious similarity to the constable.

'They still here then, master Constable?' demanded the innkeeper, much aggrieved.

'Still here,' answered the constable, looking up, losing his place and returning to the top of the pass he was reading now.

'It is not right,' observed the innkeeper, 'travelling on such a holy day. 'Tis blasphemy pure and simple. No good will come of it, as the vicar said in his sermon, and more evil's like to fall on our poor heads as a result. The crops are lost already and starvation looming for all of us in the iron heart of this icy time.'

' 'Tis the order of the Council,' soothed the constable, 'and there's a good few bishops and such upon the Council.'

The innkeeper's belligerent superstitions seemed to have caught the mood of the desperate townsfolk, for Tom could see, beyond his scrawny family, some rather more substantial and no less truculent neighbours beginning to crowd across the Great North Road. He caught Hobbie's eye and then those of the driver and his mate. The three men began to sidle towards the carriage and, looking across at the vehicle, Tom was surprised to see that the blankets were off the horses' backs and a slim boyish figure was framed in the open doorway, ready and waiting to go.

Tom stepped back, therefore, and briefly rested his right fist apparently casually on the table between the pile of documents which the constable had finished reading and the last pass, which still claimed his sluggard attention. 'Unless that is the watch that you have summoned by some exercise in magic,' he said quietly, glancing meaningfully out through the inn door, 'then you have an illegal congregation gathering, master Constable. 'Ware riot, sir. 'Ware riot.'

The constable looked up at that, and saw that, as Tom had warned, some thirty strapping farmers dressed in their Sabbath

best were crowding across the High Street, as though specta-
cularly unaware that the season of goodwill was hard upon
them. As he did so, three things happened in swift succession.

Tom reached down and gathered his papers together, sweeping them out of the startled constable's grasp. Just at the same
moment, the driver lit the first flaming torch on the right-front
corner of the coach and it exploded into a dazzling shower of
flames; and a pair of horsemen thundered up the High Street at
full gallop, hurtling into the black-clad crowd in the shadows,
smashing them ruthlessly aside with the power of their pound-
ing steeds, and were gone again into the darkness before the
first of their victims could tumble, broken and screaming, on to
the icy ground. Tom caught a flash of their impact on the
crowd: a black stallion rearing; a head split by a sharp-spurred,
stirrup-armed boot; the bulge of a saddlebag behind with an
ornate device upon it; shocked men and women hurled brutally
aside.

Then the constable really did have a riot on his hands. The
farmers went from congregation to mob in a twinkling, as
though some philosopher's stone had transmuted their essential
being. Into the inn they came boiling, outraged and looking for
a fight – after the blood of the only strangers left within their
grasp.

Stuffing the papers into his satchel, Tom swung out of the
little parlour side door that had let Eve out to ready the horses,
but he knew he would be lucky indeed to reach the carriage
unchecked. In the brightness of the second blazing torch, the
driver and his mate could see as much and the pair of them
leaped down while Hobbie steadied the frightened horses and
Eve called curses from the carriage itself, her spirit returning
through rage where gentleness and wit had failed to stir it. Then
the mob was upon them all.

Tom had neither time, room nor inclination to reach for his
swords. Even the daggers would only have added to the
bloodshed, and therefore the delay. Clutching the precious
satchel tight under his right arm, feeling the weight of the
four-barrelled bastard pistol ironically heavy against his heart,

he pushed forward, swinging his left fist manfully at the first face in his way. A stool flew past his shoulder, and smashed into the next face he was targeting. Quick as a flash he caught it and swung it upwards as a makeshift club, the threat of it enough to make his next two foemen fall back. The driver and his mate arrived on either side of him then, and the three bundled forward all abreast. As they pushed through the mob, there was much elbowing and jostling but, thought Tom grimly, a bruise or two was a small price to pay to get out of the place.

'Hobbie, leave the horses!' Tom bellowed, and his old friend obeyed at once, swinging back to take the driver's place at Tom's right shoulder even as Eve replaced the second man at his left. Then the three travellers were in the solid vehicle and the drivers, aloft, were whipping up the horses.

The hooves of the rearing, plunging leaders cleared away those last few men still on the High Street – for at the very least they had seen the damage that the sudden riders had done to their friends still lying at the roadside in varying states of disrepair. It was as well that some of these, at the outskirts of the riot, had pulled the wounded clear, otherwise there would have been a good deal of death dished out; for once the carriage was moving, neither the sharp-shod hooves nor the heavy, steel-hooped wheels would have stopped for anyone.

Seemingly lent wings by their terror, the four horses plunged up the hill, scarcely under the driver's control, and the coach behind them bounced and swayed, throwing its occupants hither and yon as though they had been dice in the hands of an energetic gamesman. In the darkness they bounced off one another, exchanging a good few more bruises before they could settle on the big broad seats. Only as the vehicle attained the straight run of Ermine Street itself, and the steady rise up to Puck's Ridge, did some semblance of calm return.

'What in God's name happened there?' gasped Eve.

'I think the constable slowed us on purpose,' Tom answered slowly. 'I think we must have an enemy somewhere capable of acting more swiftly even than we – someone who has sent messages to Ware and riders to the North, riders ordered to overtake us at any cost and perhaps to wait in ambush for us; certainly to organize some mischief for us later.'

Eve laughed aloud at that. 'You cannot know this!' she spat. 'You're simply making it up.'

'Perhaps,' said Tom. 'But even if I am doing so, would we not be wise to act as though my guesses were gospel truth?'

'Lad's got a point,' said Hobbie dryly.

'But whoever they were and whyever they came,' continued Tom more reasonably, 'they came and hoped to go in secret, for they rode with muffled hooves. In spite of the season and the terrible danger, they rode with muffled shoes. How else could they have come over the bridge and in amongst the townsfolk so sudden and unexpectedly? No. From this moment onwards, we must behave in everything we do as though we face a great and ruthless enemy.'

Tom lapsed into silence then, as though the exercise of so much logic after such an affray at the latter end of such a long and exciting day had tired even him. The coach rattled and heaved as the four strong horses hauled it up past Collier's End. The blind over the open window, knocked loose in the escape, flapped open and torchlight flooded into the box of shadow within. Tom was sitting strangely on the wide, padded seat, his cloak thrown back, his right glove held between his teeth and his right hand moving inside his jerkin.

'Tom, what is it?' asked Eve, her voice suddenly strident with worry.

'Tom?' called Hobbie, catching her sudden tone.

'God's my life, I've been stabbed,' said Tom. He pulled his hand out of his shirt and in the unsteady, golden light, it seemed almost as dark as if he had resumed his Spanish-leather glove.

Tom looked at it for an instant with frowning concentration while the other two sat riven where they were; and then he keeled over on to his side.

CHAPTER FIVE

The Nightmare Journey

N o doubt, thought Tom, looking back on it all from near the end of the affair, it was the swaying of the coach that had made him dream that he was flying at first. It was, probably, the massive howling of the gathering nor'easterly gale that had made his dream of the Barguest later; and it was, no doubt, the distant voices of the Christmas bells that had made him dream of death in the end. But when he discussed matters with Eve and Hobbie, it seemed that much of what he had dreamed was true, if others of his logical assumptions were a good deal less so.

The pain in his side and the words of his rough nurses wove in and out of his dreams seemingly at will. While they did this, the black-cloaked, huge-fisted, ruggedly inexhaustible drivers hurled them all through the night at breakneck speed, and the coach charged onwards at nearly ten of the Queen's new statute miles in every hour, north to New Castle.

Tom dreamed he was an eagle – an angel seemed so unlikely – skimming over the wild lands of his childhood home, a home drawing near again in all sorts of ways as he tossed restlessly upon the coach's seat in the grip of his nightmare vision. Below him, all clear-etched by a low sun in a cloudless sky, lay the rough rock waves of the Marches from the Cheviot Hills to Teviot Dale. Two waves of moor land moss they seemed to him, frozen waves of rock running from north-east to south-west, spanning less than fifty miles in all, with a trough of a valley between them. The Teviots stood in the north, contained mostly in Scotland, coming down from Berwick towards Dumfries; and south of them ran the Cheviots, from Bamburgh towards Carlisle. Between them was fixed the border, which wandered invisibly but vitally from moss to fell to wilderness, from sea to sea. Two rocky, mountainous walls designed by God to keep the Scots and the English apart, more effective even than Hadrian's wall skirting the southern slopes of the Cheviots away to the south on Tom the dream-eagle's left.

'Tom?' asked Eve's voice. 'What're ye doing, Tom?'

'I'm flying,' answered Tom. 'Flying away home.'

'Lie still,' commanded Eve more roughly. 'I'll not lose two men within the week. Hobbie, hold him down.'

But not even Hobbie could hold down the dream-eagle Tom had become as he skimmed away back to his home. The walls of rock had been worn away over the years. Due north and due south ran the river valleys, pathways leading easily through the forbidding highlands, allowing constant raiding and reiving from one land and law into the other – Coquetdale, Redesdale and Tynedale through the Cheviots into England; the valleys of the Jed, the Yarrow and the Elvan out of Scotland.

As he flew from east to west, into the glimmer of the setting sun, Tom seemed to settle into lower air, skimming between Kielder Heights and Hermitage Hall, England beneath his left wing and Scotland under his right, with the border under his belly as he flew; the border under his belly and the Bewcastle Waste close beneath his heart.

'Tom', whispered Eve, 'this will hurt. I've to close up your side, where the dagger . . .'

Still through the rough walls of wild wasteland, like daggers through ill-fitting armour, even through the stout breastplate of the Waste itself, stabbed the dark river valleys, wooded with cover, steep-sided, secret, shadowed and convenient to mischief, two of them running in parallel and the most deadly dangerous of all: the river-dales of the Lidd and the Lyne coming down to the Esk river and the Solway Firth, on either side of the border; between them the debatable land, neither English nor Scottish but a lordless, lawless morass of constant war, tomb of political dreams and graveyard of armies. Up and down their dangerous valleys marched warriors beyond counting, times out of number.

'There, Tom. That'll do,' said Eve. 'You'll rest easier now.'

And so he did; without disturbing his dream or his thoughts. Now Eve Graham Musgrave, it seemed, widow of his brother and his sister within the church, had the northern tributary, the Black Lyne, of a sudden, under her hand and within her dower.

No wonder the canny Captain of Bewcastle had sent her to seek the advice and the protection of the Lord Chancellor. For only a man like Henry Carey, Lord Hunsdon and Lord of the North could hold this coil, this cockpit, together.

Outside his dream, he sensed the coach stop. The driver got down and showed the passes. The door opened briefly to let in the light and the thunderous howl of the gale that came bellowing in off the North Sea over the fens to Stamford, where they had been stopped by the watch and waited to change horses. But inside his dream he was flipped out of flight, air and time. In a heartbeat Tom had lost the bewildering vista of the Borders and the silver Solway stretching towards the sun. Instead he was caged within a woody coolness. There was a leafy, deep-green, fragrant stillness all around him. And, if he had never experienced the breathless reality of flight except in his imagination, then he knew the truth of this. For it was not imagination at all. It was reality rehearsed – memory made more vivid by the dream; terror made more poignant because he knew what was going to happen next.

'My Lord's woodsmen will never catch us now. Not even Hobbie will find us here, Tom,' said John then, his voice louder, deeper, than Tom remembered it.

He turned, and John stood at his shoulder, tall and slim with his dark shock of hair – gangling and bony still, yet to fill out and square up; twelve years old to Tom's ten; both of them breathless with excitement at their adventure with Hobbie, doing a little poaching here in Inglewood Forest.

' 'Tis the best of ambushes,' Tom acknowledged. 'The heart of a yew in the midst of a forest, surrounded by trees not like to have been disturbed since the Romans needed wood for the Wall.'

'Since Noah needed wood for the Ark,' fantasized John. 'Near at the dawn of the world.'

'If the Flood ever reached here,' dared Tom, blasphemously clever even then; and about to learn a lesson from his unwise words. 'And I'll lay odds it never did! Why, there could be creatures in these woods, John, that lived before the Flood. Think of it: things hid like us in the black heart of this timeless place, never seeing the full light of day. Undiscovered. Unsuspected. Things condemned of God but never . . .'

He stopped then, for he was frightening himself and his wild suggestion seemed suddenly quite plausible, for the forest was huge and dark. It had about it that very air of infinite age, as though it had in truth stood here untouched since the dawn of Time, and theirs were actually the first human feet to disturb its ancient loam.

And the instant Tom stopped speaking, the hound howled.

It was a huge sound, haunting and overpowering; and all too close at hand. Both boys screamed at the sound and ran to clasp each other. Their screams were echoed by another fierce howl, a howl that tailed off into the guttural baying of a hunting animal.

They stayed tremulously embraced for the merest instant and then they were in full flight; but whither should they run? Whatever was out there seemed huge, seemed all too close by; seemed to be after them. The ancient yew tree within which they were hiding had reached out a massive tent of pendulous branches, each one taking new root where it touched. These branches made a tight-woven palisade near thirty feet across at whose heart stood the original growth. This was more a matted sheaf of thigh-thick stems than one great trunk, but it made easy climbing. The boys went up it side by side like squirrels – and not a moment too soon.

A huge head smashed through the outer wall at the very

weakness they had widened to come in here themselves. Tom, still climbing wildly, had leisure for only the briefest glance over his shoulder at the great black face of the thing – a head, he later swore, that must have been near as tall as he was himself; a drooling, slobbering red mouth wide enough to have swallowed him down at one fell gulp, could he have fitted past the fangs as long as wild boar's tusks. In through the hole beneath its jowls it thrust one huge black paw as wide as John's broad shoulders, armed with curling claws as long as his fingers, as grey as flint and sharp as daggers – claws that curled down into soft loam and tore at soft flesh; claws that had never been worn down by hard rock or strong foe. For Tom could imagine nothing ever standing against this monster. It would hunt wolves, gulp boars, chew bulls and shatter bears with one flick of its paw.

The thing pulled back, then howled again, throwing the massive black invisibility of itself against the creaking branches of the ancient tree, tearing them out of the forest floor, roots and all, as it ripped its way in, while Tom, screaming still, looked up for John.

And found him immediately above. John grown to manhood in a dream-instant; frozen in a scream, wide eyes bulging and staring, wild hair standing upright in the icy blast; lips blackened with the shout of horror that had burst his heart, and tongue thrust out like a slate gravestone, stark dead of terror, staring down at Tom from an inch away.

Tom screamed and fell backwards on to soft, warm ground; and the great hound bounded over him, grown like the boys to full size in the interim, reaching up twelve feet sheer with those terrible claws fit to tear out the heart of a mighty oak tree as it stood like a massive sentinel and looked from Arthur's Seat down the valley that the dead man's wife owned – down the dale of the Black Lyne into the defenceless heart of the Borders.

Down which, of a sudden, Tom saw them carry the body – flat on a wicket under a blanket out of respect; down off the high fells, away from the tree towards the little stone kirk at Blackpool Gate. As they brought the laden wicket down, so the bells began to chime, a wild peal of joy.

36

'No,' cried Tom. 'That's not right!'

'Hush now,' soothed Eve. 'What is it, Tom?'

And she was there at once in the dream, standing tall at the open door to the church with her black water running over her black land at her little white feet. She smiled, as full of joy as the bells.

Tom looked across at the men with the hurdle, and all of them were Hobbie. All of them were smiling as they walked across the water – water that came off the fell-side black as tar with the blood of the peat higher up; black and gold with the heartsblood of the oak tree, bleeding great golden angels where the Barguest had ripped it open; black and gold and red with the blood of the men that had died to get it and hold it and ride up and down it. Men who were piled up the fell-side so that their blood made the river flood at Eve's feet, the red running wildly into the kirk at Blackpool Gate. There in the kirk, in the blood with the dead he had made while Tom, in another childhood, had watched, stood Robert Devereux, the Earl of Essex himself; and the Barguest stood at his side, as big as a horse, with his shoulder at its shoulder.

'No!' shouted Tom.

'Tom!' shouted Eve.

Both seemed to be speaking in the last of the dream but the dream was fading now – fading into the heady joy of peal after peal of bells.

But the dark vision lingered, there by the Black Pool, by the kirk by the Gate, with Eve, Essex and the Barguest itself and Tom and the corpse on the wicket held by six smiling Hobbies – lingered long enough for Tom to take the dream-edge of the dream-blanket and jerk it back off the screaming face, to see the wide bulging eyes and the wide black lips and the big black tombstone tongue. But the face no longer belonged to John.

It belonged to Tom himself.

'Where am I?' Tom asked, as reality swept over him in a blaze of light and a peal of bells like the high waterfalls at the Devil's Beef Tub.

'New Castle,' said Hobbie, as terse and succinct as ever.

Tom sat up without thinking, such was his shock at the news. Some sense of movement had informed the visions of the night but nothing could ever have prepared him for the news that the coach had continued its incredible progress hour after hour all through the near eighteen hours of the night. They had come very nearly two hundred of the Queen's new miles since they had escaped from the riot at Ware.

It was as well, he realized at once, that Hobbie and Eve were both well schooled in simple surgery. His side was easy, its stiffness as much to do with tight bandaging as anything else. Further careful movement, however, revealed the familiar pulling sensation that told of several stitches. 'A long, shallow gash?' he hazarded. 'A good bleeding to sharpen my senses and restore my humours and little more.'

Hobbie looked back at him from his position immediately outside the coach's doorway. His eyes were narrow and guarded; but that, thought Tom, might have been because the Good Lord had seen fit to let the folk of New Castle celebrate his birthday beneath a clear, frosty and dazzlingly sunny heaven.

'Restore your humours but ruin your linen,' supplied Eve's voice from beyond him suddenly. 'Heaven help the Lord of the Waste's washerwoman when she sees the mess you're in. But you're in the right of it. It was a long shallow wound in the soft flesh above your hip. You've cause to thank all that easy living in London, mind. Were you leaner, you'd likely be dead.'

'In no fit condition to ride the Wall, at least,' said Tom easily; 'but I should be able to do it now, thanks to your tending.'

'If we take it slow,' warned Hobbie, 'and if we ever get to start.'

Feeling the still-damp clothing beginning to set and crisp scratchily against his ribs, Tom slid off the seat and stepped out of the coach. Light-headed still, he let the overwhelming day swirl and settle before he let go of the coach itself. He looked around, mind whirling into action.

At first it seemed to him that Hobbie and Eve had been

teasing him and they had not left London at all, for the coach was standing beside a bridge upon which stood houses and shops all brightly decked and glittering under the sun. But no: this bridge was smaller than London Bridge, for all that it seemed to bear a village on its back like its bigger cousin in the South. Seven spans served to step across the Tyne, and there were no great waterwheels at either end to pump water or grind corn; there was no great stone gateway festooned with poles and severed heads. And, of course, there was the dream-like memory of the night with its stops and starts; its pauses to check papers and change horses counting through the hours as he had dreamed.

Even as this thought occurred to Tom, so the pair of drivers returned. 'We're clear,' growled the big driver to Hobbie. 'We're to take five horses and go on. They didn't like it, mind – not on Christmas Day. They're all *Christians* down here.'

Tom knew then – knew that the two drivers were to come with them, to guard them along the Wall, likely as not, and keep them from kidnap or the blackmail. And he knew who these two were – their names and clans, if not their individual titles yet – for it was a well-known story, often told a visitor to the wild haunts of bandit-reiver heartland of Liddesdale, looking to find a kirk on the Sabbath and finding only castles, forts and peel towers, had asked, despairingly, 'Are there no Christians in Liddesdale?' Only to receive the answer, 'Na, we's all Elliots and Armstrongs here . . .'

CHAPTER SIX

Riding the Wall

They left the carriage at the south side of the bridge and crossed it on foot. Through the deserted roadway between the bridge houses over the River Tyne, the two guides led the little party to a quiet inn upon the north bank, hard by St Nicholas' Church, which seemed to lean back upon the Wall they were destined to follow west.

The whole of New Castle seemed deserted at the moment – or outside St Nicholas' Church and the others close by it did. For, as in Ware the night before, only those with special – crucial – business would be out of church at this time in this day, while the Christmas services were on, thought Tom, shivering a little with understandable concern that the imperative of this ghastly business might well be putting his soul as well as his life in some dark and deadly danger.

The inn was called The Wall's End. Here Tom and Eve were led into a small private room that had clearly been prepared for them some time earlier. Here Tom and his sister-in-law were further accoutred, while Hobbie and the two guides brought out arms and armour that clearly belonged to themselves. There were jacks for all, the quilting in the heavy leather coats well designed to keep them warm as the metal sections sewn on the outside were designed to keep them safe – full jacks at that, with skirts to guard their lower backs, not the shorter, lighter jackets that were coming into fashion. Both Tom and Eve joined the other three in setting aside the back- and breastplates that were also on offer. They were due to travel fast and light; and, in all conscience, it would be a black heart indeed that would attack poor travellers on this of all days.

By the door, however, lay five steel bonnets in the modern burgonet design, five long lances, a couple of Jedburgh axes with their peculiar, curving blades. On the wall above these jutted a shelf on which lay three unstrung bows with quivers full of arrows, a couple of crossbows with quarrels to match and a solid-looking arquebus, flask of powder and bag of wadding and shot. Tom was really beginning to feel at home.

The door opened and a solid man entered, grey-bearded, thick-haired and wild of eyebrow. His deep-set eyes fell on Eve first and he frowned but held his peace. Then he looked across at the others. 'Hobbie,' he said, with a nod. 'Sim. Archie. Food?'

'If ye've any handy and to spare, Clem,' said Hobbie. 'We'll naw be up on the Waste afore evensong. The lass is strang enough, I doubt, but the lad here lost a deal of blood in the night.'

'There's an eel pie in the baker's oven.'

'If ye can spare a crumb of that, I know the Lord Chamberlain in London himself would be grateful.'

'I'd rather the Lord of the Waste were grateful; and certain Armstrongs and Elliots I could call to mind – in the matter of cattle particularly.'

'I'll speak for the Armstrongs,' said the man called Sim.

'And I for the Elliots,' said Archie.

'And I for the Lord of the Waste,' said Hobbie.

'And I'll still speak for the Queen herself, for the Lord of the North and for Her Majesty's Council in White Hall Palace,' said Tom, easily.

The innkeeper's eyes switched to Hobbie, his bushy eyebrows raised.

'Aye,' said Hobbie. 'He can that. D'ye no mind Long Tom Musgrave, brother to the Blacksmith of Bewcastle? He's a big man at the Queen's court these days.'

'I do,' said the innkeeper, shortly. 'Ye're welcome in my house, Master Musgrave.'

'And welcome, I hope,' said Tom in reply, 'to a flagon of your good New Castle ale to go with the crumb of your fine eel pie; but not before I ask a question of you, Master Clem.'

'And what wid that be, Master Musgrave?'

'Two men riding hard on horseback overtook us in the night. Is there any word of them here as yet?'

'None that I know of, Master. And I would know if they came or if they went.'

'Good enough. And thanks for your honesty. Now as to the other matter . . .'

And so it was done. With allowances being made for the importance of the Queen's business – and Her Majesty having the right to dictate in the matter, being Defender of the Faith – food and drink were served and consumed, work done and reckonings paid all at the holiest hour of the holiest of days; and weapons taken and ponies readied and mounted. So that by the time the good people of New Castle came streaming out of the South Door of St Nicholas' Church, the five weary wayfarers were gone westwards along the North Wall – the Wall built by the order of the Roman Emperor Hadrian seventeen hundred years before, that led from here to Bowness, west of Carlisle, on the south shore of the Solway Firth.

Tom had ridden the Wall as a child. Some folk never stirred more than a mile or two from their own front door through all of their lives, but Tom had always been a restless soul. The adventures in Inglewood Forest had made John seek to stay close to home, but they had done the opposite to Tom. Where John had remained on the Waste for the rest of his time on earth, Tom had come away with Hobbie, exploring the Scottish Marches as far as Edinburgh and the English Marches up to Berwick, Carlisle, New Castle and all before he was sixteen summers old – needfully so, for he had become a scholar at Carlisle Grammar School before his twelfth birthday and had trotted there and back each day thereafter. Then for a short while before his studies took him north to Glasgow, his exploration had moved to another level and had taken him less far afield. Those had been the days of dalliance with Eve

Graham and a host of other beauties, from Carlisle Cross by the Solway in England to Hermitage Castle at the head of Liddesdale in Scotland.

Tom assumed leadership of the little band as of right, but he was the kind of captain content to let his command display their own strengths. He kept a clear eye on the disposition of the group, but was silently satisfied that Sim Armstrong took the lead with Hobbie close behind him and that Archie Elliot brought up the rear, allowing Tom himself to keep a closer watch upon Eve.

Once they were clear of New Castle, they used the break in the Wall, at Heddon, to cross to the sheltered south side after the first hour's riding; and they began to make good time over the flat country as it gathered gently up towards Harlow Hill. Their indefatigable little mounts jingled forward over the frost-crisp grass at a steady trot, consuming perhaps half a dozen miles in an hour, sending plumes of steam behind them, thinning away in the wind that whipped over the Wall. The distance travelled was quite easy to judge, for every thousand paces on the wall there was a small fort; and the Queen's new statute miles were based on the Roman thousand-pace miles. Soon they settled into the rhythm that Tom remembered from his youth – one fort passed every count of six hundred.

Unlike the ride up the Great North Road, there was light and space here, and, apart from the keening of the wind in the timeless stones and the distant clamour of the marsh birds down on the Tyne, it was quiet. Tom soon urged his pony up alongside Eve's so that they could talk.

'I've been wondering,' she said at once, her breath smoking up over her steel bonnet as though her throat were afire.

'About?' he asked, sending his own cloud of breath into the crackling cold of the air.

'About who stabbed you.'

'And I've been wondering why they stabbed me. But I admit to some surprise. Surely you must be wondering more urgently about John.'

'What wonder is there? The Barguest took him.'

43

'You believe in the Barguest?'

'You do not? Now *I* am surprised. John did. The whole of the Borders does. Those that doubted when there were only rumours on the wing are hard-certain now. Because of John. And you were right. He always believed in the thing himself. He said that you and he had seen it – once, in your childhood, away in the depths of Inglewood Forest. You were lucky to escape it, he said.'

Tom rode on, silently, framing his thoughts and his words. 'We saw something,' he admitted after a while. 'But I would be loth to swear that we saw a hound of hell lately unleashed by Satan himself.'

'You saw it again in your dreams last night. You screamed and raved.'

'There's the rub,' he said. 'In my dream I saw a dream-monster. I mind it well enough from my childhood and I can call to my inward eye a picture of it as easy as looking at you. But it is still a thing of fantasy. I see what the child saw in memory and in dream; and I am no longer that child. So perhaps the man would see something different now. Does not the Bible say, "When I was a child I understood as a child – but now I am a man I must put away childish things"?'

'Then what killed my John?' Eve asked, forthrightly, 'if not the Barguest?'

'What indeed? Or who? And why?'

'The same questions you asked about that wound in your side.'

'And no coincidence, my lady. Is it not likely that when a man comes to search out the truth of his brother's death and is greeted by a dagger thrust, there may be some link between the two? That it is rather more likely there may be a link than that it is simply a coincidence of accidents? In short, that whoever slid the dagger into my side wanted to stop me looking into John's death? And that in turn makes me question the matter of hell-hounds more closely too. For if Satan sent the Barguest after John, why should Satan not do as much for me? And if a cold blade is sent instead of a monstrous dog, then it is less likely that hell is involved at all – especially as the steel went awry and left me to be nursed back to fitness in a trice. For the Devil needs no daggers.'

'And makes precious few mistakes,' admitted Eve. 'I see where logic leads you.'

Eve was quieter after that, and Tom took the initiative, as was natural with him. As they trotted down the last of the hill into the wide valley of Tynedale towards the bridge at still-distant Low Brunton, where the Wall stepped over the North Tyne, he took her through and through the events surrounding the death of his brother as far as she knew them. She was able to give him chapter and verse of what had happened after the body had been found; but unexpectedly, unsettlingly, she was less able to tell him what had happened to John immediately before. It seemed that at this season, unlike most others, their various duties were apt to keep them apart.

Three hours after they had left New Castle, they crossed the North Tyne river and began the long, steepening climb towards Stanegate. The Wall stood on their right hands, cresting the great Whin Sill whose cliffs fell increasingly precipitously as the land the five rode gathered up, extending the Wall's barrier on the north. South of them, down the increasing slope across which they were trotting with such deceptive ease following the ancient track of the Romans' Military Way, lay a great bank running parallel to the Wall itself. Beyond that, Tynedale settled in the blue-glimmering distance into the broad valley where the South Tyne wandered, curling up towards them as they rode onwards, beginning to smoke with frost mist as the sun began to settle lower, shining directly into their weeping eyes as the fourth hour of their riding became a fifth.

Tom saw Sim Armstrong turn to Hobbie and Hobbie turned to Tom, waving and calling, 'Spur on. Spur on apace!'

Tom turned to Eve and saw from her curt nod that she had heard. Tom drove his heels into his pony's flanks and the game little mount picked up the pace willingly enough. They pulled in together as their ponies cantered up the slope, and Tom, coming up on Hobbie's shoulder, saw what he and Sim could see. Through a break in the Wall called the Busy Gap, a vista northward opened over Houghton Common and the mountainous heights immediately beyond; and on the skyline there, at the one point for ten miles and more that might command a view of anyone riding the Wall down here, there sat a horseman, etched black against a sky as blue as the Virgin's robes in a stained-glass window.

'We are looked for,' said Tom to Hobbie, reining to a stand, with the others gathering around him, their ponies stamping and steaming in the chilly air.

'Watched and followed. As we were at Ware.'

'D'ye think we're hunted?' wondered Sim Armstrong grimly.

Even as Sim asked the question, so the horseman seemed to settle in his saddle – turning, Tom decided; and from the midst of his black outline came a gleam of dazzling light.

'Hunted,' confirmed Tom; 'and if we can see the signal, then he's calling someone close at hand.'

'We should run for it,' said Archie Elliot at once, 'helter-skelter and each for himself. We should make Greenhead and mebbe Thirlwall Castle within the hour.'

'Haydon Bridge and Langley Castle in half that time, if we run due south,' said Sim. 'We're just coming up on the road south to Haydon.'

They would clearly both be gone; but they turned to Hobbie for a ruling. And Hobbie turned to Tom.

Tom was still looking north, watching the lone rider vanish beneath the skyline, heading away north into Scotland or coming south to join the men he had just alerted – it was impossible to say.

'Wait,' said Tom. 'Let us take thought before we take flight – for a moment at least,' he added, sensing the restlessness of the two guides as their ponies pawed the frozen turf. 'Let us say that we are hunted then. The horseman has signalled to a band of men nearby and they are coming to find us now. It would need to be a large band, would it not, to overpower five hardy and well-armed fighters such as we are. Also, it would need to be a well-chosen group, made up of men with strong bonds with each other and few wider ties. For look at us – an Armstrong and an Elliot, close kin to half of Liddesdale; a Graham, related to most of Cumberland; a noble, whose family lives all along the Lyne Rivers, Black and White – and who is owed a life debt by Jock o' the Side for getting him out of New Castle gaol – and by a goodly number of other Armstrongs to boot; and a Musgrave, close kin to the Lord of the Waste, who can by his patents, speak for the Queen and Council – though I know well enough how faint their voices will sound up here.

'So, unless we are hunted by Kerrs from Teviotdale or by Johnstones from Annandale or, God save us, by MacGregors or worse, then we are in as strong a position to talk as to fight.

'On the other hand, all of you know well – as well as the man who let us spot him before he signalled – that if we do take flight, then we must needs spread out – perhaps even split up. We will be easy to pick off and hard put to make any defence either with weapons or words. If the men who hunt us are reivers, then we will be easy to take in pairs or alone and will be caught for the blackmail or slavery in Scotland. If they be men confederated with the riders who overtook us at Ware, then we will be easier to take for questioning or worse – easy enough for us all to vanish like five puffs of smoke into any of the dungeons between this and Hermitage Hall.'

He mentioned Hermitage again calculatedly, for he wished to make his point most strongly to Archie and Sim, and both of them would know well enough about the haunted, Satanic castle that stood glowering at the head of Liddesdale, a place of infinite evil, to be talked of in whispers, owned by devil-worshippers and worse – at least one of whom had been boiled alive almost within living memory. And that, well *within* living memory, had been the haunt of Mary, Queen of Scots, and her doomed Bothwell, who had been, for a time, the captain of the place.

Of course, Tom wanted a message driven home to all here. For he reckoned it a fair wager that one of the other four watching him now owned the dagger that had been slipped into his side at Ware.

47

CHAPTER SEVEN

Fort and Farmstead

They went west away from the Busy Gap, therefore, in a tight group with Tom at their head, riding like the wind; and they were wise to follow him, for it was clear to all there that, with his reasons spoken or unspoken, here was a mind that could marshal such strengths as lay in their dangerous position; and that if any could get them safely through, it was the Lord of the Waste's nephew, who had clearly inherited much of the old man's genius for war.

Tom had not revealed the whole of his thinking, in any case. For he was relying on the childhood memories that he had called into question with Eve. It was the same boy who had seen and feared the massive hound in Inglewood – and remembered it now as the Barguest – who remembered a huge safe fortress a little more than a mile on up the Wall, with a two-floored bastle farmhouse solidly built against the south wall.

Just as it was with hounds, so might it be with ruins. He remembered the fort and farmhouse as being a solid refuge, easy to defend, commanding the sort of salient easily raked by fire from longbow and crossbow, armed still with heavy oaken doors that might be proof against burning and walled and floored with heavy stone to two levels with a stairway almost impossible to climb leading up to the second floor, where farmers lived above their stock; a narrow, easily defended staircase overlooked in any case by an overhanging battlement from the strong slate roof. The fort had been strong enough for Hadrian's men and the bastle farmhouse would serve the five of them, if they could get safely into it. Or it would do so if it all still stood as the child in him remembered it.

Side by side Hobbie rode with him, looking along the Wall and trusting their ponies to keep their feet. 'Who farms at Housesteads now?' called Tom.

'Hugh Nixon,' came the answer.

'If he's there, would he give us shelter?'

'Depends who's coming after us. He's an Armstrong. Pays his blackmail to Jock o' the Side; and he watches the Busy Gap for him too, like as not. He'd stand with Sim and with me for the sake of the family. Unless he's a better reason not to. But he'll be down in Haltwhistle today, I'd wager. 'Tis the nearest kirk – and the nearest tavern, if ye take ma meanin'.'

'Family?'

'None as I know of.'

'Then we have our shelter, if we can reach it before whoever hunts us comes snapping at our heels.'

'Aye. I thought as much. It's a good enough plan – and fall back into the fort itself if we cannot get up into the farmhouse? Hold out there for as long as we can?'

'And that may not be too long a time. If the men that hunt us know where we are, then, like as not, the Lord of the Waste will know it too; and know that we are hunted.'

'Ye were always a canny lad – nigh on witchcraft some days.'

They came over the crest of the hill-slope above Busy Gap as Hobbie spoke, and there before them the Wall settled down into a west-sloping valley, though beyond its broad grey eminence immediately to the north there still fell a considerable cliff. On the side of the valley, reaching southward at an angle from the Wall itself, stood the ruined Roman fort; and against the outer wall of the fortification, in the strongest possible defensive spot, stood the solid little farmhouse for which Hugh Nixon paid his rent to some local landlord living down in Carlisle, like as not, and his blackmail to Jock o' the Side Armstrong living up in Liddesdale –

and spied for him on the comings and goings through the busiest gap in the Wall.

Tom's thoughts were interrupted at once by Hobbie's urgent call of, 'There!'

Away at the foot of the slope in the hazy distance a solid group of riders was spurring up out of the frost mist over the lowlands called Beggar's Bog. No sooner had Hobbie called out than the gathering wind stopped whimpering through the Wall beside them and backed, so that the thunder of hooves on the iron-hard ground was carried up to them.

With no further word, the little group spurred on. It would be a close-run matter, for the distances looked about the same, but at least they were riding downhill. The lay-out of the fort would help them too, for the hunters would have to skirt three sides of the fortification while Tom's little command were heading straight for the foot of the steps leading up to the stout oak door.

Down to these steps they came, even as their enemies reached the far side of the ruin and began to come round the outer walls towards them. Here there was a big door that stood open, for Hugh Nixon had no stock in the byre at present. Tom leaped down and ran up the steps while the others helped Hobbie get their horses in.

At the top of the steps stood a solid door, closed tight. Tom, trained in the black arts by two London lock-picks, threw himself to his knees and pushed his dagger into the massive mechanism of the lock. He was feeling for the tumblers that would pull back the bolt when Eve reached over his shoulder and turned the handle. The big portal swung open with a scream that would have appalled the devil himself. 'He pays his blackmail to Jock o' the Side,' she said. 'No one's likely to take anything in here.

'Unless he has some secret fortune hidden away,' she continued as the pair of them stepped into the little room and were joined by Sim and Archie, 'then there'll be nothing worth risking the wrath of the Armstrongs over.'

'Sim, close the door,' said Tom and the big reiver dropped a solid balk of wood into two brackets across the door as Tom pulled up a trap in the floor – the only part of the floor not made of stone – and signalled Archie to pull up the weapons that Hobbie was unloading from the horses and passing up out of the byre below.

Then he joined Eve at the narrow window that looked due south, just as a dozen riders pulled up at the foot of the wall. For a moment words would have been wasted amid the snorting and the stamping of the steaming horses; but then a kind of quiet settled.

Tom had to break it, of course, for he did not want the riders to realize just what a range of weaponry was coming up through the trapdoor with Hobbie: 'My name is Tom Musgrave, kin to the Blacksmith of Bewcastle and the Lord of the Waste, messenger to the Lord of the North and the Queen and her Council. Is it me that you seek, gentlemen?'

In the continued silence that answered his announcement, he gave the birth, lineage and alliances of the other four as well, for he had not been speaking in jest when he had said how wide their web of family and influence might spread across the border; and if anything went wrong, there was the birth of a fair few feuds in prospect here. 'Think well what you are about, gentlemen,' he warned, 'for the shedding of our blood will beget the shedding of yours – and blood to be shed for generations to come.'

In a lower voice he said to the others as they joined him at last, 'Do you know any of these men?' – only to be answered by shakes of the head. Hardly surprising, for they all rode heavily cloaked – against the cold if nothing else. It was impossible to see either face or any significant detail of person or clothing – and Tom had been trying to the top of his bent since he arrived at the window.

Tom's eyes narrowed now, his brain still racing. The men gave the impression of having paused, nonplussed. They did not seem to be waiting as part of any plan or for any purpose, nor in expectation of any new arrival – though, he calculated, it might just be possible they were waiting for the man who had given the signal.

51

Now might be the time to test their resolve, however, he thought, as even Eve joined the other three stringing the longbows and winding up the crossbows. Before they made up their minds to action, he could test the riders' mettle, test their own armaments and start his own blood feud all at once.

'Pass the arquebus,' he ordered quietly, and his nose wrinkled at once with the stench of the match being lit even as he felt it pressed into his hand. He laid it on the sill of the narrow window and took aim at the foremost of the riders, even as that worthy swung round to direct some gruff orders to the others. The match came into the pan and the powder exploded at once, mercifully expelling most of the thunderous noise and resultant smoke with the shot.

The leader of the riders was blasted back out of his saddle and sent rolling across his horse's hindquarters into the face of the horse in his rear. That horse reared, unseating its rider in turn, and all the other ten plunged and curveted, shocked by the noise and the action.

'Did ye see that?' asked Hobbie.

'Aye,' said Tom, regressing through ten years of courtly education. 'Tartan under the cloak. They're Kerrs.'

'Kerrs right enough,' said Hobbie; and he pronounced the name 'Cur', which showed his opinion of the clan.

'Have you killed him?' demanded Eve.

'With this?' laughed Tom. 'Only if he's mad enough to rely on plaid instead of plating.' He struck the metal plates on his own chest even as the fallen man amid the scattering horses rolled over and began to pick himself up.

'Now, Master Kerr,' he called, pronouncing the name 'Car' as the Kerrs preferred. 'We have longbows and crossbows enough up here to put holes in your jacks, breastplates and hides enough. We have provender, water and a lively expectation of help at hand. Will you depart, will you parley or will you die? The choice is yours, and is only offered out of respect for the holy season.'

'You are grown into a braggart, I see,' said Eve quietly at his shoulder. He put out his hand and she put a crossbow into it.

'Hobbie, who is the man amongst the Kerrs most likely to be at the head of such a band? Do you know?'

'I know few enough of the rogues,' growled Hobbie, 'but I would say Little Dand is your man.'

'So, then, Little Dand Kerr,' continued Tom, 'I see you have recovered your wind and your wits well enough to stand. But I warn you that you stand beneath the point of my quarrel with my finger on the trigger of my crossbow here. And I still await your decision and your reply.'

He dropped his voice again. 'Sim, Archie, keep an eye on the rest of the rogues. They'll be getting into positions if they mean to fight. Hobbie, you go up and overlook the steps and doors. You prefer the longbow, I recall.'

'Aye,' came Hobbie's distant voice, from high behind Tom as though the little reiver were halfway to heaven after all. A sigh of icy wind seemed to whistle through the place and he was gone behind the battlement on the roof.

No sooner was he up there than a voice called over the restless keening of the wind: 'Ye're in the right of it, Master Musgrave. My name is Little Dand and I lead the Kerrs who stand around ye. But 'tis not my breast that stands beneath yer quarrel. So, here's the start of the bad blood between us.'

'Rider coming in!' called Archie.

Tom had already seen him, thundering in from the right hand, low over his pony's withers, reaching down to grab the man standing helplessly in the line of fire and swing him up behind him. It was a daring act, arrogant and masterful. Tom saw instinctively that he could not allow it to succeed, for it was finely calculated to give heart to the nonplussed Kerrs and demoralize his own small band.

The alternatives were immediately obvious to him: kill the man, kill Little Dand or kill the horse. It would be an act of charity to kill the beast, a beautiful but soulless section of creation, if by doing so he could preserve the lives and souls of the men involved. Just at the moment the two men took hold of each other he fired.

But at that very same moment Eve, standing close behind

him, unused, perhaps, to the tension such critical moments can bring, stirred and struck the crossbow's stock, so that Tom's aim was knocked awry.

Such was the tension in Tom's long body, however, that his aim was moved only infinitesimally; but enough to make all the difference. The heavy metal of the solid-steel quarrel sped with shocking speed and power towards a point just behind the horse's withers. Here Little Dand had grasped at once the reins and the solid pommel of the saddle with his left hand, as he reached downwards with his right. The quarrel hit hand, rein and pommel, just as Dand took his friend and was jerked right back in the saddle. The impact of the missile splintered the saddle, sundered the reins and shattered the hand all at once. The stump of the arm jerked up, all anchor and purchase gone in a twinkling. Little Dand Kerr was whipped backwards over the rump of his horse to tumble atop the man he had risked all to rescue, screaming with a mixture of shock, agony and frustration. The horse stumbled, regained its footing and ran on, leaving a heaving pile of entangled humanity in its wake, still solidly in the field of fire as Tom, silently, white with shock himself, reached back to his stunned sister for the last loaded crossbow.

'Sim?' he yelled.

'All still.'

'Archie?'

'The same.'

'Hobbie?'

'They're on their knees from what I can see. Saying a prayer, like as not, for protection against the dark arts. That shot was pure witchcraft.'

'Blind luck, helped by my sister's elbow. If there's a witch involved, then it is she,' said Tom, still stunned.

'No!' cried Sim. 'They're up. Now what's toward?'

'Hobbie? Can you see?' called Tom.

'Naw, but I can hear. There's horses coming along the wall. Coming up from Haltwhistle, I'd say.'

'The Lord of the Waste – or his men, like as not.'

'Whoever it is it's put the fear of God into the Kerrs. The whole pack of them are scurrying away back down towards Beggar's Bog.'

'That just leaves Little Dand and his companion,' said Tom, squinting down at the two of them there.

'Ye'd be best to finish the job and kill them now,' advised Hobbie grimly. 'It's bad blood indeed when a man is crippled. He'll be stirring up the Kerrs to come against you and yours until the thing is settled anyways. Settle it now and save yourself some grief.'

The slight figure Tom had struck with the ball from his arquebus and that Dand had tried to rescue had taken off its cloak to wrap it around the ruined hand. Little more than a lad, he stood tall and strong, with black hair seeming to soak up even the light of the setting sun. Tom looked at Eve and saw her frozen, horrified face, wide eyes resting on him still full of what she had done – and made him do.

'I cannot,' said Tom.

'I can,' grated Hobbie. 'Both of them in half a minute, for I have the longbow here . . .'

'*No!*' cried Eve. 'Hobbie! Think of the day!'

And so, when the Lord of the Waste arrived with his score of mounted men-at-arms reinforced by volunteers from Halt-whistle – Hugh Nixon himself amongst them – he found the little band in no need of his protection after all.

Tom tersely explained what had happened, and Hobbie advised Hugh to pass the message up to Jock o' the Side that the Kerrs had come and gone through the Busy Gap at the orders of men unknown about evil in spite of the goodness of the day – had come down led by Little Dand Kerr, but had gone back led by One-Hand Dand, which nickname would follow him through the Borders for what little time the Good Lord continued to allow him life.

CHAPTER EIGHT

The Castle on the Waste

As darkness fell, the twenty-five riders that made up the Lord of the Waste's party turned on to the Roman road above Gilsland village that led like a bowshot across the Waste to the castle of Bewcastle five miles distant. They had changed horses in Gilsland at the expense of Tom's uncle, who had been made expansive by relief and joy at the rescue, and the new ponies were fresh. They would be home in an hour. Even so, in the village itself they had bought flambards and these they lit as the last of the light bled away low on their right, and rode within two roaring, unsteady columns of golden light.

Tom would have known the uncle after whom he was named anywhere. Sir Thomas Musgrave, Captain of Bewcastle, was a tall, straight man approaching his fiftieth year with as much virile vigour as Lord Henry Carey, the Lord of the North, to whom he reported so regularly. His head wore a cap of steel grey, curling hair that seemed to make his steel bonnet unnecessary. He wore his beard in the full, square-cut fashion of an earlier time. His nose was an eagle's beak, broken out of line. His lips and eyes were narrow, the latter guarded and calculating, even when, as now, twinkling with expansive good humour. He was a kind of mirror to Tom, showing the younger man how he would look in twenty-five years or so, if he survived the intervening time.

But if Tom remembered his uncle almost perfectly, he found

he had all but forgotten his domain. He had forgotten how much of a waste the Waste of Bewcastle really was. The last glimmers of day before the flambards were lit exposed in its blood-red light a heave of desolation fit to flatten the cheeriest soul; a frost-bound desert moorland stretching up before them and away on either hand, wrinkled more than valleyed, with sparse woods where the land folded down; full of hummocks and hollows, the latter gathering mist to their grassy bottoms, low pools of mist set writhing and roiling by the bitterly incessant wind – mist that warned of water in the deadly traps of quick marsh there, bottomless bog-holes designed by the devil himself to suck the unwary to hell; and here and there above them as the blackness closed in, those gleaming little fires, lethal will o' the wisps, that had tempted many a be-nighted traveller to stumble blindly to his death.

Yet the desolation was not without its signs of humanity. The road along which their ponies trotted, though grassed over centuries since, was still a road easily discernible across the wild heave of the moorland, telling of the hand of ancient man; and beside it, moving out and away in fathomless patterns across the Waste were standing stones, great burial mounds, the half-open wrecks of ancient huts and habitations. And – who knew? – of pagan temples, where unrecorded blasphemies had been committed to the worship of long-forgotten deities before the one true God had been revealed to the long-dead inhabitants of the place.

But, thought Tom grimly, that Holy revelation had led the natives – among whose later generations he must himself be counted – to build castles, not kirks. In years to come, he suspected, when he and his were dust, there would be ten ruined forts to be counted here for every ruined church.

As darkness fell, the wind came up more fiercely than ever, setting the flambards' flames to battering and roaring, and howling in the distant crags and caverns like the Barguest out and hunting – the Barguest with its pack of spectral hounds, all in full cry together and at once. The sound – the Barguest itself – seemed the very soul of the place. It had been easy enough down in London, and even on the road north, to talk to Eve about his unreliable memories of childhood, for he simply now refused to admit such a thing could exist, even though he remembered seeing it with his own eyes. He was, in much of his thinking, a rational humanist, given that he was a man of his times – given, therefore, his solid Protestant faith. He saw nothing in his Bible, and heard nothing in the commentaries that expounded it to him every Sabbath and each holy day, about great ghostly dogs; but up here – up here on the Waste where it was said to be hunting and the devil did, in all conscience, seem very near indeed . . . things might well be different up here on the Waste.

Tom had to begin something of a reassessment of his gloomy thoughts as soon as they arrived at Bewcastle itself. The grim old fortress had been softened by a sprawl of outbuildings extending from the outer walls, whose occupants would retire within the castle itself as soon as danger threatened, no doubt. Even so, the presence of the byres, workshops, stores and dwellings bespoke a time of restful peace in the recent past at least, for they would make useful cover and dangerous kindling for any serious besieger of the fort; and the look of them, from the distance, lamps and torches lending the brightness of a golden necklace, bestowed an almost festive air to the craggy old walls.

Within the walls themselves, the first thing Tom saw and heard as he trotted with the others under the great portcullis of the gate, squarely in the corner opposite the main building of the keep, beside the stabling and the castle smithy, was the chapel. As the portcullis grated down behind them, shutting them in and the fears of the holy but haunted night outside, so he heard the bell begin to ring, summoning them all to prayer. At the door to the chapel they were greeted by the Lady Ellen whom Tom remembered from childhood, a round, apple-cheeked woman, with a warm heart and boundless good intentions that sometimes overstretched her ability to fulfil them. She gave him a hug that threatened to tear his side open and a smacking kiss that caused the priest to turn and frown –

and thus Tom recognized yet another old friend. Father Little had educated him from his first catechism until Carlisle Grammar School had seduced him far away.

It was into the chill, bare garrison chapel that they repaired as soon after dismounting as nature would allow, to celebrate an evensong extended and illuminated by a service of thanksgiving for their delivery from the Kerrs and safe arrival now. As Tom stood shoulder to shoulder with the little garrison and their guests, listening to the short sermon expounding on the Christmas text set down for the day, he was struck by the manner in which even here his uncle's old-fashioned tastes almost thoughtlessly dictated what went on. The service was from the old Prayer Book, with much less accommodation to Catholic sensibilities than the new one. The priest was a solid, down-to-earth lowland Scot, as Tom knew well, a man walking warily – sensibly – in the footsteps of Calvin and his Scottish acolyte John Knox. But little hellfire and damnation was called down, and when the congregation – and he called them his congregation – was called forward to the Eucharist, Tom saw that the priest was of that number who allowed the consecrated bread and the wine to touch the lips of everyone at worship; even of Eve and the other women, led by the Lady Ellen, not Sir Thomas's wife (the old man was single and childless), but a widowed sister who kept house for him. Lady Ellen was likely to be the busiest person in Bewcastle during the next twelve days, thought Tom, with a glow of affection. The priest was content to let them take their place where they stood in the order of communicants – not saving them for last as lesser souls, as some did.

By the end of the service, exhaustion and starvation were at war within Tom's sagging body, fighting it out to see which would claim him first. Exhaustion was not an option, though, for as they came out of the chapel into the central square of the ancient fortification, the Captain of Bewcastle clapped him on the shoulder.

'Matters of the spirit being satisfied, lad, let us turn to matters of the flesh, eh?' boomed Sir Thomas Musgrave. 'Even in these sad times. My Lady Ellen, is all prepared?'

'It is, Sir Thomas, as ever,' sang back the fair Ellen.

Three sides of the hall had been laid out for the Christmas feast. The top table sat raised on a dais and the two lesser tables stretched down the hall from the ends of that one, with trenchers, chairs and benches arranged down the outer sides only, leaving in the centre a broad area where servants could pass and entertainments be offered. Sir Thomas himself arranged those few who did not already know the order of their degrees at the table – Tom on his right hand, as honoured guest, and Eve, to her evident surprise and confusion, on Tom's right.

In the brief interim between the service and the supper, when the travellers had been shown their accommodation and allowed leisure for quick ablutions, Tom had taken a moment to rearrange his clothing, assess the damage to his linen done by the blood of his wound and readjust the bandages that held it stiff but safe. Of course, his aunt Ellen came to see how he did and to make sure he stood well aware that the offices of the fort – basic though they must seem after London and the Court – were all at his service. He warned her about the state of his linen but assured her that the wound itself was trifling. Then, fit for the court in all but his lack of face powder, he descended with her on his arm.

He did so to discover that Eve had changed out of her travelling clothes into the plain dress of green, blue and lavender squares in which she sat beside him now, which Tom recognized as the Graham tartan. Beyond his silent sister stood an empty place, in memory of his dead brother, and beyond that sat Hobbie.

Tom tore his eyes away from the vacant seat and looked around the hall. Here at the muted Christmas celebration he would expect to find the men closest to his uncle, and their wives. Order of precedence – as important here as at Her Majesty's Court – would dictate that, apart from honoured guests, relatives and their widows, the men seated closest to Sir Thomas would be the men who held most power from him. On any other occasion, in any other circumstance, he might have expected a reception line where, at his uncle's side, he would have made the formal acquaintance of these men; but things had fallen out differently tonight. Even the Lady Ellen was seated on the far side of his uncle, so any enquiries he had for her must needs be shouted across him. Tom must needs make use of Eve, therefore, in the times when Sir Thomas was not honouring him with his attention, and find out who else held what power within the keep and upon the Waste of Bewcastle.

The two that sat closest, beyond Lady Ellen on Sir Thomas's left hand, were a short, square man with a wrinkled, jowly bulldog's face, and a tall, square-jawed soldier, captain under Sir Thomas of the band that had saved them from the Kerrs.

The bulldog had not come with the rescuers, so his role in the castle was not military. Financial or organizational, then. Eve identified him as William Fenwick, the laird's factor, by which Tom understood at once that this was his uncle's agent, who ran his farms, dealt with his tenants, collected his rents and balanced his books – who took care of the business that Sir Thomas had no leisure or inclination to do for himself.

Fenwick the Factor was clearly a man of importance here, but he did not take up as much of Tom's attention as the other man – the soldier. Whenever Tom looked up, it seemed that the soldier was watching him with a brooding, almost threatening intensity. He wore a doublet of military cut – almost a jacket – and a sword. Most of the men at the table sat down still armed, a breach of etiquette that would never have been allowed in London at a formal occasion such as this; but this man's sword was unusual. It was a basket-hilted broadsword, thick of back and sharp of blade with a curve like a Jedburgh axe. Tom had heard swords like this called claymores, though the name was also applied to the big two-handed highland battle-sword; and from the look of things, this was a potent man-killer, no matter what you called it. 'That's Geordie Burn,' Eve told him later, 'captain of horse.' But no sooner had she given him the information than Tom made the more intimate acquaintance of Captain Burn, and of his claymore.

The feast itself began with a loyal toast, drunk to Her Majesty in good French wine, followed by another to the guests and a third to the season, and the feasting began when the porpoise was brought to the high table for Sir Thomas to carve. The porpoise seemed to have been baked in the bread oven recently vacated of the black bread trenchers sliced on the wooden ones before them. Sir Thomas took a fat slice of the choicest section behind the creature's head, and passed some, with due ceremony and courtesy, to Lady Ellen first, then to Tom and Eve. Then, as the fish, in increasing stages of dismemberment, worked its way down the table, those first served fell to eating. The porpoise was followed by a spiced pottage of oats and codfish. Again, the course began at the head of the table and worked its way slowly down. In old-fashioned ceremony, which seemed to suit very well with the way Sir Thomas ordered everything, the pottage was succeeded increasingly rapidly with baked herring, stewed lampreys and a huge eel pie. At this season there could be none of the sallets of fresh herbs Tom had learned to love in his Italian tutelage, and on this particular day Sir Thomas had ordered there be no flesh served; but the boiled bream and gurnards were at last succeeded with some winter-stored apples and wrinkled warden pears.

As each of the courses was removed from the bottom of the tables, so a toast was drunk, and Tom was soon very glad of the presence on table of flagons of good clean spring water with which the borderers mixed their wine – unlike Londoners, who would dare do no such thing with the foul liquid pumped out of the Thames.

As stomachs filled and the pace of consumption slowed, so conversation flowed. And when that too began to ebb, Sir Thomas called for entertainment. The first part of the entertainment was Sir Thomas's minstrel. Accompanying himself on the harp, this elderly worthy gave them 'The Ballad of Christmas Morning', then, less seasonably, 'The Ballad of Judas' Bargain'. After his songs, he juggled to great acclaim with some half-dozen naked daggers and completed his performance by executing a series of handstands on the points of ancient but sharp-looking swords. Next, one of the castle children, tutored by the priest of the kirk who accompanied him on a simple pipe, sang a pretty carol, of a dangerously Romish character, the youthful Protestant churches being as yet ill served in musical matters. A small consort of viols arrived and two pairs of soldiers got up and danced a reel. Two more got up and fell to wrestling, and it was something of a shock to Tom when he recognized them as his drivers and bodyguards Sim Armstrong and Archie Elliot. Pipers played. The last of the food was cleared. To the strains of the pipe, usquebaugh was brought, a rare treat here, and consumed both neat and – by Tom at least, and blessedly – diluted with yet more spring water.

After the whisky there was more wrestling, and another dance. This was done by two bare-footed men who leaped nimbly around swords laid at various dangerous angles upon the floor. The whole thing looked as risky as the minstrel's handstand and Tom was surprised that the floor was not littered with fingers and toes when it was done.

Then, after the sword dance, Captain Burn stood up. 'With your permission, Sir Thomas,' he said, and turned to Tom, frowning slightly. 'Master Musgrave. Your fame, sir, has come before you back to the place of your birth. You are a Master of the Ancient Masters in the Art and Science of Defence, much spoken of, I understand, at Court and upon the public stages of London itself. I wonder, sir, if you would edify us all, by demonstrating your mastery. Here. Now. Upon myself and my own blade.'

Of course, Tom could have pleaded the journey – the wound. He was exhausted, stiff and sore. In London he might have done so; but he was far from London now – as far as he had been in his youth as a volunteer in the Lowlands, at the battle of Nijmagen where his road to fame had begun. This was a garrison at the lonely heart of a dangerous place – none more so in all the kingdom, save a ship or two off the Spanish coast. This was a place where courteous pleasantries must needs take second place to the imperative of knowing your men – knowing who will stand with you and who will not, who will guard your life and who will lose it. If he was to be tested, he thought, then let it be sooner rather than later. Let it be now, in fact.

'Well, I am for you, Captain Burn, with all my heart,' he said and rose. 'With the licence of the Lord of the Waste and the Lady Ellen, of course.'

Sir Thomas nodded, smiling slightly with his narrow lips if not quite with his narrow eyes. Lady Ellen's eyes were anything but narrow, and her face was a picture of motherly concern.

Tom walked slowly round the right side of the table as Burn came round the left. As he moved, Tom unloosed his doublet so that as he came on to the piste between the tables, when all eyes were on him he could pull it off and lay it aside. A hiss of shock whispered round the table as the expectant audience saw the great red-brown stain on his shirt where his blood had dried. The Lady Ellen screamed – though that, mused Tom with an inward smile, could well have been the thought of the washing.

'You have been wounded, sir,' observed Burn.

'A scratch, Captain. Part of last night's adventurings. Sewn closed by the lady Eve and by Hobbie Noble there. Think no more of it.' As he spoke, he eased his back and shoulders, stretching the long-stiff muscles there, and made a pass or two as though he held a sword to see how his legs would react. They held up commendably and he began to think he might still do himself some credit. Escaping without being crippled would be a good start, he thought. 'Your blade is not protected, Captain, and neither is my own. Would you prefer to rely on skill? Or take assurance with a jacket, perhaps.'

'Oh, a pass or two at play, sir. Surely we may rely upon our skill?'

'As you wish.' Tom took off his sword belt as he spoke and slid the long Solingen blade out of its scabbard with a lingering hiss to echo the sound that had gone round the room at the sight of his bloodstained clothes. He wound his hand into the intricacies of the Ferrara silver basket of the hilt and wrapped fingers and thumb into their allotted hooks and handles. With his back casually to his opponent, he performed a series of more testing passes, frowning with concentration as he assessed what his saddle-sore buttocks and thighs could stand and what his side was like to allow him to do before it tore open again. Faster and faster he moved, easing and warming his muscles, only distantly aware of the hypnotic power his flashing point seemed to be having on his audience, particularly at the high table.

When at last Tom turned, he found Captain Burn ready and waiting for him, a little stiffly, in the high ward, as befitted such an elderly, heavy weapon. Tom moved to his own guard, and chose the hanging ward, with his point deceptively low. As soon as he was in position, he said to his opponent, 'Are you ready, Captain?'

A nod in reply, as slight as Hobbie Noble's jerk of the head; and following the action, the claymore came down in a blow that would have made old George Silver proud. But the fighting technique was as out of date as the sword and the English fencing master whose *Paradoxes of Defence* was the bible for an earlier generation. Tom turned the edge of the heavy weapon aside with the surprisingly resilient length of his own sword and stepped back – rather than stepping in to run his opponent through in the *coup de main* that would have ended the matter had this been a fight to the death.

Captain Burn recovered and resumed his guard, seemingly unaware how close to death he had passed. Frowning, he assumed the same dangerous high ward as before. Tom this time settled into the slightly more forceful open ward. His eyes focused on the point of the claymore as he waited the one beat Burn would take before launching his second attack. It came, cunningly flashing out to the right and swinging in to Tom's head as it came; but Tom's head was long gone. The instant the blade point stirred, Tom threw himself forward. He had the measure of the man and of his weapon technique now. As he moved, so his left hand reached out blindly but unerringly.

So that when Captain Burn completed his blow he found that his sword hilt was held by Tom's firm grip and the needle point of his opponent's rapier stood within a hair's breadth of his right eye, so close that when he blinked he felt it with his lashes. He disengaged and stepped back, shocked, unable to overlook how close he had come to losing much more than an exhibition bout. His mouth opened, but if he said anything the words were lost beneath the applause of the audience.

'But this would never serve in battle, Captain,' said Tom quietly as the clapping died. 'My blade is all very well for a show on the stage or the piste – for an exhibition or a duel. Were we to front each other on the battlefield, however, then yours would have the edge.'

What the embarrassed captain would have said to that Tom was never to find out, for as Burn drew breath to answer, a servant burst into the hall. 'There's fifty Kerrs at the gate, My Lord, and they want the man that crippled Dand.'

This time, when the Lady Ellen screamed, Tom knew it was nothing to do with the washing.

CHAPTER NINE

The Price of a Hand

During the feasting and the entertainments the wind had strengthened and the temperature had plunged even further. The sky was speckled with fiery brightness overhead and the moon was westering behind them, almost full and incredibly bright in the crystal clarity of the wind-scoured air; but something huge and threatening was stamping out the stars in the northern sky, over the lands whence the Kerrs had come.

They sat in a great black mass outside the Bewcastle gate now. Because of the massive moon it was possible to see areas of brightness – steel bonnets agleam and cold eyes glittering just beneath; pale faces with down-turned mouths. Above them a great cloud of smoke and steam gathered palely, as though they had brought some of that threatening cloud cover south with them.

Tom stood atop the great gate with Sir Thomas by his side. Both had come – with the others – straight from the hall, and were dressed for feasting not fighting. Tom and Sir Thomas stood up here apparently alone in the bright moonlight, but on Sir Thomas's other side a stream of quiet men came and whispered and went, and in the keep behind them, everything was silently astir. Much of the action, Tom noticed, seemed to centre around the rear of the silent smithy and he surmised there must be a secret passageway of some sort there.

Tom still wore only his bloodstained shirt, carried only his naked blade, and the cold cut through him like the blade itself, seeming to strike at his bones and his vitals; but the tension of the situation, the sudden, overwhelming danger he had brought on Bewcastle almost the very instant he arrived did more to snatch his breath away than the ice-laden wind.

'Who speaks for the Kerrs?' bellowed Sir Thomas.

' 'Tis I, as ye well know, Sir Thomas: Hugh of Stob,' came a cold, calculating, elderly voice from the anonymous heart of the mass of horsemen, 'and I call for the man that took young Dand's hand.'

Tom would have stepped forward at that, but his uncle's hand held him hard back. 'Ye make it sound like a wedding, Hugh,' said Sir Thomas easily, not at all disturbed by the stirring of outrage that went through the squadron of warlike reivers below.

'And if ye make light of the matter, Sir Thomas, then ye'll find that yer wit's not the only thing will catch light this night.'

'You mistake my purpose, Hugh. I meant that, were the affair to be seen as a wedding of sorts, then it might be amenable to a marriage settlement, of sorts.'

'A settlement, ye say?' A hint of avarice affirmed both the age and the Scottishness of the man in Tom's eyes; and just at that moment someone came close up behind Tom himself with his great travelling cloak, so that he stepped back into the shadows and became one with them as he wrapped the heavy woollen warmth around himself.

'Everyone pays the blackmail to someone, Hugh,' continued Sir Thomas. 'Some men pay it to prevent such matters arising, and some men might pay it in reparation for damage done; but call it a settlement for the sake of fair words this holy night.'

'A settlement. And how much of a settlement had ye in mind?'

'He's your lad, Hugh. 'Tis your hand, therefore. Name your price and we'll get down to business. Or is young Dand there with you? He may name his own price if he is.'

'He's not here,' came a new voice, young and clear; 'but I'll speak for him. He lost his hand saving me at Housesteads.'

'That's for you to decide, Hugh. I'll settle with you or with the lad, but when I settle, I settle for all and there's an end to the matter.'

Sir Thomas stepped back at that and dropped his voice. 'That'll give them something to think over, but it'll not keep them occupied for long. We must stay here to keep the pretence alive, but your jack will be up soon with a breastplate and backplate to boot. I'd hoped young Eve would stay to help you slip into the gear quietly, but she and Hobbie have disappeared. D'ye use those pretty pricks of yours in battle or would ye rather a man's sword like Geordie Burn's? I'd stay clear of Geordie if it comes to close work, mind: he'll not have forgiven you for besting him at those passes just now.'

There was time for no more speech, for Hugh of Stob was calling up again: 'He'll no be able to farm again, mind.'

'He never farmed in his life, Hugh. He reived and he whored and that was the sum of it. He can still hold a sword and he can still clasp a wench. It was his hand he lost, not his prick.'

'But a hand's a hand for all that. And there's the saddle to be thought of . . .'

'He's making time, sir,' breathed Tom. 'He has spies out, engineers coming among your outbuildings with petards like as not.'

'Aye,' breathed the Captain of Bewcastle, every inch the fighting commander. 'That, or he's sent elsewhere for more men.'

'Or both,' answered Tom, every inch his kin.

'We've saddles aplenty here, Hugh – the equal of Dand's, I've no doubt. Why, he can even take the great saddle I keep for my great black stallion when I go to the hunt with my hounds. Take it and welcome, though it would spoil my plans for the morrow; but I see you hesitate, for the saddle's not the issue. It's the matter of the hand, man, and the settlement for that.'

Tom felt a stirring at his back and slipped the cloak off his shoulders, then surrendered his rapier to shrug on a quilted, steel-covered jack like the one he had worn along the wall. Backplate was pressed in place as he fastened it, then breastplate slipped on and belted tight as his rapier was retrieved before a freezing bonnet was placed on his head, the thick leather lining as cold and hard as if it had been steel itself.

'One way or another we're out of time, sir,' he said to Sir Thomas.

'A moment more, lad,' said Sir Thomas, glancing back over his shoulder. 'We need a moment more . . .'

Tom took his cloak, wrapping it over his armour as he pulled off the bonnet and stepped forward in front of his uncle, apparently dressed for the cold, not for battle. 'I'm the man you seek, Hugh of Stob: Tom Musgrave, Master of Defence.' He thrust himself into full view and saw the ghost of his shadow before him, knowing he was framed against the moon. 'I took One-Hand Dand's hand because he sought to take my life. He was lucky I let him live, for he was set against me and he knew as well as you all do that I am a messenger for the Queen and the Council, carrying letters from the Lord of the North. Be careful what you stir up here, for you will follow the fate of Kerr of Ferniehurst, who marched with the rebel Dacre when I was nobbut a lad, and find your own Hell Beck at his hands. You sound like an ageing man, Hugh of Stob. You saw, I doubt not, what the Lord of the North left of Dacre's rebel army after the battle at Hell Beck; and I'll lay you were lucky indeed not to be amongst those left to rot there or strung up later by himself and Lord Scrope. Think on this, Hugh of Stob – and the rest of you. Is one Kerr hand worth a hundred Kerr necks?' He pronounced the name as Hobbie had done – 'Cur' like a worthless dog.

The Kerrs gave a great shout of outrage at this and all surged forward, every eye among them fastened on the turncoat Musgrave, who had started out one of their own but changed into an arrogant southern courtier now.

And that sat perfectly with the Captain of Bewcastle's plan, for, echoing the shout of rage with a great whoop of attack, the Bewcastle garrison's horsemen came thundering up the little valley that led round from the secret Gully Hole exit on the south side of the castle and debauched on to the flat area outside the main gate. With Geordie Burn himself in the lead, and the shrug of a little hillside behind them to shadow their numbers, the twenty horsemen hit the fifty Kerrs like a thunderbolt. The power of the charging Bewcastle horses shocked the sedentary Kerrs terribly. Tom had bewitched all their eyes so that the wild charge came as a complete surprise. The reiver ranks broke and the black phalanx of the Scottish horse shattered into a morass of melees down the slopes away to the south and east of the ancient keep.

The portcullis of the main gate screamed up at once and Sir Thomas led the foot soldiers out with Tom at his side. In the moonlight it was impossible to tell friend from foe – particularly for the men on foot. Sir Thomas showed the way, however, for every time he threw himself towards a fighting knot of men he called 'The Gravel', and one or other of the combatants answered 'The Waste!', and the hardy old soldier struck at once at the man who did not answer.

'The Grave!' called Tom, charging past Sir Thomas at the nearest group of riders. 'The Waste!' answered the nearest, and Tom thrust his rapier unerringly through thigh, saddlebag and horse of the next man beyond. The effect was so swift and spectacular that he lost his weapon at once – and near lost the hand that held it, like Dand Kerr had done. The pony collapsed, stone dead upon the spot, trapping the rider's good leg while the other jerked spasmodically, emitting a throbbing spring of blood. The dying man clamped his hands over his wound and let fall a ten-foot spear as he did so. Tom grabbed this and drove the butt end of it against the fallen man's forehead, stunning him as he jerked his rapier free once more; but then he slipped his sword into the belt of his breastplate and held on to the spear as being better suited to attacking horsemen – and easier to replace if lost in the fray.

Then his better angel prompted him to check on the state of his late foe. As he bent to do this, a blade whispered past his head and smashed into the armour on his shoulder where breastplate and backplate met. He turned, and for an instant could have sworn he was looking up into the face of the man he

71

had just helped – Captain Geordie Burn; but then the battle eddied like a river in spate and the two were swept apart. 'The Grave!' he called again, and was off into the thick of it once more.

So things proceeded for an uncounted time. Call and counter-call led Tom from one little melee to another, and he stabbed upwards with increasing confidence and accuracy, unseating horseman after horseman. But the battle was by no means going all one way: the little garrison were heavily outnumbered and the Kerrs had not ridden in alone – as both Tom and Sir Thomas had known all too well. Nor were they stupid or slow-witted men. At last exhausted, Tom called out, 'The Grave!'

'The Waste!' came a hoarse voice from across a little space. Tom turned towards it, eyes busy looking for enemies he might help his companion overcome; but instead he saw with horror that the outbuildings behind the horseman were alight. His attention distracted and his own wits slowed by fatigue, Tom was slow to see what was happening. The horseman who had answered him swung round into the charge and came full at him. Like Tom, he was armed with a lance, but this one was thirteen feet long and was couched four feet up from the ground and pointing unerringly at his breast.

It was at that moment that Tom remembered riding with Hobbie as a young man, learning from the old master how to spear salmon in the Black Lyne river – spearing quick wild salmon in the brown water, from horseback, with a spear exactly like this one; and he knew that he was dead, but he also knew what he must do to die with honour. The butt of his own spear slammed to the ground and his right foot stamped down upon it. Out stretched his left arm, angling the spearpoint down so that its solid, steel-tipped length pointed directly at the pit of the galloping pony's throat. He raised the Jedburgh axe, turned his body a little to offer a surface that a spear might glance off, gritted his teeth and stood ready for the shock.

CHAPTER TEN

Hobbie Noble and the Barguest

Tom was ready for a shock from the front – and was within an instant of receiving it – when he was hit from the back instead – hit from the back and ridden down. The muscular chest of a pony knocked him aside and he spun away to slide across the icy ground as the two horsemen met like thunder above him. The moon shone on the face of the newcomer who had ridden him down and saved him: it was Geordie Burn.

'Back to the castle,' yelled Geordie. 'The Captain is calling for ye.'

Tom picked himself up and ran back through the gate, which was no great distance away. It was lucky the gate was so close at hand, for the ground beside it was littered with dead and dying, men and ponies. The last of the moonlight and the growing brightness of the flaming buildings showed the grim guards beneath the portcullis who he was; otherwise, like many of the bodies littering the flags, he would have been blown back out by the guns they held trained on him.

As he entered the courtyard, so his uncle turned to greet him. At the same time, the dog-faced factor Fenwick – a useful man in a battle after all – said, 'That's all in now, Captain, save for Geordie Burn and the others that you know of.'

'Lower the portcullis,' ordered Sir Thomas. 'We'll send out spies through the Gully Hole at once. I want men to find our wounded, guide Geordie and the others back, and discover what in hell's name has happened to Hobbie Noble and the girl and my black stallion.'

'Hobbie's a law unto himself, as ye know, Captain,' said Fenwick; 'and the girl's a Graham. Did ye not see the plaid she wore tonight? Mebbe the Nobles and the Grahams owe the Kerrs some settlement of their own that can be paid with the price of a little treachery and a good horse.'

'If they meant mischief, they'd have led the Kerr spies in through your Gully Hole already,' said Tom breathlessly. 'And there'd be more than your outbuildings afire.'

''Tis a secret way,' said Fenwick frostily.

'Have ye any secrets Hobbie doesn't know the truth of?' asked Tom, all innocent surprise.

'The boy's right,' said Sir Thomas. 'If Hobbie was with the Kerrs, then their horse would be among us as we speak – instead of assembling outside the gate again.'

'To continue our discussions about Dand's hand,' said Tom: 'you should let them have me. I'm worth preserving for the blackmail alone.'

'A gallant offer and well meant I am sure; but ye must see that I cannot let them have my kin, nor the Queen's messenger: the names of the Lords of the Waste and the North would never stand the shock. My standing and reputation on the Borders and in the Court would be dead on the instant, and even were I to settle the matter of Dand's hand as I mentioned, there would be no end to the Kerrs, Armstrongs, Johnstones and such who would suddenly find grievances also needing settlement.

'But let us see what's toward, shall we? And draw our next plan of action accordingly.'

There were only five Kerr horsemen now, and they sat well back from the gate where arquebus, gun, crossbow and long-bow were likely to do them little damage, out of the light of the blazing buildings around the outer wall of the fort; but Tom and Sir Thomas both knew they had never killed or wounded forty-five – probably no more than half a dozen in all, given the way melees usually came out. So there were forty more of them

– with the spies who had fired the outbuildings – all out there in the stormy darkness; and up to mischief, no doubt.

Of Geordie Burn and the last of the garrison horse there was no sign.

'Hell Beck is it, Master Musgrave?' called Hugh of Stob, his voice shaking with rage. 'Ye's'll have me remember Hell Beck? Well, sir, if I might take the liberty, I'd ask you to think on Lord Buccleuch's work in the Middle March with the Kerrs of Stob and Ferniehurst and Cessford at his side. Remember Redesdale and Tynedayle and Coquetdale, sir, and where was your Lord of the North then?'

'Yet to be born, my wee mannie,' bellowed Sir Thomas, 'for 'tis more than seventy years since; and if ye mind the raids Buccleuch did on Redesdale, Hugh, then ye're an older man than I thought ye. As well tell us to remember Bannockburn; and I'll call down the battles of Berwick and Solway Moss and the slaughter done at both, if it's a lesson in history ye want. I'll call down Flodden Field!'

'No lesson in history, Thomas Musgrave,' spat back Hugh Kerr. 'Not from the likes of you. But I'll give you a lesson you've needed this twenty year and more. A lesson in tactics and terror!'

As Hugh Kerr spoke these last words, so he jerked his horse's head in a prearranged signal. The little group split up and scattered now that the negotiations were done, and the five horsemen sped along well-planned lines, each to a prearranged destination.

But, just at the very minute Hugh of Stob moved, as though released by the very same signal, something huge and terrifying came over the western skyline and stood framed against the setting moon on the ridge above the valley that led from the Gully Hole.

It was the size of a horse, and a proper horse at that – higher by far and heavier than the hobbie horses here: black – coal black – from massive muzzle to sweeping tail; a huge, hulking monstrosity, all massive misshapen head, mouth agape and belching fire; eyes ablaze as red as hell and bright enough to send beams out over the snarling wrinkles of its slobbering muzzle. It raised its head against the moon and such a howl came from it as never was heard on the Borders. As tall as a tall man to the shoulder with its head nearly a yard higher still, it reared and howled and capered on the skyline while round about it gathered a pack of smaller, man-sized hounds, all of them glowing and gleaming with a hellish, baleful light.

Tom stood, thunderstruck, watching the worst of his nightmares take life before his eyes; and he was by no means alone in that.

Then, still screaming and howling, the whole wild pack of them turned and came down the valley into the heart of the attacking Kerrs. A secret squadron of Kerrs that had been following Geordie Burn's surprise attack back towards the Gully Hole came screaming out again, wild with terror; and all the others, creeping on their own pre-planned missions, saw the horror overtaking their clansmen, kith and kin.

Even Hugh Kerr of Stob, their oldest and wisest – and most fearsome – froze upon his horse and sat struck with horror like Lot's wife turned to salt. Like some victim of the Gorgon, he stayed until his horse reared in simple terror at the ghastly horror rushing down on him, burning through the shadows with its huge, howling muzzle seemingly all alight.

'The Barguest!' screamed Hugh of Stob. 'Gods save us, it is the Barguest!' and at his words the whole clan of them took flight.

Wisely so, for their plans were in ruins and their valour broken; and down behind the howling horror came more of the garrison horsemen, led by Geordie Burn still, regrouped, rearmed, and taking no prisoners. As the wild hunt streamed past the gate, so the portcullis went up again and the rest of the garrison ran out on foot to send the fleeing Kerrs upon their way with shower after shower of arrows, quarrels, shot and curses.

Tom ran out with the rest, his head ablaze and his mind in a whirl. The others slowed at the edge of the light, but Tom plunged on into the darkness after the monstrous dog and its

wild pack of hounds. For it was the very creature he had come
here to hunt – the thing that had killed his brother John, that
could set the Borders alight more swiftly even than godless
Kerrs come marauding and reiving and out for revenge on
Christmas night itself.

As he ran, he reasoned – he could not help himself. For what
sort of a hell-hound was it that one night terrorized an innocent
man to death, and a few nights later frightened off an army set
to kidnap and ransom his brother – perhaps even slaughter his
uncle? And why had Hobbie and Eve both vanished at the
moment they were needed the most? Where were the hounds
with which its Lord would hunt the Waste on the morrow? And
where oh where was the great black stallion Sir Thomas kept
for the hunting?

Tom slowed to a walk, winded and exhausted. The light from
the burning outhouses sent a long, unsteady shadow, just
visibly, down a slope of frozen moorland in front of him,
visible only because it was frozen white and his eyes were
adjusting to the starlight; and there they were, in the valley
bottom, surprisingly close at hand. He knew it was them
because of the dogs, and because of the shape of the great
black horse, and because he could hear Hobbie laughing.

'Hobbie!' he called, and the laughter stopped.

'Is it yourself, lad?'

'Who else?' came Eve's cool voice. 'I told you. It's as well we
were dealing with old Hugh Kerr of Stob instead of young
Thomas Musgrave of London town. There now, boy, you were
wonderful,' she crooned to Sir Thomas's great black hunter.
'The mask is off and you're all right, see?'

Something shapeless fell to the ground, giving off in the
restless air a smell of candle wax and sulphur. Tom understood
almost all of it then, and what he still wondered about could
wait until morning, he thought.

'Some hay and some rest and you'll all be ready for the
Lord's great hunt in the morning,' she said.

'He'll still go hunting, even with Bewcastle as it is?'

'Some clearing up, but no rebuilding – we'll all live within the walls until the matter's settled once and for all,' said Hobbie. 'For it won't end here. There's Kerrs must pay for disturbing Bewcastle; and there'll be a good few more widows made on both sides by this night's work. Blood and vengeance: the law of the Borders.'

'Blood and vengeance and pride. And yes, he'll hunt,' said Eve. 'He's the Lord of the Waste. It is Yule. He'll hawk and he'll hunt and he'll scour the moss, for there'll be wounded Kerrs out there, if they make it through this bitter night alive; and the stags he's been saving – if the live Kerrs overlook them – and foxes and hares. All for the hunting by the Lord and his guests on the day after Christmas Day. It's what's expected and he'd never open himself to shame and scorn by doing any less.' Was there bitterness there? It was difficult to tell in her cool, measured tones.

'Naw,' said Hobbie, exultantly. 'There'll naw be any Kerrs to hunt. With horse or without they'll be back in their bothies in Stob before daybreak! And under their beds and shaking wi' fear – those that has beds, at the least. Did ye not see them run, little Eve? I swear one or two took wings and flew they were so overcome with sheer stark mitherin' terror!' He clapped Tom on the shoulder and slid a fatherly arm round Eve as she led the big black stallion back towards the guttering fires of Bewcastle; and the hounds trotted cheerfully at their heels. 'There'll be ballads about this night, mark my words,' continued Hobbie gleefully: 'how a girl and a horse and a cunning old reiver put the whole of the Kerrs to flight. The Lord of the Waste'll get his minstrel to write it, like as not, and we'll sing it at supper on Twelfth Night after the mummers' play. We'll call it "Hobbie Noble and the Barguest" and they'll sing it for years to come!'

Hobbie threw back his head and laughed; and, as they crested the rise and walked into the light, he threw back his head and howled at the top of his lungs, repeating the terrible sound he had made for his make-believe monster.

Out in the darkness, quite close at hand, something answered him.

CHAPTER ELEVEN

The Master of the Hunt

The portcullis would have remained safely down in any case, after the last fires amongst the ruined outhouses had been extinguished. The Captain of the Castle would have talked to his men, hale and wounded, congratulating them on this night's work and warning them to remain on their guard. The women of the castle, led by the Lady Ellen, Eve amongst them, would have succoured the wounded and laid out the dead, two from the garrison and four unrecovered by the fleeing Kerrs. The full garrison would have had to sleep doubled-up on a war footing, with straw palliasses blanketed with plaid replacing tables in the hall. Bewcastle's priest, Father Little, would have celebrated midnight mass in any case.

But all these things were lent an extra flavour by the ghostly echo that had answered Hobbie's last great Barguest howl. That echo, and much that had caused and surrounded it, gave added flavour to the festivities that began early on the morrow, too – especially to the Lord of the Waste's great Christmas hunt.

Tom, as honoured guest, retained the little chamber assigned to him alone, though in a flash of insight he realized it was probably the quarters of Geordie Burn, consigned to the main hall now with his men. As he prepared for bed, deciding wearily to leave his disturbance of his aunt's washerwoman until the morning, he saw that the bandages at his side were damp and glistening. Weary as he was, therefore, he went back down to that area of the kitchens that had been set aside as a hospital.

Even though the chamber in which Tom was housed seemed quite isolated, and finding his way back to the main areas seemed to necessitate his passing a surprising number of open doors and manned guard points, he really never doubted he would find his way to the kitchens. Even could he not follow his nose, he could follow his ears, for he had thought he would find the place by following the screams: he remembered battlefield hospitals too well from his youth. But the whole area was quiet when he got there, women softly passing from one man to another with warm drinks, which seemed to be calming even the severely wounded and offering a kind of oblivion.

Aware of his own standing and importance here though he was, and well schooled in the exercise of precedence and consequence by simple observation of such luminaries as the Earl of Essex at court, Tom was nevertheless content to wait in line. Although all he needed to do was catch the Lady Ellen's eye – or Eve's, come to that – and he would be tended first of all, nevertheless he stood and waited. There were men here with heads open to the bone, arms cut and broken, with stab wounds, spear gashes, hoof-clubbings and the like. His own wound, treated but torn open by the wild activity of the last few hours, seemed hardly worth worrying the women so busily nursing.

Yet as he turned to go and do the best he could for himself, two things conspired to stop him. Eve looked up from the man she was tending and softly called to him: 'Tom, have you ever seen a wound like this?'

The wounded man was Archie Elliot, the second driver from the coach, companion on the ride along the Wall, and champion wrestler of the evening. He had been one of the footsoldiers running out into the melee after Geordie Burn's great charge, evidently, although Tom had seen little of him during the battle itself. He lay face-down now, his shoulders and back uncovered, as Eve completed a neat job of simple stitching on him. 'Have you seen wounds such as these?' she repeated, pulling a cloth out of a bowl of steaming water liberally afloat with dried herbs, and mopping the drying blood from the swollen flesh.

Tom looked more closely. It seemed at first glance that Archie had been cut by three strokes of the same sword, for three wounds ran in parallel across his back and shoulders. Tom tried to imagine how accurately and how swiftly a single blade would have to have been wielded to cause such an effect. A master such as himself would have been hard put to reproduce it on a subject standing still. How it had been done in the heat of battle to a wildly fighting soldier, he could not begin to guess.

'Have you asked him how it was done?' he enquired quietly.

'Before he fainted. He has no idea, save that he was hit hard and thrown down.'

'Hit once, or hit and hit again?'

Eve shrugged, in the French manner. She signalled to a couple of lightly wounded to carry him away. 'Now, what about you?' she asked.

He showed her his wound, self-consciously among so much more mortal damage, but she frowned. 'This may need re-stitching,' she said, her voice severe. 'It needs washing and re-bandaging. And I have an unguent here will ease the inflammation.' She called softly to one of her helpers – and Tom realized with a little start that the other women were all deferring to the Lady Ellen first, as a matter of course, and then to Eve. Then, like any cadet after his first battle, he fell to prodding the cut in his side, surprised by how well it seemed to be healing, how neatly it had been sutured – before his activities had torn the stitches – and by how carefully it had been filled with powders and unguents to speed its recovery.

Or he did this until Eve slapped his fingers away like a mother correcting a child, and handed him something instead. He took a little horn cup.

'Drink this,' she said as she fell to working on his side again. 'It will help you sleep in case the pain disturbs you in the night.'

He sniffed it and looked at her with his eyebrow slightly raised.

'A weak infusion of mandragora,' she said. ' 'Twill rebalance your humours and by easing the fiery elements assist rest and recovery, for it is governed by Mercury.'

He did as she bade him and was lucky to make it back to his little chamber without dozing off on the cold stone stair; though he himself thought that he would have slept like the dead without the bitter little potion, and woken just as refreshed and energetic to greet the bright, brokenly clouded morning.

In fact it was the hounds, not the daylight, that woke Tom. Their well-tuned baying seemed at strange variance with the wild howling they had made last night as they charged down the valley behind Sir Thomas's great black stallion so cunningly disguised. Now it was clear that the pack had been chosen for their mouths, the treble barking setting a pleasant line over the tenor and bass baying. Tom thought wistfully for a moment of his friend Will Shakespeare. For while Tom himself had been in that vicious little battle yesternight, Will himself, or Dick Burbage, in the person of Theseus the Prince of Athens, would have been standing before the Queen and all her court, boasting of the well-tuned voices of his hounds of Thessaly. The words of the play, beautiful though they were, seemed worlds away from the fierce reality outside in the freezing morning – as the dream of midsummer was far away from the reality of Christmas; and, indeed, as Blackfriars was from Bewcastle.

Thus philosophical, Tom heaved himself out of bed, wrapping his cloak – warmed by serving as a blanket – about his shoulders at once. There was a bowl of water by his bed, fortunately fashioned of pewter. He had to punch the surface of the liquid twice before the ice would break. His toilet, therefore, like his dressing, was necessarily brief. Only the razor-sharp Solingen steel of his daggers would have allowed him to make as good a fist of scraping the beard off his jaw as he did. Not for the first time, he thanked God for the prevailing fashion that dictated a point of beard over the cleft in his square chin and a curl of moustaches on his tender upper lip.

As Tom clattered down the stone stair from his quarters,

Uncle Thomas met him and offered him the services of his personal barber.

'Perhaps on the morrow,' answered Tom cheerfully. 'It is your washerwoman I need today . . .'

'Fear not,' he answered. 'It was the Lady Ellen's last word before she went to bed last night and it will be among the first of her thoughts this morning, I am sure.'

The main hall was astir, and Lady Ellen's other concerns were clearly legion. Last night's bedding was being packed away and preparations were in train for the busy social occasion that was the Lord of the Waste's Christmas hunt. Noting in his mind the way in which there seemed to be three levels of authority within his uncle, one to suit each title, Tom passed out of hail of his family relative, Uncle Thomas, through the domain of his social and courtly uncle, the Lord of the Waste, and out into the command of his warlike, battle-commander uncle, the Captain of Bewcastle. Here, in the castle yard between the keep and the gate, he met Geordie Burn returning from his first patrol of the day.

'All quiet?'

Captain Burn glanced down at him and Tom felt last night's enmity still smouldering there; but Burn was content to be civil for the time being. 'Quiet on the Waste,' he said. 'Not a Kerr or a Barguest in sight – as far as a swift sweep can descry.'

'Good,' called Hobbie Noble, stepping out of the long kennel that stood along the wall beside the stable. 'Then the hunting will proceed unchecked. I can finish preparing my hounds. And you, Captain Burn, if you would be so good, may release a couple of your riders to swell the ranks of my men. For I am Master of the Lord's Hunt and this day of all days that puts me in the highest standing.'

Burn's usually severe face broke into a swift grin. 'After last night, Hobbie, if your standing was any higher, you'd be talking to St Peter at Heaven's Gate.'

'Good,' Tom echoed Hobbie. 'Then I too may be about my business.' Tom called for a pony from the garrison stock, saddled it himself while the groom that brought it looked to the rest of the tack and called across to Captain Burn, who was performing the exact opposite of the offices on his own steaming mount. 'The road to the right leads straight to the town still?'

'It does,' confirmed Captain Burn, his smile long vanished.

'And the smithy ten minutes down?'

'Halfway to the town, as it ever was,' confirmed Hobbie.

'Good. I have a visit overdue.'

'You'll need to be quick,' warned Hobbie. 'The Lord of the Waste may forgive your absence at the early meal – may even wink at your face missing from early services; but if you miss the first reception or the Hunt Mass, then you will be struck off the list of his relations. Even though you be the last of them left, lad.'

'You waste your time in any event. Mistress Eve remained in the castle through the night,' said Burn, possessively.

'It is not my sister I mean to visit,' said Tom, swinging into the saddle as he spoke. 'It is my brother.'

In spite of the advice of both Burn and Hobbie, Tom swung easily to the left as soon as he got outside the castle gate. He rode thoughtfully up the slope above Kirk Beck that flowed down to Bewcastle town, then he swung away up towards the Waste itself, his eyes busy on the ground. Only when he had gained a little ridge and could look away across the main section of the Waste itself towards the Scottish border did he pause and sit, still deep in thought. He could see both the forbidding, frozen emptiness of it and the slow gathering of the black cloud above it, but his eyes remained fixed on the vastness as though he could see things otherwise invisible up there. Only after a few long moments did he turn and begin to direct his pony's steps across the fell behind the fort and down towards the town itself.

As he rode down the hillside, he suddenly began to address his thoughts to the sure-footed little chestnut, as though it had been the man with whom it shared its name.

'Ye see, my little hobbie horse, the first part of my own especial hunt must be the Barguest itself. Does it exist or does it not? If it does exist, then how and why did it kill John? If it does not exist, then who killed John, how and why? And who then pulled the Barguest into his murder, how and why?'

The horse gave a soft whinny, as though it was content to mull over these musings with the Master of Logic on its back; but in fact it wasn't. Like all of the animals in Bewcastle fort, it was on edge, high-strung with the excitement engendered by Hobbie Noble, his hounds and his preparations for the other, more physical hunt.

'Have the adventures of the last two nights moved us any further forward?' the Master of Logic continued quietly. 'Silent horsemen following us means that this is not some little local matter – that there are powers here involved; more than just the Lord of the North growing nervous at a lack of snow in the reiving time and a trusted servant's servant dead. Someone else at court is involved – someone who is not close to the Lord of the North, or, therefore, to the Council; but someone with power and influence that can reach even to this godforsaken place. And whoever is not with us must be against us.

'But that is speculation which lies beyond calculation at present. We have other, sharper matters near at hand – a dagger in my side for one, that makes murder more likely, as was explained to Eve; and that explanation calculatedly offered. For is she not the most likely culprit in the matter of John's murder, having the most opportunity, being married to the victim, the most of gain, in the reclamation of her inheritance, the valley of the Black Lyne? And, clearly, having the ability, for she is a strong and intrepid woman and a fearsome herbalist. And the support, should she have chosen to call upon it, for either Geordie Burn or Hobbie Noble would clearly dance all the way down to hell for her. But she says they were not together on the day John died – that he was about his business and she was about hers. Here is a matter to be examined further. And here is a second: why would she call in the Barguest and all this wide, dangerous interest, when she might have done the thing privately and secretly with none the wiser?'

The little horse whinnied then, and Tom looked up to see that there, by the road in front of them stood the smithy where John and Eve had made their home – where Tom's father and mother in their turn had made their home, and where John and Tom themselves had grown through boyhood. The square grey house with the smithy built into the hillside behind stood halfway between the castle and the town. For John, like his father, had been the castle's battle-smith in time of restlessness and the town's blacksmith in times of calm.

Tom would have stopped there, but mindful of Hobbie's words – and of his more urgent mission – he decided to return later, and so rode on down the hill, drawing nearer to the gurgling brook of Kirk Beck, which would become the White Lyne when it attained riverhood further downstream, and over the bridge that was the heart of Bewcastle town. As he rode, he continued to examine the reasons for his sister's guilt, but silently now. Of all the investigation so far, this was the area that he did not wish to discuss at length with the man he was going to visit.

Then he began to speak again, moving on to another topic that might be painful also. 'And Hobbie. What of Hobbie last night? At a stroke he proved he might at will bring the Barguest to life. This was no doubt a skill he would have kept close secret had the Kerrs not called it to light. But it is a cause for concern, is it not? And he could have been as swift with the dagger as Eve the night before. Only I cannot see that they could be confederated together in the matter of the stabbing or I should be stark, not stitched – dead, not deliberating.

'And there's another thing, for I have tested Eve herself now. She could have completed her killing work last night, had the dagger been hers and the stitches the result of Hobbie's presence in the coach. Indeed, she could have despatched me earlier still, I believe, with her unguents and her physics, without waiting for mandragora last night.

'And I have tested Hobbie, too, in case the situation was the opposite within the coach. For if he had stabbed me at Ware and dared not finish his work in front of Eve, then he could have despatched me in the dark last night and blamed the battle or the Barguest as he chose; but, again, he did nothing of the sort.

'Or it could have been an Armstrong dagger in the hands of Sim; or an Elliot dagger in the fist of Archie. Or a dagger of one of the rioters in Ware, confederated to the horsemen with muffled hooves, as were the Kerrs, like as not, or One-Hand Dand at the least, as is someone in Bewcastle fort as well. Someone like Geordie Burn, perhaps, who would have killed me in the melee last night but saved me instead. His motives need untangling, as do all of their motives, I fear – but carefully, like a nest of vipers . . .'

The kirk after which the beck was named, like the kirk at Blackpool Gate, stood a little back from the stream, and the churchyard that belonged to it stood up the hill behind it. Tom, therefore, was able to tether his pony at the churchyard gate under the sloping hillside and go in without disturbing the services in the kirk itself – services slipped in by a busy Father Crawford Little between the imperious demands of a less than heavenly Lord.

'They've not been able to lay you deep, then, Johnny,' Tom said, looking down along the length of the new-made grave. There was no marker as yet, but it was the only new grave in the yard. Sunlight swept across the place like blades stabbing between the clouds and, as it came and went, it cast the shadow of a great cross over the new-turned earth. The bitter wind came sobbing out of the north, bringing tears to Tom's eyes and making them seem to be freezing upon his cheeks.

'Of course, with the earth like iron, it's a wonder they managed to lay you in its bosom at all. A shallow grave's no bad thing, Johnny, for I may have to summon you up and out of it long before Judgement Day. But let us proceed a little more with logic before we resort to picks or shovels.'

'And to bishops, come to that,' said a familiar voice behind him. 'You'll need the word of a bishop to touch that grave.'

Tom turned to see Father Little standing by the great ancient cross upon which the Musgrave boys had played like Barbary apes in times past.

'I have an order of the Council,' he answered easily, 'signed by at least one archbishop. I am, in effect, the Queen's Crowner here, should I exercise the full extent of my power. That will do in this case, I think.'

'You are grown to high estate then, my Tommy – a great man at court.'

'No, Father. It is the matter, not the man, that is deemed to be great.'

The old priest smiled, his open face crinkling and his blue eyes twinkling. It was not a merry smile, as might be suited to the season, but a smile that took account of the way the world went when one brother stood at the grave of another, talking over the matter of his murder; and yet it was a smile, and it warmed Tom's heart.

'But I interrupted,' said Father Little, softly.

'An exercise in logic, Father,' said Tom, equally softly. 'A chopping through of the matter here in the manner you first taught me, that I carry on in my generation merely like a dwarf on the shoulder of a giant.'

Father Little laughed at that. 'Did I teach you the wisdom of the ancients that you quote them back at me? I had thought I taught you only the catechisms of your own true faith – and the commandments, so that you might be sure to break them all at some time or another, I fear.'

Tom looked down at John's raw grave. 'You told me that it was a saying of Bernard of Chartres,' he said; 'but, good Father, how many commandments have been broken here?' Then he continued speaking before the priest could answer him. 'The sixth – that's for certain: *Thou shalt not kill*; the seventh, like as not . . .'

'Adultery. Your favourite, as I recall . . .'

'Or if not the seventh, the tenth – the coveting, if not the taking, of thy neighbour's wife. The eighth, stealing . . .'

'Stealing is the Borders' sin. And so, before you add it, is the ninth.'

'But here especially, Father. There has been a deal of false witness here; and much that has been sworn to – and sworn to on oath – is nevertheless false, so the name of the Lord has been taken in vain. The Sabbath, indeed Christmas Day, has been neither honoured nor kept holy. And there is an image abroad, is there not? – An image of a creature that is under the earth. If the creature itself is a demon, then the image is a sin – and people coming very near to worshipping it, this Barguest, real or manufactured.'

'So, all that stands unbroken is the honouring of fathers. On earth and in heaven,' said Father Little sadly.

'But the chain of logic is not yet complete; indeed I have hardly begun to forge it,' said Tom grimly. 'There are sins here yet to be uncovered, Father. And, like as not, more deaths to come.'

CHAPTER TWELVE

The Laird of Hermitage

I t so befell, and by apparent coincidence, that Father Little
had the liberty to accompany Tom back to Bewcastle fort –
and the need to go thither at once, or he would be late for the
Hunting Mass. Of necessity, therefore, they travelled together,
and both in turn astride Tom's pony, for priests in the Borders
went on two feet, no matter how urgent their mission, while
bishops, archbishops and cardinals went on four. It was a
mildly subversive variation on the riddle of the Sphinx that
Father Little had taught to Tom, along with so much else,
before releasing him to the grammar school in his youth.

It took a good deal of heated negotiation to decide they
should take turn about. Then, while they went up the hill with
some urgency towards the smithy and the fort, now one
walking now the other at the bridle like the veriest groom,
they continued to talk.

'You have never taken against your sister Eve,' said Father
Little at once. 'You cannot believe her guilty.'

'I have not and do not; but I can see how a man might have
reason to,' answered Tom forthrightly, then spent the next few
minutes explaining his reason to his new confidant.

'But she loved your brother more than life itself,' answered
Father Little, sweeping away logic with all the practice of a
priest whose faith is founded in belief before reason. 'Did ye not
see the flowers on John's grave?'

'Aye. Christmas roses.'

'Hard to come by. Brought and laid there at great cost of effort, pocket and spirit. A sign of miraculous love, Tom.'

'Father, d'ye not know Eve for a wise woman? I've no doubt she has gardens of herbs and physics behind the smithy though I've scarce had leisure to look. She has packed this wound in my side with secret physics. She put me to sleep last night with mandragora, much beloved of witches. And you point out her sign of love to me . . .'

'The Christmas roses, aye . . .'

'. . . also known as black hellebore – more deadly even than mandrake roots and crocuses and daffodil corms, the juice of poppies and half the toadstools in the darkest woods.'

'You speak with authority, lad.'

'With some. I made the acquaintance of Gerard the Herbalist some six months since over the matter of some poisonings.'

'With hellebore?'

'With belladonna, aconite and such. I'll lay odds we would find nightshade, monk's hood and wolf's bane beside what's left of the Christmas roses in the smithy's physic garden, as surely as we would find rosemary and sage in the herb garden.'

'If they are there, lad, it is because they can help as well as heal. You have yourself said that the infusion of mandragora she gave to you last night helped your wound.'

'It did. It helped my slumbers at the least. And had I been constipated 'twould certainly have helped with that. I am purged, blood-let and balanced in humours; I am a new man altogether.'

'When it could just as easily have torn your soul from your body and destined you for poor John's side – made you new-born with a vengeance,' countered Father Little severely.

This conversation served to carry them as far as the smithy and, had they not both been too well aware that the Lord of the Waste would be impatient for his mass and his hunting, they might have lingered a little, to test the truth of Tom's words; but on they trotted, Tom up and Father Little panting at the pony's head. 'If not Eve, then who next?' puffed the priest.

And Tom took him through his thoughts about Hobbie Noble and Captain Burn.

'Geordie Burn is a proud and stubborn man, short of temper and long of memory,' the priest allowed. 'He has reasons more than most to feel threatened and ill-at-ease when he stands with the Captain of Bewcastle. But I see no marks of evil ingrained within him. He would serve you ill, I've no doubt, for you bested him at the swordplay last night and, he fears, you may best him again with Eve, of whom he hopes great things now she is free to give her heart once more. He has waited in John's shadow this ten years and more. I believe she is the reason he remains when he has so many good reasons to go.'

'Waited? No more than that?'

'Eve would allow no more, even had he proposed it. She loved John; and Geordie feared him a little, as he fears you. So he was with John as he is with you, but that he had no immediate cause to kill him.'

'Except for the hope of Eve's hand.'

'Now where is your logic, Tom? To kill John would be to lose her for ever. Would she marry the man that had killed the husband she loved – though she loved the murderer still?'

'Ho! Now there is a question fit for the Borders! Or for some twisted tale in the telling of Kit Marlowe, Tom Kyd, or their like. Not even Will Shakespeare could untangle such a knot as that one!'

'But your answer, Tom. Ye see that Eve could never love him then?'

'Aye. I see it.'

'Good. But remember, you do not sit in that blessedly safe seat. Geordie might think he has reason to kill you – especially if Eve's eyes turn more kindly towards you; and it was to yourself, remember, that she ran the instant John was underground.'

'Not to me – to the Lord of the North. And she didn't run; she came south with Hobbie at my uncle's direction.'

'Indeed. So you may believe. And there are two more powders for this potion of suspicion you have abrewing.'

'Hobbie, yes, as I have said, though I have known the man longer than I have known yourself, Father. But my uncle . . .'

'Your uncle is a desperate man, Tom – a desperate man in a desperate situation.'

'What do you mean by that?'

'Did I teach you nothing, my son? Use your eyes. But if I were to ask any man to explain the deeper, darker matters to you, then here comes that very man now.'

As Father Little spoke, so a band of horsemen topped the ridge above and ahead of them, and went cantering down towards Bewcastle fort with banners fluttering, all gaudy gold, deep blood-red overlain with lavender and green tartan, white-squared, breathtakingly colourful against the frost-dark sky and the frost-white ground.

'And who is that?' asked Tom with a frown.

'That is the Laird of Hermitage, your uncle's opposite on the Scottish side, the Warden of Liddesdale – Black Robert Douglas himself,' said Father Little; and, as though he had said *That is the Lord of Hell, Lucifer, Satan himself*, he needed to add no more.

No sooner had Father Little spat out the answer, than, as though the Black Douglas were indeed a devil to be summoned from hell by the calling of his name, he turned, saw the pair below, held up his hand and wheeled. His whole company followed him around out of their straight path to Bewcastle fort to come cantering down the hill.

Father Little continued speaking very rapidly, dropping his voice as the horses approached until his last words, a fierce, hissing whisper, were lost beneath the stamping and the whinnying and the Black Douglas's cheery greeting. 'Tom, beware this man. For all his gentle Scottish speech and courtly manners, he is deadly dangerous. Were I to choose any man nearby likely to be responsible for all of this, it would be he. He is lord over the Armstrongs, who obey him out of simple terror. He can call to his banner the scum of the Scottish Marches, the Elliots, the Grahams and even the Kerrs. From his eyrie at Hermitage he looks over the Scotts and the Johnstones, the

Maxwells and, some say, even the MacGregors. If there is no God in Liddesdale, then it is because this man drove him out! If anyone could steal away Eve Graham, now she is widowed and free, with or without her consent, it is he; and if he should decide to do so, then never look to see her in this life again. If anyone has the heart or the power to snatch the Waste away from your uncle, or the North away from Lord Henry Carey, it is he! And as for the Barguest, he . . .'

'Halloa! Father Little! Afoot while another rides. Not while Robert Douglas has horse, sir! We treat our churchmen better than that in Scotland. Come, Father, up on my black hunter now, and let us all trot over to the Lord of the Waste's abode.'

'And you, sirrah, who ride while the good father puffs at your bridle, you must be the master come up lately from Her Majesty's Court, to the wonder of all men from here to Berwick. Master Musgrave, is it not?'

'It is, sir. Lord Robert Douglas, the Laird of Hermitage, I believe.' Nothing abashed, Tom swung easily down and faced the Black Douglas, offering the courtliest of his bows – widening the sweep of his arm to take in all assembled there, for the instant Lord Robert stepped down from his hunter, so all of his company swung down from theirs. Except, Tom noted, for two. Guests, then, he surmised at once, hoping his bow had hidden his look, for he recognized at least one of the men at once.

Not from the Douglas it hadn't. 'Ah, Master Musgrave,' Lord Robert continued smoothly. 'I see you observe my guests. Allow me to perform the briefest of introductions: Senor Sagres and Master de Vaux, both lately of London.' The two men bowed in their saddles, then both, reluctantly, followed the lead dictated by their host and his men, swinging down to stand at their horses' heads.

Very lately, thought Tom as he straightened. De Vaux had been standing behind the Earl of Essex's shoulder when his lordly blade had rested on Tom's throat and the Queen's screams still echoed at the rehearsal of *A Midsummer Night's Dream* two days since at White Hall. And his saddlebag had an unusual pattern upon it – familiar from that flash of clear sight he had gained of the riders kicking the farmer's aside at Ware.

Then he turned back and fronted the Black Douglas. They were big men, Tom and Lord Robert, able to look each other in the eye, able to look down on the others around them. The Laird of Hermitage earned his nickname from the long hair that he wore gathered at the nape of his neck, from the beard he wore barbered to the finest point, and the moustaches that curled down to join it on his chin, all of which were so black that they seemed to take a tinge of blue from the dancing glitter of his eyes. His brows, raised in amused quizzicality now, rose to points then swept up across his temples almost to the tops of his ears. His lashes were thick and dark, like those of an Italian girl.

In his looks and in his vanity, in his consequence and dangerous affability, he reminded Tom of that other Robert of his acquaintance, so recently called to mind, the deadliest of his enemies – friend to de Vaux and no doubt to Senor Sagres too, for there were always Spaniards in his train – Robert Devereux, the Earl of Essex. The Earl of Essex was just such a man as might have the power, the will and the wish to bribe a constable at Ware while he despatched his men to stir up the Kerrs and warn the Black Douglas against him.

'Put up the father, Tam,' ordered Black Robert, his eyes never leaving Tom's as he spoke. Tom glanced over to his companion and exercised his mastery in self-control once more as another piece of the puzzle fell into place so unexpectedly. The man called Tam, moving to obey his master's command, clearly the Captain of Horse to the Laird of Hermitage, was the image of Geordie Burn. Two brothers, then, each holding the same post, on opposite sides in a brewing conflict – who must come face to face and steel to steel, and soon. The same two brothers, like as not, as had fallen out over Eve all those years ago.

Eyes wide and innocent, Tom turned back to Lord Robert and smiled. Behind the smile and the innocent eyes, even as he listened to Lord Robert's conversation, Tom's mind whirled in speculation – speculation as to how all this tangle of confused loyalties and dark motives could have called up the Barguest to kill his brother – and why.

Father Little's protests were cut short and replaced by the sound of the saddle creaking; then Black Robert himself took the bridle and the rest of them all walked up towards Bewcastle fort together as the priest, alone, rode.

'I hope you will be amongst the number to whom I may repay this visit soon,' the Laird of Hermitage continued to Tom as they walked. 'It is a tradition that has grown up during the days of your lamented absence from the Borders, so you may not know of it, but in the season after the Lord of the Waste has his hunt, the Warden of Liddesdale has his hawking. The game does not compare with the fine red harts that your uncle offers for sporting and feasting, of course, but I have hawks, buzzards and even eagles with which we can pass a merry afternoon, and a range of birds from herons to capercaillie that we may kill and feast upon. In return we request only the detail in the matter of Dand Kerr's hand. What a story that must be! Hermitage keep is only rarely graced by courtiers and adventurers such as yourself, Master Musgrave, though we are fortunate that Master de Vaux and Senor Sagres have graced us.

'Ah now, Tam, look where the story carried by those fleeing Kerrs we captured this morning is not true. The outbuildings are burned down indeed. There must have been a sharp fight here last night. I had hesitated to believe them, Master Musgrave, for the Kerrs are notorious liars and these ones told us that the Barguest itself came down and ran them off. But now I see that it is at least partly as they said.

'I assure you, sir, and I will assure the Lord of the Waste, that you shall find them hanging at Hermitage gate when you grace us with a visit – them and any other Kerrs I discover nearby.'

Lord Robert got his chance to assure the Lord of the Waste on the matter of hanging Kerrs almost at once, for the band of walkers with their thoroughly embarrassed rider went through the main gate to be greeted by a reception line. Drawn up in due order, it was headed by the Lord of the Waste himself, the Lady

Ellen at his side. The first formal section of the day began at once as the Lord of the Waste and the Lady conducted the Laird of Hermitage along the line of precedence, making formal introductions. Lord Robert in turn introduced his party and all with apparent amity, disturbed only by the threatening looks exchanged by Tam and Geordie Burn. Tom noted also that, while in the Bewcastle garrison there were a good number of women, the visitors from Hermitage were more like a war band, being made up exclusively of men.

The introductions led across the courtyard and into the little kirk, which could hardly in all its history have held such a magnificent company. Here they all stood shoulder to shoulder, lords and lairds, Scotsmen and Sassenachs, soldiers and reivers, courtiers and commoners, men and women. They bowed their heads when they should have knelt, for there was simply no room to bend the knee. Standing, therefore, together, they spoke the words of commandment, creed, confession; they echoed the blessing and the breaking of the body and bread, the shedding and the mixing of blood and wine. All of them stepped forward to the Communion, the order of precedence breaking down so that there seemed to be no particular order in the celebration. Sir Thomas and the Lady Ellen went first and Lord Robert and his guests came later, soon before Fenwick the Factor and Archie, then Tom who stood beside him. Finally, Geordie and Eve brought up the rear. They tasted the bread and sipped the wine. This was never designed to be a full-sung celebration, so the only music came from the well-tuned hounds outside; and that was apt enough, for, holy worship or not, it tempted them all to hurry through.

Out in the courtyard there had been a bustle during the service. The mass had been for the hunters only. When the Lord of the Waste led them all out into the restless morning, therefore, all the horses were saddled, the hounds leashed but ready. As they mounted – even the women going astride for the going would be hard and hectic – so the Lady Ellen disappeared. The hunt was not for her. Her other responsibilities were fully met, however, for on the instant she reappeared with the castle's entire kitchen staff bearing great platters of steaming food and bumpers of smoking punch.

In spite of his boast that Eve's medicines had made him a new man. Tom partook of little. He could hardly get the taste of the communion wine out of his mouth and the residue seemed to make his lips and tongue tingle irritatingly. A draught of punch and a baked chicken wing simply added to a mild sense of discomfort within him, though they eased his mouth and throat. And he thought no more about it.

The hunt breakfast was a feast of baked chicken, boiled eggs, filled pastries and sliced haggis. The punch was a fragrant mixture of herbs, spices, wine and sugar. It was taken in the saddle and the bones thrown past the hounds to the castle's domestic dogs. Wild with excitement and hunger, straining so that Hobbie and his men could hardly hold them, the hounds led the way out of the castle gate with the riders in careful precedence behind. The musicians from the Christmas festivities swapped lutes and pipes for horns and, as the hunt began to climb the hill to the crest above the Waste, they echoed the music of the hounds. At the crest of the ridge, with the waste rolling away before them, Sir Thomas gave the signal and the horns sounded the commencement. The hounds were unleashed and every heel there spurred into the heaving flank of an expectant horse. In a charge every bit as wild as the charge Geordie had led on the heels of the Barguest against the Kerrs last night, they were off across the Waste.

CHAPTER THIRTEEN

The Kill

T om was sick of this inaction. He had not yet reached that part of his exercise of logic where he had assembled all the facts and could begin to test them through observation of suspects or manipulation of their actions. He was still caught up in the tangle of events and could see but little of the pattern as yet. His gift for suspicion was being exercised to its limit, but his genius for logic had too little to work upon unless he got down to some serious action: *doing* must take precedence over reasoning. Finding out the truth of the matters that had been described to him must be done at once, before he try any more conclusions.

Tom had been on the Borders for less than a day, admittedly, but he was used to taking decisive action. He still felt that he had been sluggish in the pursuance of his task. His slowness of action, of course, was partly due to exhaustion and weakness from the blood-letting, and perhaps from Eve's treatment of it; but it also had its foundation in the fact that he was being watched wherever he went. It was also because he was being delicately but carefully enmeshed in toils of social expectation whose effect – and, perhaps, whose design – was to tie his hands and hamper his work here. At every turn came circumstances that tempted him to look away from the simple act of his brother's murder itself and into the causes and consequences that might or might not surround it.

The hunt came as blessed relief to this queasy sense of inactivity. It gave him the opportunity to take a little freedom through the simple exercise of some calculated rudeness and careful intransigence – freedom that started now, even though the morning's nagging sickness lingered.

The other horses streamed away after the hounds, heading up on to High Waste and away over Hazel Gill and Calf Sike towards the forested sections of Hart Horn, where the Lord of the Waste had kept his carefully nurtured herds of hunting deer since long before Tom was a lad learning his logic as well as his catechism at Father Little's knee. Everyone, including Tom, knew where they were going; everyone except Tom galloped away to the south-east, therefore.

Tom waited for an instant to make as sure as possible that he was being neither watched nor followed, thoughtlessly wiping the back of his hand over his burning lips. Then he jerked his pony's head to the left and galloped off at a calculated angle designed to take him, at first imperceptibly, north. He was cantering across country he knew as well as he knew the direction of the hunt. He was headed over White Preston and then along the ridge past Whiteside End, Crew Cragg and Watch Rigg, the five miles to Arthur's Seat, some twenty minutes' riding time away.

Tom's destination was the birthplace of the Black Lyne river, its spring in the little coppice dominated by the great oak where his brother had been found dead almost a week ago, the huge tree that they said was clawed to the heartwood to a height of two full fathoms from the ground. The Lord of the Waste, Eve and Hobbie had all said it, but Tom needed to see the thing for himself. Second only to John's body, which must be dug out of its grave to tell him more, that tree must be as full of secrets as all the rest together.

Yet as Tom galloped more freely and urgently along the skyline between White Preston and Preston End, he was unsettlingly aware that he was also compounding the mounting risks he seemed to be running lately. The idea of the danger into which he was so wilfully thrusting himself suddenly made him feel actually, physically, sick.

Simply starting on this journey had earned him a knife in the side, he thought – perhaps provoked by de Vaux and Sagres at the behest either of the Earl of Essex or the Black Douglas; possibly delivered by one or other of his closest childhood friends; or by an Elliot or an Armstrong, either or both in the pay of the Laird of Hermitage as well as in the employ of the Council.

Then, getting as far as the Wall had called down a troop of Kerrs, again probably directed by de Vaux or Sagres – therefore in the employ of the Black Douglas, who was, like as not, confederated with Essex in any case. Escaping them had called forth half the clan and near destroyed Bewcastle itself. In the melee there, death had come its closest yet. Next, this very morning, perhaps by coincidence, visiting his brother's grave had called up Father Little with his distractingly far-flung suspicions, and then called down the Black Douglas himself with Essex's friends as his less than welcome guests. What, Tom wondered queasily, would be the consequence in this deadly game of coming to the ancient oak that stood at the very heart of the matter?

Suddenly the chicken wing and punch, which had been sitting so ill on his stomach after the hunt breakfast, gave another unwelcome stirring, and he leaned over clear of his trotting mount and was copiously sick down the cliff at Crew Cragg. Then, lighter in spirit as well as in body, he spurred up the crest towards Watch Rigg.

Tom paused for a moment on Watch Rigg, for, as its name implied, the little hill summit gave a wide view of the surrounding countryside. Especially against the white heaves of the frosted moorland with which he was surrounded, it was obvious that he was not being followed, unless he had pursuers hidden in the black depths of the wooded river valleys with which the place was surrounded – into one of which, after all, Tom himself was heading.

Due north he continued, into the very teeth of the wind, which had swung round further in the night and was bringing the clouds now, lower and lower, like the Black Douglas straight out of Scotland over the border that lay all too close at hand. Yet, when he paused at last on the shoulder of the cragside above the rounded hollow of Arthur's Seat, a rift in those same dark clouds allowed a brief beam of sunlight as bright as midsummer to rest on the coppice below him, so that the great bare oak where his brother had died seemed a thing of gold and fire. Light-headed with shock and anticipation, at being at the tragic place at last and ready to learn – and avenge – its secrets, Tom spurred down the hillside.

As he rode, he pulled his eyes from the hypnotic horror of the ruined tree and looked at the ground itself. There was nothing soft about the place. Thin earth covered stony ridges, the one as hard as the other in the grip of the unrelenting frost. He could have marched an army over here and left almost no mark, he thought. He reined his pony to a standstill, dismounted and walked back along the track of his own progress. The thin grass and moss lay beaten down by wind and rain uncounted months since and frosted over now so hard that he could find no evidence that his steel-hoofed pony had ever crossed this ground. Thoughtfully, he climbed back into the saddle and trotted on down.

The oak stood exactly as he remembered it. It rose to its majestic height well clear of the little wood further down the hill where the floor of Arthur's Seat folded into the beginning of a valley, deep-throated and steep-sided seemingly before there was even a rivulet to occupy it. Such was the thinness of the earth over the rocks even down here where the soil was at its thickest, the roots rose out of the thin grass like huge serpents frozen in the midst of some writhing battle; and it was a wonder of this particular tree, as Tom recalled from childhood, that when the leaves and acorns came down at the fall of the year, so they were swept away by the torrents of autumn rain that gave birth to the Black Lyne itself. You would find more oak leaves and acorns at Blackpool Gate, so the saying went, than you would ever discover on Arthur's Seat. The fodder for pigs was the best in the county down there.

Above the wild, weird, writhing roots stood the trunk of the

tree, so wide it had taken Tom as a boy the better part of five
minutes to walk around it, as he remembered. Tom the man
had longer legs, but it still took him the better part of a hundred
paces. Up above the trunk, truly fifteen feet above, nearly twice
as high as Tom could reach, the huge branches sprang out, the
least of them as thick as his thigh and most of them as thick as
his body.

Between the roots and the branches the tree stood horribly
naked, and in place of the bark that he remembered being thick,
grey and crusted, there was only the pale gold of the sap-teared
wood. That wood had reason to weep its thick amber tears, for
it was exactly as Eve had described and he had seen in his
fevered vision on the coach: the pale wood had been clawed,
torn and splintered. Claw marks gouged in series, overlapping,
crossing, hacking, chopping, until the tree's flanks, which
should have stood as smooth as any woman's, resembled
instead the hide of the bristling hedgehog. Twice as high as
Tom himself the wild, bewildering madness reached – higher by
far than he could touch on tiptoe; higher than he could reach
standing in his stirrups; higher even than that by a yard and
more; so high that even the lower branches seemed to be in
danger of that savage, satanic clawing. But they were not, for
they remained untouched. Indeed, for a good yard beneath the
lowest of them there hung a sorry series of shreds and tatters as
though the great tree's bark were reduced to a beggar's rags,
and what had been stripped away lay strewn in a great untidy
circle all around.

The sunlight was gone now and the low clouds threatened a
thin, sleety rain. The wind trapped beneath them seemed forced
by the wild contours of the place to come sighing like a dirge
down to the tree. This creaked and groaned in agony, stirring
even to its foundations as its naked twigs and branches set up
the most doleful range of sobs, screams and howls.

Tom knelt down beneath the worst-torn section of the trunk.
High above here there stood a pair of branches that forked out
from the trunk itself like the double tip of a snake's tongue.
Here, evidently, John's body had been found, kneeling with one

hand and one knee on each of the branches. The ground beneath was clawed, Tom found, after he had cleared the shreds of bark away – clawed almost as badly as the trunk was clawed; and that gave Tom cause to frown thoughtfully, for the ground up on the slope had given no sign at all of the passage of an iron-shod pony bearing a heavy man. This ground was no softer, and yet it bore the claw prints of the creature that had torn the tree. The roots and the thin-grassed soil between them both carried the marks of the claws. Out in a circle around the tree, further and further apart, the marks tore up the ground as though the monstrous hound had been trying to bury something – or to dig something up, perhaps.

Tom followed them, seeking for single tracks, until he found enough to examine individually. Lost in thought, he lay full length on the frozen moss. He brought his face as close to the ground as the steaming of his breath on the white grass would allow.

There were no pad marks. The hound might have come straight from hell, but it was by no means brimstone hot, therefore. Yet it must have had well-spread pads and great weight in itself to drive the four clear claw marks into the thin soil. Tom pulled out his dagger and drove it down beside the marks, and could hardly get the Solingen steel to penetrate the ground. Were these the forepaws or the hind? Tom looked further back, but there were no more marks upslope. He looked further forward, but the mess of claw marks began too soon – he could not find the pattern that would betray the size of the thing.

Yet, he mused, returning to the tree, sinking into deep reflection beneath the ghostly wailing of its agonies within the howling wind, he knew the size of the Barguest to within an ell. With its hind legs resting where his own feet rested, it was big enough to reach up with its forepaws to a point fully twice as high as he stood.

Thank God, he whispered, that John had been up in those branches a safe yard higher still. Then he stopped all thoughts for a moment and tried to clear his mind, for he realized with a

104

sick lurch that he was starting to believe in the Barguest after all.

Then, out of the thin air of his blank mind, the most obvious of thoughts occurred to him: how in God's name had John climbed up there in the first place?

'How did he do it?' came a cold, quiet voice from immediately behind Tom.

Tom whirled, too startled to maintain his facade of imperturbability.

'How did your brother get himself up fifteen feet into the air? Perhaps the Angel Gabriel gave him a helping hand – what do you think?' Lord Robert Douglas enquired.

Tom's mind echoed Lord Robert's first question: how in all the world had he, de Vaux and Sagres come so silently down on him? Then Tam Burn's horse gave a quiet snicker from behind the tree and Tom realized that a combination of the wind in the tree, his own preoccupation and the captain's tracking skills would easily have been enough for the task.

'Or,' Lord Robert continued silkily, 'perhaps his fear of the beast that hunted him lent him wings before it frightened him to death.'

'I doubt, My Lord,' said Tom, as steadily as he could – 'I doubt that he died of fear.'

Lord Robert smiled. 'Do not doubt too surely,' he said. 'People do die of fear. I have seen it happen.' He leaned forward suddenly, so that his lean and handsome face filled all of Tom's vision. 'I have *made* it happen.'

Tom licked his lips. 'I do not doubt *that*, My Lord.'

The Black Douglas sat up straight in his saddle then, with a bark of laughter that put Tom in mind of the Barguest with a vengeance. 'But let us not talk of such dark matters,' he said lightly. 'Let us talk of much more pleasant things. Let us discuss, in short, exactly how you would like to die, Master Musgrave. And, perhaps, how *soon*.'

Tom's eyes flicked from Lord Robert's hypnotic gaze to the stony faces of the three that sat beside him. He opened his mouth.

And a hunting horn sounded. It sounded the view. The sound of it was brassy and thin, strident, raucous, echoing – the sweetest sound that Tom had ever heard. Over the shoulder of hillside above Arthur's Seat came the great hart the Lord of the Waste was hunting, a red deer stag full fourteen points of antler, a prince of its species and fit for such sport. The hounds were close upon its heels with Hobbie close on theirs and his horns close behind him calling to the hunt; but they were no great way behind either, for, as Lord Robert Douglas tore his eyes from the skyline every bit as surprised as Tom had been, so the wild mob of horsemen came galloping over the rise and pounded down upon them.

The stag, seeing men and horses before it as well as behind, threw itself sideways and ran to the north; but the northern arm of Arthur's Seat was steep, as befitted the last ridge before the border itself, and slowed the tired beast still further. Down it came relentlessly, back to the illusory shelter of that little coppice at the head of the Black Lyne; and the well-trained hounds, as keen as they were well matched in voice, saw how its path must go and ran straight down the hillside just before Hobbie, closing to cut it off.

By the time the whole hunt came past the little group by the oak, there was nothing left for Tom to do but swing into the saddle and join in. By the time he reached the rest of them, the stag was at bay with the hounds snapping at it. Tom looked for Eve and, when he could not see her, he crossed to Sim Armstrong, as a familiar face that might answer a question or two.

'A good run?'

'Aye. Though we lost the beast once or twice. And there's a good few of the hunt lost still, I'd calculate. Did ye not see for yourself?'

Tom smiled and shook his head, thinking that Sim's news was to the good. His absence might not have been remarked at all. His standing in his uncle's eyes might remain safely high for a while longer yet.

But where was Eve? Tom glanced around, seeking her

familiar shape amongst the last few riders as they cantered down the hillside – seeking, for the moment at least, in vain; but he could not imagine her far parted from Hobbie or from the hunt itself, especially now that they had reached the climax: the kill.

The beast was trapped by the thickness of the undergrowth and the precipitous sides of the little river valley behind it. The hounds were keen and ready to tear into the hart at Hobbie's word, but tradition dictated that Sir Thomas himself should make the decision. The hart and the hunt, like the Waste itself, were his, after all.

'Call them back, Hobbie,' he ordered as he rode up. 'Now,' he continued breathlessly as the master of the hunt obeyed, 'my crossbow. And you may sound the kill.'

CHAPTER FOURTEEN

After the Kill

The great red hart seemed to leap to meet its death as the black steel quarrel flew from Sir Thomas Musgrave's crossbow and pierced it unerringly through the breast and heart at once. Then, having leaped up, it crashed back into the undergrowth and lay still at once. All the men and women there clapped and cheered the clean, accomplished kill – even, noted Tom, the Black Douglas, whose lean cheeks seemed flushed with sport and excitement.

Hobbie's men, having leashed the dogs, rushed forward again and pulled the dead stag into position so that they could lash its hind legs together. They threw the rope up over the branch of the nearest tree so that it could serve as a gallows and they pulled the dead beast high enough so that its antlers just whispered across the frozen grasses of its deathbed. Sir Thomas stepped down and, taking a knife, he turned to Lord Robert. 'Will ye do the honours, Lord Robert?' he asked, and the Black Douglas, all affability again, stepped down and cut the deer's throat with all the delicacy of a master surgeon at work. Then he handed the knife back to his host with the most courtly of courteous bows.

The very instant that the stag's thick blood began to flow, Hobbie was there with a great metal ewer. The horns were sounded again and again as the blood drained swiftly into the smoking bowl. Then the Lord of the Waste stepped forward once more and, with Hobbie deftly helping him, he stripped the carcase of its hide. So delicately was this done that neither man soiled even the finest parts of his linen with blood at all, and so swiftly that the breathless hunters had little time to do more than pass around the stirrup cups of golden usquebaugh and congratulate each other on another successful day's sport before the head, hide and hooves were off and the next part of the ritual began.

Bread was thrown into the bowl of blood while Hobbie, no longer the gentleman hunter, rolled back his sleeves past the elbow, then deftly opened the deer's belly and slid the intestines, liver and lights on to the ground. The blood was added to this steaming mess and the whole lot was covered with the deer's head and hide. Then, at the master's sign, the strident horns sounded again and again while the antlered head was lifted clear and the dogs were unleashed to feed.

The whole howling pack of them, sounding very much more like the hell-hounds they had figured last night, rushed forward to their grim feast; but even as they did so, a terrible screaming began. The sound was louder than the howling of the dogs – almost as loud as the howling of the oak's branches, but this sound was undeniably human. It was issuing from the undergrowth that had held the stag at bay.

Tom and Hobbie, who was nearest beside him, dived into the bushes at the sound and all but tumbled over the cliff concealed behind them. Here they found, at bay just as the stag had been, the youngest of the Kerrs. Tom recognized at once the arrogant, black-haired youth who had been caught beneath his own crossbow at Housesteads fort and farmhouse, who had cost Dand Kerr his hand and who had spoken up so bravely for him at the castle gate last night.

By no means so brave today, the youngster was near to tears with terror, rage and frustration when they dragged him out into the light. Silent now, if struggling still, he shot a fulminating glance at the dogs whose terrible sounds had frightened him and tricked him into giving himself away. They, however, were too preoccupied with their own vast meal to spare him even a glance in return. Not so the other hunters here. The garrison men sprang down at once and went into the undergrowth, searching in case the boy had any companions.

The Lord of the Waste leaned forward and looked down at the writhing lad from the height of his saddle – and the height of his position as the law in this land. 'How came ye here, lad?' he demanded, gently enough, thought Tom, for a man that might apply any form of punishment, torture or execution with no questions asked.

'I rode,' came the grudging reply, elicited, Tom noted, by a quick turn of the wrist that Hobbie was holding.

'Ye were lucky to make it this far in the dark without breaking your neck – or your pony's. Where's your hobbie horse?'

'In the burn. With a broken neck,' the youngster admitted grimly.

'And how did that happen?'

'We saw . . .' the youth began, but then thought better of the confession clearly. 'We stumbled in the darkness.'

'We?' The Lord of the Waste was on to the word at once.

'Selkie and I. Selkie was my hobbie horse.'

The Lord of the Waste was not convinced, though the lad looked young enough to be giving names to his horses yet. 'Are ye sure ye rode alone?'

'I did.'

'And ye're still alone now?'

'I am,' came the stout reply; and Sim Armstrong, returning from the undergrowth, nodded in confirmation.

'Then we'll be taking you back to Bewcastle with us and holding you till I talk to Hugh of Stob. And mayhap One-Hand Dand himself,' decided the Lord of the Waste. 'There was killing and wanton destruction of property last night, and someone has to pay.'

'Oh let me take the lad,' said Robert Douglas suddenly. 'I've a couple of his relations up at Hermitage. I could bring the family briefly together.'

That suggestion seemed to lend the slight captive the strength of Hercules. One arm tore out of Hobbie's hand and the other nearly broke Tom's grip. Quick-thinking as ever, he held tight for an instant more, then released his grip as the arm tore back again. The captive stumbled, thrown off balance by the unexpected freedom and Tom, swapping one defensive art for another, knocked him cold with a single blow.

Tom stood over the fallen body, panting slightly. His gaze swept over the two men in command here. 'Sir Thomas,' he said. 'If I could beg you to consider for a moment more before you answer Lord Robert's request. The lad has seen something – seen it by his own admission, and seen it here; and this place lies beneath the tree where they found my brother. What he knows may help me in my quest for the truth. Take him to Bewcastle, I beg you, where I may question him.'

Sir Thomas looked at Lord Robert and Lord Robert shrugged. 'It makes no matter to me,' he said with apparent affability. 'Let Master Musgrave ask his questions.'

'Very well,' said Sir Thomas. 'You may take the lad.'

'And,' added Lord Robert, 'as the hunt is done and the day is darkening, I think we will also take our leave. Ah now I know, Sir Thomas, that you have a feast in the making and the hart here to be roasted and eaten, but if I may do so without incurring your wrath, or that of the good Lady Ellen, I will decline. This place is nearer my door than yours and our parting would be convenient now.'

They split into the groups that had composed the Christmas hunt – the Black Douglas's men and guests, the Captain of Bewcastle's men and their guests, and Hobbie and his huntsmen, who still had business here.

That done, the hunt all turned and rode away.

Hobbie and Tom were left with the hart, the hounds, the unconscious Kerr and half a dozen helpers. Up went the deer's carcase on to Hobbie's saddle-bow, for it was his privilege and duty to carry it back. Up went the hide, carefully wrapped under the head, on to his senior helper's horse. The hounds were leashed and secured to the pommels of the other helpers' horses; and, last, the youth was lifted by Hobbie and Tom himself and lain like the stag over Tom's saddle.

'Lad be damned,' said Tom quietly. 'It's a lass we have here. Do all the ladies of the borders dress as boys to go roistering over the place? It was never so when I was a youth.'

'More's the pity,' said Hobbie, mounting beside him. 'But ye're right. 'Tis a new fashion. If ye want to know more, then here's the lass will enlighten ye.'

For over the ridge came Eve herself, her horse at full gallop. She met them halfway up the slope and simply looking at her told Tom that something terrible was in train.

'There's a terrible plague struck the hunt and the fort,' she gasped. 'Archie Elliot that wrestled so well is dead. Geordie Burn is close to death. There's others sick all over the place and I . . .'

She slid from her saddle and tumbled to the ground, twitching, with a little thread of foam leaking out of the corner of her mouth. Tom swung down beside her and caught her up at once.

'We'd best get her back,' said Hobbie. 'I'll take the Kerr lass at my saddle-bow and you take Eve. The hart'll go over the extra horse and we'll ride him in gently. There'll not be any urgent need of him this day, if what she said is true. But hurry, man. Hurry! Whatever's abroad, Eve has it and the least delay may cost her dear!'

CHAPTER FIFTEEN

Plague and Poison

E ven after the canter up over Crew Crag and Arthur's Seat,
Tom's pony was still fresh. It had been at fighting pitch,
after all, and ready to join in the hunt and gallop until its legs
gave out. It gave of its best now with great heart, running back
along the way it had come as though it was in truth pursuing the
greatest of harts, the double load notwithstanding.

As much by judgement as by luck, intuitively associating his
own illness with Eve's news – and his vomiting with his
continued health – Tom heaved his fair, fainting burden over
on to her belly, and after a while the low swinging motion of her
head and the bouncing of the pony's downhill gallop set her to
puking weakly. As he galloped, he speculated.

Eve had said plague: *There's a terrible plague struck the hunt
and the fort . . .* But she could not mean the word literally. Tom
had seen the plague and knew its symptoms. There were none
evident here. She used the word in its figurative sense, therefore.
This was not the Black Plague but some sweeping, overwhelming sickness, swift of onset and fatal of outcome. Strength and
heartiness were no great bastions against it, for Archie Elliot
and Geordie Burn had been rude, healthy and of soldierly
fitness. Both had been robust this morning, therefore the onset
must have come since the hunt breakfast. And thinking of the
hunt breakfast, of course, put him in mind of his own sickness
again.

Accidental poisoning was by no means unusual. In London, particularly, he was often mildly surprised that it was not far more common than it seemed to be. But even up here, away from all that filth, humanity and vermin, in the midst of chilly spaciousness, clean water and careful, prudent lifestyle, it could never be ruled out.

Any of the foodstuffs in the kitchen, most of which would have been preserved for some time, could have become tainted: ill-preserved apples or pears; ill-smoked pork, hanging since the winter slaughter several weeks since; fish, perhaps becoming sick-making on their journey from the river or the sea; oats or barley going damp and musty in the store – or infested in the field before harvesting. The local sheep – gathered in winter folds at the moment but still providing mutton to the rich that could afford them – could become tainted through tainted feed. Even the chickens that ran around the kitchen door until they were forcefully invited in could become dangerous through bad food, careless cleaning, faulty preparation. Was it not for wholesomeness as well as taste that the prudent housewife stuffed them with that natural poison-killer, sage? – as had Lady Ellen for the Hunt Breakfast, remembered Tom.

Of all the possible culprits in this case, the chickens were at once the least likely, for they were the only elements of the hunt breakfast that had been slaughtered freshly – last night or this morning, in fact. On the other hand, they were also the most likely, for, as chicken was all he had eaten, Tom thought the guilt must lie there if anywhere; and, unlike the rest of the food on offer, the chickens would have been handled and roasted individually – allowing one to do the damage to a limited number of people – as seemed to be the case here.

If not the food itself, continued Tom grimly, then tainted utensils, perhaps. But again, not likely, for he had actually been impressed with Lady Ellen's housewifery thus far and she had an abundance of clean water nearby, and a good staff with which to work. Even using the kitchen as a hospital last night had not seriously upset the domestic arrangements, as far as Tom could see. Tainted utensils would logically have spread any sickness further – unless, of course, it was widespread and the hearty huntsmen who had killed the hart were now, like Archie, Eve and Geordie, dead or sick unto death.

Yet, he persisted as he rode wildly down the slope above Kirk Beck, if one of the chickens were the cause of the problem, again, it had passed between fewest hands. It had come under the least number of knives and through the merest bucket or bowl in any case. It had simply been killed, plucked, cleaned, stuffed with dry sage, baked in the oven, sectioned and handed round. Where could any sickness spring from in such a simple ritual as that?

The punch, then – a possible contender, certainly. A capable housewoman like his aunt would be trying to use up the last and worst of the castle's wine supply – without letting Sir Thomas or any of his guests know, he thought. The water added to it and boiled would be twice potable – clean from the well and purified through boiling. The herbs and spices might be tainted, ill-chosen, or . . .

And that was where logic had taken Tom as he rode under the stone gateway and into the castle itself. If he had expected chaos, he was pleasantly surprised. This was a front-line fort, used to crisis piled upon disaster. True, there was no sign of the festive feast, the ritual roasting of the skinned hart. That, of course, would have to wait – as would Lord Robert's invitation to go hawking at Hermitage. In the meantime everyone had a job to do and went quietly about it, while those whose job was to heal the afflicted went skilfully about that business too.

Tom threw the reins to the stable lad who had been waiting since the keen-eyed sentry called down. He swung down off his horse and pulled Eve into his arms. The same sentry had warned the castle of his burden and the Lady Ellen came fluttering out of the keep as he turned.

'Follow me, my dear,' she said at once. Only when they were inside the building and alone for an instant did she enquire, 'Dead?'

In truth, thought Tom, it was hard enough to tell. 'Fainting. She has puked, an act that helped me, for I believe I have been tainted too.'

'If it helped you, then let us pray it will have helped her. And it must have helped you if you are right, for otherwise we would be carrying you like we had to carry the others, living and dead. Not the kitchen,' she continued sharply, for Tom had turned that way. 'Wounds are one thing. This is quite another and I want it nowhere near our food.'

This brought Tom back to his own train of thought and so, as he carried Eve in Lady Ellen's footsteps towards the back of the keep, he asked, 'What do you think it is, Lady Ellen?'

'I think it is poison,' she said forthrightly.

'I agree,' said Tom.

'What do you know of poisons?' she enquired sharply.

'Little enough,' he admitted. 'I have talked with Gerard the Herbalist over some such matters, but I am far from wisdom myself. I had simply applied logic, for I believe some part of the hunt breakfast unsettled me and I only had a bite of chicken and a sip of punch.'

The Lady Ellen fell silent at that. She led the increasingly breathless Tom through into a small, warm room not unlike the chapel, right at the back of the keep. It was lit by several lamps, for it had no windows and its one other exit, a door with a pointed lintel in the old Gothic style, was tight shut against the cold; but there was a chimney to the outside against a second wall, and beneath it blazed a good fire well stocked with logs and winter peat. Here lay Geordie Burn, white and feverous, but sweating profusely. He lay in a little truckle bed, plaids and skins piled up on him. A three-legged stool stood by him and upon it stood a little horn cup not unlike the one that had held the mandragora Tom had drunk the night before. There was another bed convenient for Eve's still form.

'You were expecting more patients?' asked Tom as he laid her down.

'This was Archie Elliot's,' said Lady Ellen severely, 'but he rests in the chapel now. We'll need to get Father Little to bury him in proper form when he gets back from Blackpool Gate.'

'Why has he gone there?' asked Tom.

'To say a service in the kirk. He's a busy man this season. Let me look at you a moment.'

'But Eve—'

'I cannot give her the tending she needs with you here. I need to see you're well enough to get away from here and let me work.' As she spoke, Lady Ellen was examining Tom's face and eyes. She looked into his mouth and smelt his breath.

As she did this, Tom himself looked around and was struck at once by the way the little room was filled with little pots and jars, how the rafters above the pointed door were hung with drying plants and herbs; by the little cauldron convenient to the fire.

'You'll live,' said Lady Ellen. 'Take a sip from that cup and then you may go.' She indicated the cup by Geordie's bed.

'What is it?' he asked. 'Not more mandragora.'

'It is infusion of all-heal. It's eased Geordie's breathing so it may settle you as well. If ye want to know more, go ask your friend Gerard.'

Thus dismissed, Tom went back the way he had come, his lips pursed in thought. Apparently at random, he wandered unhindered out across the courtyard and through the main gate. Round the burned-out ruins below the walls he went, looking for that unusually shaped door. The thing was of wood and, though heavily barred and bolted, from the inside at least it had shown no sign of fire damage. Yet if he had understood the layout of the castle correctly, it must lead to the outside. Where was there, therefore, an area beside the castle wall untouched by the Kerrs? Where and why?

It was a little graveyard. Edged with a low dry-stone wall and marked with one or two mouldering monuments, it stood green and undisturbed among the charred wreckage of the little stores and outhouses. At the uphill end, there was a little gate and Tom came in through this – necessarily so, for immediately inside the wall all around there grew a strong yew hedge to shoulder height. But it was not so much the wonder of a place so undisturbed that called Tom in, nor the sense of eerie calm and sense of timelessness here; it was the fact that at the castle end, where the soil was richest and deepest, over the bones of the very dead had been planted a garden – not just any garden: the very garden he had told Father Little he would find behind the smithy. He might have known it by the winter form of any of the herbs and plants he had discussed with Gerard himself, but he knew it at once, and with absolute certainty, by the little clump of Christmas roses with all the blossoms gone.

Then, wondering how much difference to his calculations might be made by the fact that it was the Lady Ellen and not Eve herself that was the wise woman here, he wandered back into the castle.

His next object would no doubt await his attention too, for it was Archie Elliot. In that apparently wayward and unfocused mood that Ugo Stell or Talbot Law, his friends in London, would have recognized all too well, he strolled across the courtyard. Hobbie raised a hand from the stables where he was unloading the deer and their insensible captive alike, but was surprised to receive no reply. Sir Thomas, glancing down from the in-facing window of his little study, caught his eye but again received no sign of recognition. Yet when that vacant eye fell upon the tiniest thing that seemed strange or out of place, it fastened on it as though riveted.

The courtyard had been swept since the departure of the hunt – necessarily so, given the predilections of excited horses, well fed and watered and brought to their highest point in the areas of urine and manure. The manure had mostly been added to the pile beside the stables, convenient to the midden chute that led out through the wall beside the Gully Hole, to the only other area near the wall not torched by the Kerrs the previous night. Straw had been scattered over the flags and probably swept up again after the rest of the hunt had returned. Yet over there, beside the door Tom was approaching, between the well-worn, well-swept flags, there lay a little black scrap, spurned by the brooms, obviously, and pushed back towards the doorstep instead of over towards the manure heap. Why it attracted Tom's eye only Tom could tell – perhaps because it looked so strangely out of place; perhaps there was even some spark of recognition too deep ever to be registered. Or perhaps it was his Better Angel once again. Tom stooped and picked it up, wondering at first what on earth it could be. It was a little tube of black leather, stitched to a point but open at an end. It was of a size to slip over a finger. Tom almost slipped it over his own finger – but refrained at the last moment and put it into his pouch instead. For he had recognized it. He knew what it was, at least. It was the finger of a glove – cut off and cast aside; the finger of a black, Spanish leather glove.

It was just at that moment that Hobbie Noble's hand closed on his shoulder and recalled Tom to himself.

'Come, Tom,' said Hobbie. 'No more of this waking dream. We've work to do and a Kerr to practise it on.'

CHAPTER SIXTEEN

Selkie

'We have dungeons of course,' said Sir Thomas, looking at the young woman. 'Were you the lad you appear to be, then I would lock you there.'

'Were I a lad,' spat their prisoner, 'then no doubt I'd be in the Black Douglas's dungeons by now.'

'You're lucky not to be there in any case,' said Tom equably. 'I know little of the Laird of Hermitage, but I cannot suppose you would be enjoying the experience.'

'I'm not enjoying this one,' she hissed back.

'At least it involves no direct discomfort, yet,' said Tom. 'And mind also that you're likely to survive it. Lord Robert says that when we visit Hermitage next there'll be at least a brace of Kerrs hanging by the door to greet us.'

'Come,' said Sir Thomas shortly. 'You know the reputation of the man as well as I do, lass. He's famous through the Borders. If you were in Hermitage instead of here with us, d'you think you'd be sitting in Lord Robert's private chamber with a glass of sack to steady you and Lady Ellen to look to your bruising as soon as she is free – whether Lord Robert is truly associated with your clan or they with him?'

'And d'ye think if I was safe home in Stob with Hugh and Dand I'd be worried over either of ye?'

'I do,' said Tom forthrightly. 'I know nothing about Hugh of Stob, but I know that Dand and the others of his band – including you – were called down to Housesteads on the urging of a man that's guest with Lord Robert and that ye were called down there to put a stop to me. For all your saying, hissing and snarling, you answered the Black Douglas's call swiftly enough, did ye not? So at home or abroad and with Dand if not with Hugh, you are worried about the thoughts of the Laird of Hermitage – and if not you yourself, then those whose orders you obey.'

'Ha!' she spat. 'D'ye think I obey . . .'

'Of course not. If you obeyed anyone – parent, priest or the elders of your clan – then you'd never be roistering around the Borders dressed as a lad and getting into worlds of trouble. If it were not for you, then none of this coil would be wrapped around us. Dand would still have his hand.'

'It was you that took it!'

'It was you that he was helping when it was taken; you that was trapped out on the moss and likely to die there and then.'

'D'ye think I don't know that?' she shouted in return. 'That's why I came out last night and braved the Barguest!'

'Ha!' This time the derisory laugh belonged to Hobbie. 'Did ye not know it was a trick, girl? A horse done up with a false head?'

'No! Not that one, the other one!' Her voice trailed away and she frowned back in silence at the three awestruck gazes resting on her pale, determined countenance.

The sound of that second howling echoed in Tom's memory, certainly, and he saw that it echoed also in the minds of the other two.

'You cannot have seen it,' he said. 'Child, it would have killed you on the spot as it is said to have killed my brother, through simple terror.'

'I did not see it, no,' she answered. 'But I heard it.'

Hobbie laughed aloud at that. He laughed with relief, thought Tom, that an explanation might be offered after all; for they were all, it was clear, afraid of the phantom dog.

The girl thought that he was laughing at her. 'I heard it hunting me,' she snarled, stung into more truth yet. 'Only the strength of my little Selkie kept him off. I went away north along the ridges past Crew Crag, but it hunted me to Arthur's Seat and I could ask no more of Selkie. So we went under the great oak and into the undergrowth there, for there is a cavern there . . .' She tailed off and they watched her in silence, for once again her tongue had worked faster than her mind and betrayed her.

After a moment she looked up at them defiantly. 'There is a cavern above the spring there, in the little cliff below the bushes and I thought to be safe and mayhap a little warmer there. And so I was, by the luck of the Good Lord; but Selkie fell and I lost her. And *it* . . . it came on down after me. I could hear it outside the cave mouth howling . . .'

The place was obvious enough, under the clawed oak tree and behind the bloody pit left by the disposal of the stag. Still Tom said, 'Here?' and the girl Janet nodded. Because they were all confederated upon a larger, more disturbing quest, she had lowered her guard to the extent of her name and her word that she would attempt no escape. Though there remained in Hobbie's mind, as he made no secret, a question as to the worth of a woman's word. Still, he kept his concerns fairly quiet, secure in the certainty that if she broke it, she wouldn't get far before he caught her and taught her the lesson so clearly lacking in her upbringing so far.

Tom looked down, wondering whether he should call for the rope he had thought to bring with him this time; but then his manly pride asserted itself. Janet Kerr had made it down here without a rope last night, he thought – in the dark and in the grip of a good deal of well-warranted terror. The undergrowth at the lip of the cliff was torn away and, now that he was looking for them, he could see twin sets of marks – of Selkie the pony falling to her doom and of her mistress – scrambling down and up; down last night out of the reach of the Barguest, and up this morning and into the teeth of the hounds. No wonder the child had screamed.

Well, then, he thought, let us see what we shall see, deciding against further questioning when his own good eyes could tell him all he wanted to know at the moment. Holding on to a strong-looking branch that leaned out over the little abyss, splintered at the bottom as evidence of Selkie's passing if not the Barguest's, he swung down.

At once Tom found himself hanging, one-handed, over a drop of ten feet or so. Fortunately, near seven feet of this was covered by his own stretched body and so it was a fall of only one yard more before his feet hit the slippery slope below. He skidded a little, but then stood firm and turned to look around. The bank rose immediately behind him with a narrow crack showing just enough disturbance to mark it as the cave mouth. There were bushes around it that would have hidden it perfectly in the summer and he wondered that he did not know the place himself, for it was a very heaven for children down here, he thought. Or it had been before the Barguest came abroad.

That thought made him shiver. He had seen the thing in childhood, and yet he had questioned his own memory. The thing had clawed the tree above – and yet he had convinced himself there must be some other explanation. He had heard it last night and supposed it an echo of some kind, and now this girl had seen it

Yet, his rational mind persisted, even if the beast existed, was that proof that it had killed his brother? And the word of a girl, terrified and on the run . . . What was it Will had made Theseus say in his new play of the midsummer dream, about being out in the woods?: 'Or in the night, imagining some fear, | How easy is a bush supposed a bear . . .'

Even as these thoughts attempted to distract him – like Father Little yesterday morning before Lord Robert had arrived – he was busily at work. Here, clearly, poor Selkie had fallen, only to slither deeper down the vale with legs broken for certain and neck, too, most likely. He would follow that broad pathway later, for he had a more immediate focus now. Here had the girl leaped free of the horse and, in a panic, run inwards into the cavern; and here, something had followed. But what, precisely? The Barguest, if she was to be believed; and it had been here twelve hours since, its huge pads scratching where his good boots scuffed.

Where were the marks down here like the ones that its claws had made above? Where were the sharper-than-a-knife incisions into the ground where it walked? There were none. But something had been here, for the bushes by the cavern mouth were torn; some of the branches seemed to have been chewed. What looked like drool was frozen among the icicles, thicker and yellower than they; and everything around the narrow entrance certainly smelled of dog – dog and loam and mould and . . . something else? What else? Something metallic perhaps? His mind closed down in concentrated thought . . .

So that when Hobbie dropped like a petard exploding right beside him, he jumped and slid away from the place again. But Hobbie, ever practical, just reached down and pulled him back, and that he did one-handed, for Hobbie had brought a torch with him.

'Sir Thomas?' he called up, 'do ye wish to see the place? It's slippery but safe enough. No Kerrs in waiting to kidnap any of us after all. Shall we bring the lassie down?'

'I'll guard her here for the present,' came the answer.

'Wise enough,' said Hobbie; 'there's no telling what else may be down here even if there's no more Kerrs. Shall we in, Long Tom?'

Thus warned to mind his head on the roof at least, Tom nodded, and the pair of them squeezed in. The little cavern opened out and upward into the cliff immediately behind the deceptive little door. They stepped over a low sill into a great crackling nest of leaves and branches, thick and springy enough to provide a warm, safe bed.

'The child's right,' Hobbie said in wonder. 'This is a sizeable place. It's as well the entrance is so narrow,' he continued, 'or we'd be like to waken a winter bear! That would remind the pair of us how to hop, skip and jump, eh, Tom? Or is there magic in those great long swords of yours that would bring even a bear to its knees?'

'Are there bears still?' asked Tom, paying Hobbie scant attention as he searched the place with narrow eyes.

'So they say. In the deep woods still – the wild woods that still lie even at the hearts of Inglewood Forest and some of the others up here. Bears like the ones they bring to be baited from Russia into Berwick and New Castle with the grains from Gdansk; and big black boar such as they still hunt in High Germany; and a wild grey wolf or two, left from the days of Robin Hood, like as not.

Ye can hear them howling on full-moon nights, I'm told, in the last deep thickets as the ironmasters and the metalworkers clear the forests for charcoal for their furnaces and the shipwrights come in deeper and deeper, looking for heart of oak and straight, tall pines for the fleet to answer the next armada when it comes. Or maybe the wolves are all as dead as Robin himself and it's the Barguest they've heard instead.'

Tom was still paying scant attention, though it was unusual to hear Hobbie wax so sad and lyrical. The walls of the little cavern were consuming his lively attention. They were strangely banded with ridges, and the ridges seemed to glitter in the light. Following the gleaming glitter down, he stirred the thick-piled bottom of the cave.

'Looking for smuggled goods – such as the Kerrs would leave convenient in a secret place like this?' asked Hobbie more brightly.

'I don't know what I'm looking for,' said Tom. ' 'Tis likely a distraction to be looking for anything at all. And yet . . . Hobbie, do you know what sort of rock this is?' Tom straightened with a piece of rock the size of a crab apple in his hand. It glittered dully, a greeny golden colour.

'Nay, lad. I know about reiving, not metalworking.'

Tom nodded and slipped it in his pouch.

'Mind,' continued Hobbie without thinking. 'If ye want to get an idea, then ask John the Blacksmith . . .' He stopped, frowning. Tom nodded.

'And failing my brother John? Who should I ask then?'

'I know of no one else to ask about the rock. But you could ask your sister Eve, who John would have asked if he did not know the answer.'

'Later perhaps, when she is stronger, if I feel the toy has import.' Tom tapped his pouch dismissively. 'But to the matter in hand. Is that opening proof against something of the size and power of the creature that clawed the tree, d'ye suppose?'

'Not if it was hunting. It'd be in here like a terrier after a rat.'

'But if the lass is right, then it was hunting. It had chased her for nigh on five miles.'

'She's mistaken, then. 'Tis not a likely tale in any case.'

'Yet you heard the hound echo your own wild call.'

'I heard an echo, aye.'

'Then, my master huntsman, let us grant her a grain of truth. And let us exercise some logic. We heard the cry, therefore there was something that cried. The girl heard it too and heard it follow her. Therefore it followed. She glimpsed it and she heard it over five long miles. Therefore it hunted. It brought her to bay here and could have dug her out if it wanted. But it did not. It left her and it went away. Therefore, old friend . . .?'

'Therefore it's all a lie. Therefore she was not hunted. Therefore 'tis all moonshine, man.'

'Therefore it was not the rider that the great hound hunted. Therefore it was . . .'

'The horse!'

'Indeed. Let us look to poor Selkie, who may indeed have saved her wild young mistress's life.'

As they slithered down the icy slope after the unfortunate horse, Hobbie said, his voice low, ' 'Twould needs be a monstrous hound indeed to hunt a hobbie horse.'

'Thus are we come full circle, are we not? 'Twould need to be a monstrous hound to do that to the great oak, and to kill John through pure fear. 'Twould need to be a monster such as you released against the Kerrs last night.'

Hobbie, slightly in the lead, pulled back the last of the bushes and froze. 'Why Tom,' he said, his voice unsteady, 'I think it may well be.'

There in front of them lay the place where Selkie had fallen. It was a little clearing, made wider by the thrashing of the unfortunate animal's body. Everything was stained with blood – the exact opposite of the ritual cleanliness of Sir Thomas's hunt this morning. That was all. The little clearing had been turned into a very shambles and then left empty.

Tom and Hobbie looked at each other, lost in wonder. For whatever had hunted Janet Kerr's pony had brought it to bay here and slaughtered it; and then it had proved big enough and strong enough to carry poor Selkie's body away.

CHAPTER SEVENTEEN

Spate

A ll four of them went after it.

The three men would have fain left the girl but none of them wanted to stay with her – and Janet needed restraining as well as guarding, thought Tom with his usual insight, for her warlike blood was up. She wanted as much as any of them to go after the creature that had so terrified her in the night. She wished to be in at the death of the monster that had slaughtered and stolen her poor beloved Selkie, though she knew the experience of finding the pony would test her to the limit, let alone the experience of finding whatever had carried it off. The knowledge deepened the respect he felt for the girl into something different.

They tethered the four restless ponies beside the clawed oak. Tom unloaded rope, spears, Jedburgh axes and the pistols he had still kept in his panniers. The four-barrelled bastard pistol Ugo Stell had warned him against remained, regrettably, in the satchel containing his papers in Sir Thomas's study, but under the flap of his saddle instead was the very arquebus that had nearly despatched young Janet Kerr, in the time before Tom had known her or liked her. He exchanged this for his swords. Hobbie and Sir Thomas both had crossbows like the ones that had claimed Dand's hand and killed a full-grown fourteen-point red deer stag with one shot. Tom smiled grimly at the arsenal they thus revealed. No one rode unarmed in the Borders, he thought – except for captives, like Janet herself.

She went unarmed, though mutinously, for she was clearly accustomed to getting her own way, beyond reasonable expectation.

Tom took the lead with Hobbie, falling into old ways with unsettling swiftness. The whispered exchange of monosyllabic signals, the silence of sign and countersign were things born of poaching expeditions away south in Inglewood, away down the years; but they all came back in a flash, he thought. To be fair, though, they needed few enough of these, he knew, for they were crossing a part of Sir Thomas's territory that no one even bothered to patrol; and if the land belonged to anyone other than the English knight who was tracking carefully through it, then it belonged to the woman currently being tended by the Lady Ellen.

Tom soon saw that they needed few of their tracking skills either, for the Barguest and its victim had left a considerable pathway through the rough foliage and the low coarse bracken and winter-thin fern with which it was interspersed. They followed this pathway, therefore, which was to Tom as wide as the primrose path to the everlasting bonfire, down the gloomy little valley towards the head of the Black Lyne river itself.

Every now and then Tom's eyes glanced up from his feet to the higher spheres above. The heavens, increasingly distant above them, were covered with restless, roiling clouds and, although the wind which set the sky all adance was kept off their faces by the high walls astride them, nevertheless it still caressed them at unexpected moments with icy little tongues of air. It still brought strange, unsettling threads of scent, smell and stench that set Tom's hair, for one, to prickling uncomfortably; and all the while in the tree tops near and far, it whimpered and howled.

As they followed the pathway so clearly marked by the drag-marks of a heavy body sluggishly bleeding from a range of gashes, so Tom found himself being distracted by the simple ease of the tracking. Any one of them could have followed poor Selkie's final passage without exercising any real skill at all. The only thing that kept even part of his busy mind on such an easy task was the fear that he would round some bush or boulder and walk into the Barguest's supper – a situation, in his opinion, likely to result in them all joining the feast themselves: as an extra course.

Yet Tom found that the way the little spring bubbled up out of the frost-bearded moss from under two great boulders, bleeding so thinly out of the earth, and battling at once to break free of the ice that sought to bind it, made him frown with distant wonder. Its very pathetic gasping seemed to be the breathing of a new-born babe – a dwarf child all but lost in the heart of this valley fit for giants. An apparently unconnected thought drifted into his mind, of the way that the acorns from the damaged oak behind them at the head of this great valley were most often found away downstream around Blackpool Gate – a thought placed there, perhaps, by the first drops of rain that attained sufficient size to batter through the branches, twigs and winter-sere leaves all so tightly packed above him. He realized with a start that it must have been raining for quite some time. And raining hard at that.

Immediately, rain was everywhere, draining over the frozen slopes across their path along the Barguest's track down into the little rivulet on their right. The water of the stream was dark in colour, as though the sudden myriad of tiny tributaries slithering under their feet were washing Selkie's blood down into it. Abruptly Tom was finding that the silent signals between Hobbie and he were more useful. It would have required a considerable shout to rise above the hissing and the howling with which they were surrounded. A new urgency entered their movements, even as the noise – to Tom at least – urged caution. For, apart from the track they were following with such ease and speed, everything around them was retreating behind impenetrable shadow and overwhelming sound.

The little river valley too, he noted with a frown, made speed more inevitable, for the slope down which they were tripping steepened beneath their feet. The whole valley seemed to tilt downwards at a greater angle while the narrow floor dropped more precipitously than the walls themselves, making the place seem deeper and darker still. The valley walls had not spread out to any great extent, but the river had widened and had carved a broader, fertile little plain. The trees between which the Barguest had lugged its increasingly tattered prize were taller, thicker, more full of branches, the undergrowth more hardy and virile.

They came to a cliff over which the river jumped in a waterfall ten feet high; and Tom, then Hobbie, stopped – signalling to the others to stop as well. For the trail ended there, at the edge of the cliff.

Tom and Hobbie stood shoulder to shoulder. 'The beast's dropped Selkie over and she's fallen into the pool down there,' said Tom.

'Aye,' concurred Hobbie. 'But then has the thing gone down after her – or has it simply gone?'

'Or is it still waiting here, in shelter somewhere?' Tom looked around with narrowed eyes, thinking, *How dark it has become!*

'We need to look and be sure before we proceed,' decided Hobbie. 'It's one thing to be hunting the thing . . .'

'And quite another to be hunted by it,' agreed Tom. 'Well, we'd better split up and make a search – in pairs, I think.'

Tom took Janet. If there was reasoning in the choice, it was slight and soon forgotten but, as is often the case, it made a deal of difference. It was bitter cold. They were wet but not yet soaked to the skin, for their cloaks were thick, made of oiled wool, and near watertight. Beneath them both wore jacks and the metal saw off any moisture making it through the cloaks without even disturbing the well-tanned, quilted leather, which was again effectively waterproof. Both wore high boots over thick, oiled-wool tights. Both wore steel bonnets that would rust before they leaked, strapped tight beneath their chins nevertheless. Even in the downpour, therefore, their first instinct – and that so strong and with such good reason that they never thought of giving up and going home to the warm and the dry – was to proceed.

Tom gave Janet a spear and took the other for himself. He laid his arquebus against a tree, for its matchlock would be useless in the rain, and Hobbie gave him one of the two crossbows. He gave one of his Solingen daggers to Janet, and having the short weapon to go with the long one settled the woman's tight-strung nerves, as Tom had planned that it should. With the arquebus useless, Tom reckoned he could no longer rely on the pistols either, but he kept them, dry, tucked in his belt, safely against the back of his shirt – and the flint and powder he needed to set them off, all, again, in a waterproof oiled-leather pouch under his jack against the breast of his blessedly still-dry shirt.

So they made a few simple plans in sign and snatched phrases, then parted company. Tom waved Hobbie and Sir Thomas out to the right, where they would search up the valley slope of the bank that they had been following so far. Then he and Janet, in their high boots, splashed across the shallow, six-foot width of water-fall's head and struck out upon the left bank.

Tom noticed that things were subtly different here and, if anything, worse. There was no track to follow now, and Tom found all his skills in woodcraft suddenly being tested to the limit. Fortunately, Janet seemed to be as adept as he and they formed a team as he and Hobbie had done, using the same simple code of signals. They stayed close together of necessity, for there was too much noise for them to hear anything less than a shout at more than two fathoms' distance and the afternoon had darkened down as soon as the clouds had thickened and the sunlight had left the little valley. More than once Tom looked up to find himself alone with Janet one step too deep in the shadows for him to see her at all.

They had other reasons to stay close together, too, thought Tom grimly. The bank they were exploring led across a very little level area to a steep, forbidding slope. The narrow, overgrown winter-dead woodland had a haunted atmosphere. It was the sort of place where it was all too easy to see enemies behind every tree trunk and become convinced that there were movements in the restless patterns of sound immediately behind your back.

Although the Black Lyne's first waterfall filled only the centre section of the little cliff, the ridge of solid rock reached out in a precipice that jutted right across the valley. Quashing his rebellious nervousness, Tom led off to follow this first, reasoning that it would be easiest to spot whether the Barguest had found a path on downstream along this line. As they worked, however, he found himself easing back from the edge of the cliff itself, for his feet were forever being swept towards it by the gathering runnels of water flowing in crazy motion down the valley side in front of him and down the valley slope from his right to his left, as though the very ground were haunted here, and trying to drag him down.

Had he not been focused so fiercely on the twin distractions of Janet and the monster they were hunting, his agile mind might have warned him that these were signs of considerable danger gathering; and that it was a real, physical danger, not a spiritual or spectral one.

Instead, having followed the cliff edge to the valley wall and found it too difficult for man or beast to climb, they struck back in a semicircle as agreed at the outset; they were hoping to check for caves. There were none. So, in spite of their careful wood-craft and near-waterproof clothing, it was a disappointed and bedraggled pair of monster-hunters that returned to the top of the waterfall an hour later.

Tom knew that it was exactly the right place, for he could just see his arquebus, still leaning uselessly against the tree; but of Hobbie and Sir Thomas there was no sign at all. It seemed to be near night, so thick had the shadows become, and Tom had decided to return to their horses with all possible speed, when the crisis was upon them.

There was no warning. Such sound as the thing might have made was lost in the sound of the storm around them. If the ground quaked, why they were on the bank of a river at the head of a waterfall – of course the ground quaked. They could not even see it coming, for it was black water among dark shadows beneath thick-set trees. And so it took them: a wall of water chest high, blessedly lightly armed with branches; a wall of water with a full spate of the river behind it, strong enough to throw them over the waterfall that grew on the instant from a fathom wide to five fathoms wide.

CHAPTER EIGHTEEN

Gate

B ecause they were standing side by side, Tom just had the chance to drop his spear and grab hold of Janet before they went over. Because they were standing on the bank of the original stream, they were swept inwards as well as downwards into the deep pool at the waterfall's foot. Because of a great deal of quick-thinking and a good deal of luck, they went locked together and feet first.

They plunged down to the very bottom of the first pool and here their luck still held, as fortune favours the brave. The hard rock of the sill had been worn smooth over the centuries by a collection of rocks and boulders, also by the waterfall's cease-less action. Down the back of this giant ladle they slid, there-fore, and into the bowl of its spoon. Here they plumbed the depths before they were lifted up, over the forward sill of the riverbed and into the next slide into the next pool and the next and the next downstream. Water foamed around them, alter-nately inundating them almost to the point of drowning, then hurling them high above the surface so that they had a chance to catch their breath, so that they did not drown after all.

Tom held on to Janet with all his considerable strength and found that she was returning the compliment with all of hers. On their sides they stayed in feverish embrace. The clothing that had been designed to keep them dry now conspired to keep them safe. The steel bonnets, particularly, guarded their heads and faces against rocks – sharp as well as smooth – while the steel-covered jacks protected their backs and sides. Long legs fared less well, but both pairs of boots were stout and shrugged off splinters of branch and stone that would otherwise have stabbed them to the bone; and they managed to do this in spite of the fact that they soon filled, first with water and then with pebbles.

Finally, they were fortunate in Selkie. As Tom and Hobbie had surmised at the outset of this, the body of the little horse had been lying at the bottom of the first pool. There had been just enough light and reason in the whirling madness of that first wild plunge for Tom to see her and work out what she was. As they slid down the back of the spoon-shaped pool to the boulder-dancing depths, so the body of the pony seemed to spring against the sky above them. The sky was dull and the water thick, the situation hardly conducive to reasoned observation, but the outline of a horse's head was unmistakable and the rest elementary.

Tom and Janet struck bottom amid the dancing pebbles and very nearly lost their grip on one another; but then the pony, seeming to show the way in the grip of the rushing water, leaped over the rocky sill of the pool and on away down to the next. So they followed in her wake, protected by her bulk, through pool after pool and along runnel after runnel, down to the point where the valley widened abruptly and the spate washed suddenly into a last great pool where it began to lose its force. The lighter matter in the flood, the tree branches, leaves and acorns, swept a little further still. The heavier matter, such as bodies and boulders, stopped its journeying here. This was the deep dark pool at Black Pool Gate, where the river ran beside the little half-ruined kirk.

Battered, breathless, Tom pulled Janet up the pebble-strewn river bank. He was numb with cold and shock. All he could think of was the need to get the girl out of the river, the wind and the rain. So cold was his face that the torrents pouring out of the icy heavens seemed warm against his cheeks, and he was an old soldier, wise enough in the ways of death to suspect that this was a very bad sign.

The storm proved Tom's friend in more ways than this, for the near-darkness of the evening was suddenly rent by a huge flicker of lightning. The brightness was dazzling, almost golden, and there for only the briefest of instants; but it outlined not just the edge of the Waste high above but also the black edifice of the little kirk immediately in front.

As he dragged Janet Kerr towards the place, Tom sought to kick his mind and memory into some kind of motion. He knew that if he slipped into the deep lake of sleepy lethargy that beckoned at the heart of it, then the pair of them were like to die. He knew to within an ell where he was. Who was there lived nearby? And where? Headgate, Todholes, Nook and Knowe were the nearest farmsteads. They all lay at some distance – though a determined man might walk to them, even through this; but half of them had lain untenanted through his childhood; and things had grown worse since then.

The kirk had fallen into some disuse, too, though Tom remembered someone saying that Father Little had been working to re-establish the little congregation there; and had even come over here this morning after the hunt. He would never have waited, however. There would be no one in the little kirk now – no one near enough to help them at all, in fact; no one nearer than God himself.

Even so, thought Tom grimly, aware that the shivering that possessed his frame was rapidly becoming an uncontrollable shuddering, this was their only chance: shelter first; then dryness; then the heavenly prospect – heavenly in distance as well as beauty – of warmth.

First he had to open the churchyard gate. In fact Tom found this first step quite easy, for as he pulled himself up off the pebbles at the churchyard wall, so he leaned against the crazy wicket and it collapsed back off its ancient leather hinges, inviting him past at once. Had he not still been wearing his steel bonnet, his face would have suffered when he fell forward; but the shock of the fall roused him further and gave him the wit to discard the heavy helmets from both his own head and Janet's before he dragged her onwards.

135

Half-up on his knees and left hand, with the right hand clasped round Janet's wrist, Tom laboured up the pebble path towards the old church door. The kirk at Blackpool Gate was small; so was the churchyard, and the path was miraculously short. It seemed that Janet's heels were scarcely in through the gate before Tom was pulling himself up the first of the two steps into the ancient porch. The storm was coming from the north and the church faced south, so that the porch gave blessed relief at once. Blessed also was the fact that the big old Norman door, solid enough to have withstood siege as well as time, was unlocked. Tom pushed against it and it creaked open.

He pulled Janet through the doorway and into a little chamber, littered with rubble and wet with rain, that stood at the foot of the half-ruined bell tower. The state of the place was worse than Tom remembered it from childhood and it was certainly much more of a ruin than the church he had called into his fever-dream in the coach coming north; but the rubble had been cleared to one side and a path led through to the weatherproof little chapel beyond. The Good Lord had smiled upon them so far, thought Tom, and he hoped most fervently that he would continue to do so – and indulgently. For now that they were out of the storm itself, they needed warmth. Tom had to find in this place enough matter to burn as a fire and something to set it alight.

As soon as they were out of the rain – out of the room beneath the open tower – Tom left Janet lying on the cold flags of the little nave and pulled himself to his feet against the wall. He discarded his sopping cloak and immediately felt almost that he was floating' spirit-like, so heavy had the sodden wool become. The jack came next, and another great weight was gone. Would that he could just add some natural warmth, he thought grimly, to this fire-like, airy lightness he seemed suddenly to have about him. Would that he could stop this juddering in his near-frozen limbs. He would fain have removed his boots too, for they were so full of stones and water that they were almost impossible to walk in; but he wisely calculated that the simple effort of getting them off would use up the last of his strength, and that must still be put to better use.

Tom staggered back out into the room beneath the open tower. If there was the rubble of stones here, he calculated, then there would also be the rubble of wood. If the stones had been piled out of the path, why the wood might be neatly stacked as well. So it proved. Over in a corner, as much by feel as by sight in the near-pitch of the darkness, he found great balks standing – a well-chosen corner too, selected by a man with an eye to re-using such matter and conserving God's gifts to men. If stone didn't perish with the action of water, wood most certainly did. The balks were stored in the one dry area of the room, there-fore; and, at the cost of a stab-wound or two, Tom discovered splinters and kindling beneath.

Tom marked where the makings of the fire of salvation were and left them there. He was wet himself and feared he would flood their natural elements with his current icy state. Further-more, though he had the makings, he still lacked the vital spark. Festooned with powder and shot though he was, it was all, like himself, inundated. He had flint and stone about him too, but his tinder was as wet as the rest of him. He must dry his hands, therefore, and explore a little further still; and time was running out. His body was still feeling some relief at being out of the jaws of the storm, but the body of the church itself was still icy-cold and the last of the heat was coming out of his juddering frame at a terrible rate – so much so, that a distracting element of self-doubt, a disturbing fear of death began to lurk at the outer edges of his mind; and yet he fought on against the inner demons and the outer.

At the far end of the place there was a little altar. Father Little's care had placed a little white altar cloth upon the plain wood of the simple table. Tom noted its pale glimmer in the thick darkness of the place leavened a little beneath the high plain glass of the northward-facing window. He touched it, felt its dryness and left it alone as yet. Once dry, his hands would remain so only for an instant or two with the rest of his clothing down to the fine lace of his shirt cuffs still sopping. He needed one more thing – had great hope of finding it. For there were two great candles there, the white columns of their pure wax bodies seeming to glimmer. If Father Little had left candles in the place, then he might well have left the means of lighting them.

And so he had. There, on the altar itself, a black square in the last of the light, lay a little tinder box. Tom picked up a candle and used the stand that held it to move the tinder box aside. Then he took the altar cloth in shaking fingers and brutally scrubbed life into the quaking flesh of his hands and forearms as he dried the water out. Last of all, in a moment of blessed clarity, he swept the thing over his face and forehead, pulling back the dripping mop of his hair.

The instant Tom felt dry, he put the cloth aside and arranged the candles and the little box of wooden spills that sat beside them convenient to his shaking hands. Then he opened the tinder box. He had been using devices such as this since childhood – and in the dark at that. Why were his fingers so clumsy now? Why could he not hold the flint at the right angle? Why not raise a spark against the striker? His breath hissed in and out between his tight-clenched teeth as he struck and struck again. Wetness of cold sweat as well as running water was oozing past his wrists now. He dared one more strike, and raised a spark.

With all the concentration of a drowning man as he fastens his fist around a straw, Tom bent forward and controlled the jumping muscles of his belly so that a slow, steady breath of air fanned the tiny spark in the heart of the tinder until it flamed. With shaking hand, he reached for a spill and slid the end of it into the little smouldering ball, blowing as steadily as he could until the flame spread from the one to the other.

Slowly Tom straightened, unconsciously hunching over the tiny spark of life, protecting it from wind and rain while it ran unsteadily up the shaft of wood, and carried it across the tiny distance to the candle wick.

Even when both candles were well alight, Tom could not relax. He stumbled down the echoing, weirdly dancing chamber of the nave, past Janet, who lay as still as a fallen monument in her spreading puddle of water and out into the room beneath the tower. Like a leper, he skinned his insensible knuckles against the wood as he shifted the bigger balks aside and carried the makings of a fire into the nave. There were no pews – not even a private area for the great and the good. Had the tower not been half-ruined, there would have been nothing in the sparsely furnished place to burn except for the altar, and the priest's chair that also served as pulpit. Then, likely, they would both have died before the bitter night was out.

The tower had fallen, though, and Father Little had piled the smashed wood in a dry corner, and so Tom built his fire in the very heart of God's little house and, with candle flames and a spill or two he set it all alight – set it so and kept it so, all through the long, cold night; but that was by no means all he did.

Once the fire was safely alight, Tom looked to Janet. He stripped her of her cloak before he moved her and placed her cloak with his over the priest's chair, which he pulled as close to the flames as he dared. Then, thinking more clearly as he began to warm a little, and having desecrated the altar cloth in any case, he pulled the solid table over and set up a simple rack between that and the chair using wood from the room outside. That rack conveniently went between the door and the fire, cutting down further on the draughts, especially after he hung her jack beside his upon it. Belts were next – with such daggers and guns as the Black Lyne had left to them – and shirts, though this left them both naked to the waist. The desecration of the altar cloth was compounded as he tried to rub some life and warmth – and dryness – into the marble of her shoulders and back. He did not touch her front, for three reasons: two were soft and white, pink-tipped and tempting even in his icy condition. The third was exactly between them and it was an ugly black: the great round bruise. That mark showed her fortitude, for it must have been a source of potent agony from the moment his shot had struck her to the moment she had fainted of the cold in the rushing river.

The fire was blazing merrily now, the ancient timbers spitting and crackling as the tall flames consumed them. It gave off brightness as well as warmth, allowing Tom's wandering eyes to see the walls and roof of the place. The roof was high and pointed. Just as it kept the rain out, so it kept the smoke in, and already the highest point was beginning to fill with fumes – but, Tom thought, even eventual damnation for this sacrilege was preferable to instant death now. Below the sharp slope of the roof, the walls were rough – roughened, in fact. In the days before King Henry and the split away from Rome there had apparently been beautiful paintings of saints and Bible scenes there. They were gone now, and simple Bible texts etched in black against the rough white were all that remained. Idly, Tom wondered what had happened to the golden candelabra and great gold cross that were said to have decorated the place in the legends of his youth, long forgotten until this moment – until the necessity had arisen, in this place of all places and at this particular time, of distracting his lower spirits from the fact that he was alone with a near-naked woman.

Even this close to the fire the flags of the floor still struck icily through their sopping clothes. When he was sure he could bring no more life into her upper body working as he was, therefore, he lifted her and sat her on the steaming cloaks in the priest's chair. Then he fell to easing off her boots, allowing the warmth of the fire to bring further life into his lower back and buttocks as he worked. Her boots were not quite as long as his, but they were equally full of water and pebbles, both of which slopped out of them as soon as they came free. He emptied each with almost drunken care and stood them as close to the fire as he dared.

'So, this is ravishment, is it? It's a sight more gentle than my mother warned me. And a sight less hot to boot.'

Tom sat back on his heels and looked up at her. In the firelight she seemed a thing made all of gold – above the waist, at least, and below her raven hair. He opened his mouth to rebut the accusation. Then he recognized the tone of her voice. He glanced up further. Her eyes were resting on him like the eyes of a night-hunting cat, as huge as though she had been drizzling belladonna into them. He looked up further still. On the wall above her head it said: THOU SHALT NOT COMMIT ADULTERY; and for some reason that struck him as exquisitely funny.

'Janet Kerr,' he said, his voice atremble with strange hilarity, 'you are safe from me this night. What with the river reminding me of the closeness of death and the place reminding me of the nearness of heaven and, most especially, these boots reminding me of the torments of hell, I fear I would never dare to transgress.'

She sat for a moment, looking down at him. Then she smiled and said, 'Let us remove your boots at least, and see what might follow then, in the matter of heaven at least.'

The morning sun came late and dull. It found them enmeshed in a tangle of cloaks and clothing – and of each other's limbs. Nothing was dry, but everything was warm and, such had been the length of their attempts to visit heaven and their repeated little brushes with exquisite death, the fire was still ablaze. Tom woke first, stirred as ever by his stomach. He opened his eyes groggily, for he had not been asleep for all that long; and the first thing he saw was a pile of pebbles from his boot. In the absence of pillows such as soft southerners were growing used to, they had used blocks of wood, but even so his face was close down to the floor. The pebbles seemed quite a little mountain to him, therefore; and, in the brightness of the fire as it struck across his shoulder, they seemed to be gleaming a little. Still held by the rags of last night's sensual dream, he reached out and felt the gleaming pebbles with an idle finger. They were warm. He stirred them. They were smooth – almost as smooth as Janet wrapped against him. He picked one up. It was heavy. It was very heavy indeed.

Slowly, carefully, gently as though in a dream, Tom sat up. The cold whipped at his shoulders at once but he paid it no mind at all. Even shadowed from the fire, with nothing but the dull cobweb-grey of the morning, the pebble seemed to glitter;

and it slid down into his palm with almost sensuous slowness, like quicksilver. But it wasn't silver at all. What in God's creation was it?

Janet stirred against him, coming awake. Gently, even in his dazzled state of mind, he extricated himself from her and began to sort through the gleaming pile. Still almost asleep, as though sleepwalking indeed, Janet pulled herself away from him and stood. She caught up some covering and padded away towards the door. Cold struck again and bore upon him most urgently that they had best get dressed and moving at once; but the gleaming pile distracted him – so that Janet had to scream twice, and at the top of her lungs, before he ran out to see what had frightened her.

Even when he reached her side she had to gesture twice again before he looked up and saw: halfway up the tower was a little balcony, floored with wood and edged with a rough banister. Here stood Father Little staring down at them – staring down and screaming, eyes and mouth spread wide, tongue rigid and protruding; screaming with stark terror.

But screaming silently, for he was clearly dead.

CHAPTER NINETEEN

Post Mortes

They had not buried John Musgrave in a coffin but in a winding sheet. So it was that Tom could begin to make observations about the true state of his brother even as he oversaw the manner in which his body was eased out of the shallow grave. A coffin would have been unusual, for John was not an important man, but in any case, thought Tom, given the state of the ground it would have been impractical, and given the state of the corpse it would have been impossible.

It was after noon on the third day, the dawn of which had brought Janet's discovery of Father Little's corpse. In the interim, Tom had discovered the father's little pony tethered securely in the churchyard behind the kirk and had used that to make contact with one of the groups of men the battered Lord of the Waste had sent out to search for his still-missing guests in the dawn. He had accepted Lady Ellen's assurance that the kitchen at Bewcastle fort had been cleaned and scoured in case the sickness visiting them now had arisen from some failure there. He had fed, dressed – in a clean, neatly mended shirt for a wonder – and left Janet mutinously in Lady Ellen's charge.

Then he had returned to oversee the removal of the old priest's body from the rough wooden balcony where it stood. Doing this had allowed the Master of Logic in Tom to make certain observations and deductions that he was keen to prove now. For, although Eve and Geordie were beginning to show some recovery, and he himself, although touched by the sickness, had hardly been hurt by it, he had three corpses to compare, and every reason to believe that they had been killed in the same way.

Although he had spent yesterday, the feast of St Stephen patron saint to horses, proving to his own satisfaction that something very like the Barguest must exist, nevertheless he was also certain in his own mind that it had not after all killed these men. For he could say with some certainty that Father Little had not died of fear, and with great certainty that Archie Elliot had not, for everyone said the man had just fallen off his horse of a sudden, calling and convulsing.

Yet if the Barguest had not killed Archie, Father Little and, therefore, John, then something else had – or, more likely, some*one* else. Some person, or some secret confederation of people, was a more likely proposition as the origin of these deaths than, say, a repetition of simple accidents; or they seemed so in Tom's mind. This was because of the attempts on his own life, because of the generality of the sickness within Bewcastle fort, and because he could conceive of nothing that his brother John and Father Little could have shared, other than the company of the same, limitedly local people.

Certainly, thought Tom, checking his logic by assessing it from another angle, the Barguest had left no sign of being in the kirk at Blackpool Gate, though Satan himself might have stood close once or twice in the night, in the persons of the demons of lust. Nothing had clawed the stones or the rubble or the balks of timber beneath Father Little's balcony. Yet something had clawed the great oak – and again, if not the Barguest, then something else, or someone else. Finally, therefore, that person or confederacy had struck time and again, covering their tracks for reasons of their own; but now they must be found and stopped and made to pay. For with the Father's death, all ten of the commandments had been broken now.

Yesterday's torrential rain had ceased. This morning had been brighter but ice-bound once more. Now the freezing afternoon threatened snow. The water of yesterday's flood seemed hardly to have penetrated the earthen clods of John's grave. Perhaps just enough to mould the rough cloth of the winding sheet more tightly about the body and give it a crisp patina of ice. Even to make it almost transparent in places – over the face, particularly. And here the outline of the cloth showed John's face still frozen in his dying scream, but there was no great staining of mud; nor, to Tom's relief, was there any great icy puddle out of which the body might have to be chipped like a precious stone in an open mine.

That had been a particular worry to Tom, who was still castigating himself over the length of time it had taken him to come to this necessary point in his investigation. The God of the Borders was not a forgiving God, and Tom was quite sure that laggardness was almost as much of a sin as the manner in which he had passed last night.

Then again, no: there could be few things worse than the list of desecrations he had committed, finishing with carnal knowledge of a Kerr in the chancel of a kirk.

Tom gave himself a mental shake and called his straying wits, blessed with enough self-knowledge to understand that his thoughts were wandering because of the horror of the work at hand. This, though, was the horror he had been sent into the North to face. Therefore Tom jumped into the icily dry and solid bottom of the grave as soon as he was able. Even as he did so, he was struck by how wide the hole was – something that had not been obvious with all the rough clumps of earth piled neatly on top of it; and he saw at once why this was so. John's body, lying reverently on its back, eyes fixed on heaven, was still spread wide at hand and knee. It was still frozen in the attitude in which they must have found it, kneeling with one knee on one of the two spread branches and the other on the other one. He had remained frozen in that attitude for more than a week now – frozen literally since his burial, perhaps, for all the world nearby had been in the grip of frost and ice for at least a month now; but frozen in other terms than being gripped by ice.

For, thought Tom, taking hold of the marble-solid arm within the winding sheet, Father Little's arm had felt no softer;

and, although Tom might allow the kirk at Blackpool Gate to have been icy-cold in all areas except one, it was obvious that the good father had died on his feet, and remained frozen on his feet most unnaturally. Every dead man that Tom had seen had fallen at the point of death, if not before; but not Father Little. He had locked into some kind of seizure, had set like a rock as he died, as though he had seen not the Barguest but the Gorgon itself.

As Hobbie had said while they fought to free the good old man from the balcony, they could have carried him to one of the empty chapels in his church and stood him up as the statue of a saint.

As Tom climbed into the cart beside the solid body of his brother, he was aware that he would have to be quick about the rest of his investigation. It was all very well for the Lord of the Waste to oversee John's post-mortem swiftly and quietly, slipping him into the ground with a minimum of fuss before sending Eve and Hobbie south; but with Father Little now added to the death-list, it would only be a question of time – and little enough of that – before the Bishop of Carlisle became involved. Then, no doubt, the Archbishop of York and all the rest.

Bewcastle fort was an unseasonably gloomy place. Three tragedies within little more than a week, a serious attack by the Kerrs, and the Barguest abroad made everyone tense and jumpy; but all of that was nothing compared to entertaining these three corpses in the chapel – one of them recently exhumed at that.

Having dead men about the place was nothing unusual here. There were other dead men in the chapel now: the dead from the skirmish with the Kerrs. They were laid out reverently, awaiting burial as was due and natural – natural if unfortunately delayed now, given the circumstances. But there was nothing natural about the three corpses Tom needed to examine; and, so the rumour would no doubt go, Tom suspected wisely, there was nothing natural about the things he was proposing to do to them. In fact, all he really needed to do was to use his eyes and his intellect, to call upon the expertise he had to hand, if he found a problem beyond his own experience. To complete a theory – or call upon the Master of Logic to do so; to test it if he could; to prove it true so far as he was able. And to act.

As chance would have it, the recently dead from the attack by the Kerrs would also in their way be of use to him, thought Tom, for they were normally, almost naturally, deceased. There would, Tom suspected, be differences between them and the three he was examining most closely – or two of them at least, certainly – and these would begin with the rigidity of their limbs.

These thoughts filled Tom's head as he hesitated in the doorway of the little chapel and looked in at the six corpses lying there, the unnaturally dead nearest the altar, the naturally dead at the back. This was nothing to do with superstition. It was how Tom had ordered things. His experiences of the night had taught him – amongst much else – that the brightest part of any church is likely to be beneath the window and therefore above the altar.

Tom's orders, disseminated via Sir Thomas and the lady Eve, had been obeyed in other things as well – also adding to the sense of outrage in the fort. Father Little lay exactly as he had been found, except that he was lying down, placed here with no reverent preparation such as was fitting in the face of the Lord – fitting especially in such a holy and popular man, so respected, indeed well-beloved in the place. Tom was all too well aware of the cold and angry stares that were being directed at his back; so that when a hand fell on his right shoulder, he actually jumped.

'Fear not, Tom,' whispered Eve's ghostly voice; 'it is merely myself. And in the flesh, for a wonder.'

'You're lucky it's not her ghost, I think,' continued the Lady Ellen more robustly on his left side. 'But we are come to help.'

'To listen at least,' said Eve wryly, 'if I know my Tom.'

Having the pair of them there gave Tom the strength to proceed; but Eve was right, at the outset at least: they had little to do but to listen and to confirm his observations.

'Let us look at this man first,' he began slowly. 'Killed in battle and prepared for burial but not yet in his winding sheet. His name?'

'Walter Milburn,' said Lady Ellen.

'Very well. What might we expect to see about the man? Even with poor Walter thus attired in his best, we have his face and hands available to us, and we may observe without disturbing him too much. His face is livid, you will agree. His eyes, though closed, are black-ringed and protuberant. You can see that more clearly if I lift the pennies here. His cheeks are sunken. We can see, even though his jaw has been bound, for his jaw is slack and prone to fall open . . . There! We can see that his beard is of two days' growth or so.'

'He was clean-shaved as we laid him out,' said the Lady Ellen.

'A hairy man like Esau, then, for that's merely a day since. He has been dead a day and a night.'

'Even so,' agreed Lady Ellen, sadly.

'It is a mystery of nature, My Lady. I have seen it in the unburied dead of battle. I am told that even the nails continue their growth, but that would be impossible to prove here, I fear, in so short a time as this. But let us look at his hand: it is also cold and livid like his face. It is weighty, certainly, but not stiff. See, I can move the fingers with hardly any force applied, and bend the hand back at the wrist – straighten the arm at the elbow, indeed, and rotate it at the shoulder; and I have no doubt that I could do as much for his legs, were that needful. Thus much for our eyes and our fingers. What of our noses next? Is there not about the man a smell of anything untoward?'

'Of the lye soap with which we washed him, when we had him laid out by the fire in the kitchen,' said Lady Ellen, 'and little more than that.'

'I agree, save that I had no knowledge of the soap. Certainly no stench as might be expected from bodily effusions . . .'

'When we lay them out we stop their passages,' said Eve suddenly, 'or else they leak and stink, as you observe.'

'Even so? My own experience in the matter, sadly, consists of throwing dead friends into pits on battlefields; and, I have to observe, they leak.'

'Then why, pray,' asked Eve tartly, 'are ye come hither to lecture us?'

'Because if that is the extent of my experience with *natural* death,' said Tom lightly, 'my experience with *unnatural* death is far wider.'

As he said this, Tom led them over to the first of the three corpses by the altar. 'We see at once a difference with poor Archie, do we not? He has been prepared for burial but not yet fully dressed, for he was a visitor here and died in the one set of clothes he possessed.'

'Which are being cleaned and mended as we speak,' said Lady Ellen.

'With the last of your shirts,' added Eve with the ghost of a laugh.

'And he is dead for exactly a day. But from the outset we can observe the differences: the man's face is full, almost flushed; his eyes bulge, true, but there is no sign of dark rings here; his lips are set and near as ruby as your own, Lady Ellen; his jaw is bound but needlessly so, for see, his teeth are clenched – quite rigidly, even in death. The cloth is damp here, however, below the corner of his mouth; and he is clean. Has he been cleaned? I see he has – which is why we await his clothes. His hands are folded, but again quite rigid – but in a strange position . . .'

'He clutched there at his left pap as he died,' said Lady Ellen.

'That left pap where heart doth hop,' quoted Tom thoughtlessly, his mind miles away – and equally far from Will Kempe's speech as he played Pyramus in *The Dream*; but he echoed the words nevertheless.

He rolled the rigid Archie on to his side so that he could examine the wounds on his back again. They were still there, of course, just as he remembered them; but this time he had leisure – and strong motive, indeed – for a closer look. There across the darkly furred back of the dead warrior lay the three parallel wounds, stitched at their deepest parts, livid and crusted. 'I still do not see how this could be done.'

'You're holding the only man that could have told you,' said Eve tartly.

'Not the only one, no. There is still the man that gave him the wounds; but he is likely to be hidden away in Stob with the Kerrs.'

'Unless you can think of a way,' said Eve, 'to seduce the truth out of your fair captive Janet.'

'Well, as to that . . .' said Tom – and stopped, shocked by how near he had come to confessing all that had transpired in the kirk at Blackpool Gate.

'And as to that?' asked Eve, suddenly suspicious.

'Why, that is an inspirational idea. I stand ashamed I did not think of it myself. She was there. She might well have seen; though what there was to see I cannot think . . .'

Tom's voice tailed off as he looked even more closely at the livid back presented to him. 'Lady Ellen,' he said more quietly, 'if laying out involves shaving the face . . .'

'Unless it is bearded, of course . . .'

'Aye, I see that; but if it involves shaving the cheeks, it does not – does it? – involve shaving any other parts?'

'Such as where?' demanded Eve intrigued.

'Such as the back,' answered Tom. 'Look here . . .' Sure enough, there, on the hair of Archie Elliot's back, visible now that the thick black fur was slick and wet, there was a line exactly parallel to the other three wounds where the hair on his brawny back had been shaved away.

Janet was dressed in a plaid that Tom scarcely recognized. To be fair, it was not the plaid that took his notice but the transformation the woman's clothing made in the girl. Their eyes met once and hers registered his reaction, then fell. She would not look at Eve or the Lady Ellen. Nor, indeed, would her wide eyes meet Tom's again, over the breadth of Archie Elliot's back. 'I saw nothing,' she said. 'I know nothing.'

'And if you did know something, then you would not tell in any case,' said Tom, sounding more severe than he meant to.

'But even your silence can be made to speak, if we will it so, my lady.'

'Did you just threaten to torture her?' asked Eve, agog, when the girl was gone again.

In fact Tom had meant something deeper and more devious than that, but he shrugged. If Eve thought he was willing to torture the girl, then any suspicions aroused by his careless tongue earlier were likely to be abeyed if not allayed. It did not at that moment occur to him to think what Janet herself might suppose.

That was hardly surprising, for he was turning to the next part of his task, the one that both he and Eve were going to find the most difficult – if not quite the most unpleasant.

'We found it hard to dress poor Archie,' he said as he moved, using inconsequential conversation to cover pain and stress, as he often did. 'How have we dressed that child so well?'

'It is an old dress of my own,' said the Lady Ellen. 'I've not worn it since my husband died.'

'A lovely thing,' said Tom. And he might have been talking of the clothes – or of the girl who wore them.

The men who had carried John's body in here from the cart had taken the winding sheet off it and covered it like the others with a plain blanket. Tom folded this back now and found himself staring into his brother's eyes; and John was still screaming. As silently as he had seemed to do in Tom's all-too-vivid dream, John's face remained frozen in that wide-eyed, wide-mouthed rictus that looked like the most utter, most abject terror; but still of good colour. Still, seemingly, dead so recently that his screams might be echoing somewhere yet; but wilder of hair, thicker of beard than Tom had ever seen him.

Tom folded the blanket back further still. John's hands seemed to reach up towards him. 'Dead a week and more, yet still set like marble,' said Tom quietly. He turned to Lady Ellen, who watched him over Eve's silently heaving shoulder. 'Have you ever seen the like?'

'Never,' she said.

'Eve?'

151

'Never, Tom,' she answered, though he had to strain to hear, and he noted she did not need to turn and look.

'Could it be the cold? I have heard of sheep found up on these very hillsides, gone missing in winter, then dug out of snow-drifts in spring still fresh enough for the dogs to eat.'

'Aye, and for humans too, these last few years,' said Lady Ellen, sadly.

'So it could be the cold that preserves him. But then again . . .'

Tom turned to the last of his corpses and lifted the blanket from Father Little. Apart from the shapes into which the bodies were frozen, they were identical. Eyes and mouth wide, tongues out, strings from jaws to shoulders stretched taut. Cheeks flushed, noted Tom; flesh full. Except that he was dead of terror, Father Little had never looked so well – except that, at the very corner of his mouth, disturbed no doubt by the process of bringing him here, a finger of foam, slow and slick as the trail of a slug, was winding back across his cheek. Frowning as he did so, Tom folded the blanket back again and the same hands reached out, frozen, clutching at the air as though it were a banister rail.

Frowning still, Tom turned back to John's hands. What had they been clutching when he died? After a few moments he turned back again. It was impossible to tell.

'Now, I need you to summon up your courage here, Eve. You prepared John for his laying out and burial?'

'Of course,' she answered dully. 'Immediately after Sir Thomas's inquest. Who else would do it?'

'And that was soon after they carried him down from Arthur's Seat – from the oak where they found him itself?'

'Hobbie and the others brought him. Sir Thomas held his inquest at once and he was buried within the day. Aye.'

Tom pulled the blanket back off Father Little. 'Like this?'

'As you see him. That was all.'

'But you washed him and you dressed him?'

'As well as I could, for he was as you see him now, set like marble even then.'

'But,' said Tom, with fearsome concentration, 'answer this, Eve. Did you have to wash him before you stopped his vents? Wash his body, his face?'

'No. I hardly needed change his clothes, and that was lucky as you see . . .' She gestured to the arms and legs that might have made it all but impossible for one woman alone to dress and undress the corpse; but Tom had turned away in something like triumph, and was covering the bodies again.

'What? said Lady Ellen. 'Tom, what is it you have learned? What can you tell us?'

'This, My Lady: that these three men died as near as I can tell in the same manner and of the same cause – though the force of it was lesser in Archie's case. They did not die of the Barguest and they did not die of mortal fear; and I can tell you more. I can tell you that, although I can say to within an inch where Archie Elliot died, I cannot say where Father Little or poor John died.

'The one thing I am certain of is this. Wherever it was my brother died, he did not die in the great oak up at Arthur's Seat, whether it was clawed by the Barguest or not.'

CHAPTER TWENTY

St Thomas's Eve

T om watched the Lady Ellen supporting Eve away across the courtyard, then he turned back into the little chapel. He might have finished talking, but he had not finished looking and he didn't want to lose the light. Swiftly, silently, he pulled back the coverings over John and Father Little. He hesitated as though torn – but really he knew what his priorities must be.

He started with John. Beginning at his brother's throat he loosened the neatly bowed bindings of his shirt and pulled it wide as far as the first button of the dark jerkin. Then he began to unbutton the horn buttons that held the stout leather closed, pulling that and the lawn of the shirt wider together as he worked. Soon he had exposed his brother's torso as far to the sides as his armpits and as far down as the corrugated ridges of his belly.

Here Tom paused in his manual labour and leaned forward. Like his own upper body, John's was only slightly hairy, though less sinewy and more massively developed, as befitted a blacksmith. The skin, in common with many Borderers, was quite fair and almost feminine in its delicate smoothness beyond the lightly forested breast and belly. The armpits were an amalgam. Fine hair sprouted modestly and fair skin stood on either side; and this was particularly important to Tom's investigation because that fair skin and – when he rolled his brother over as he had rolled Archie Elliot, pulling the shirt out of his belt – the fair skin on his back were very faintly marked.

The marks were so faint that he only saw them because he was looking for them – so faint that the shocked Eve would easily have overlooked them as she washed him ready for burial. Certainly she had never mentioned seeing them. Tom looked further, now that the pale expanse of his brother's back was bared. He had half-expected to find the same parallel scars that disfigured Archie; but no – not even a close shave. Frowning, Tom turned to examine the shirt more closely in case that had been cut; but again, no.

Because of the closeness made necessary by the rigidity of John's body, Tom found the lawn of his brother's best shirt almost wrapped around his face; and so, just for an instant, he caught an odour he was not expecting at all. Surprised, he paused, his mind seeming to tick like one of the new Dutch watches Ugo had shown him a month ago at Van Der Leyden's house; but he could make nothing of the matter as yet, and so he left it to one side – and would have forgotten it altogether, except that, when he went to rearrange his brother's clothing and fit him for heaven once more, he noted that the tail of the shirt he was tucking back beneath the belt was very slightly brown.

After John was restored to proper order, Tom crossed to Father Little. He had used a quiet moment in the kitchen earlier to purloin a couple of little pots. Into these, with the point of his dagger, he scraped specimens of the foam that surrounded the dead priest's mouth and then, crossing to Archie, of the dampness that soiled the kerchief binding his jaw. When they were both full, he stoppered them and cleaned his dagger with equal meticulousness. Then he covered the bodies once again.

He turned, ready to exit the icy little chapel; but then he turned again for one last time. He uncovered his brother's hands. They were huge, the massive fingers flat-ended and horn-nailed from years of work in the smithy. The growth of nails within the week had clawed them a little, but Tom could still see that the best efforts of Eve's cleaning had left some blackness beneath them. The point of his knife traced the blackness until little scrapings of soot came out. Tom took these on the ball of his thumb and rolled them with his index

155

finger, squinting at them in the last of the light, sniffing like a gardener judging a rose, easing out the point of his tongue tip to taste and spit before he re-covered the body.

'I cannot tell what you tried to grip when your final moment fell upon you, brother,' he said gently as he worked. 'Nor where they were when the quietus came. But I can guess what your hands were doing a little time before that.' Then he turned and went in search of Lady Ellen.

Lady Ellen was in the kitchen overseeing the evening meal. Although it was usually reserved for a feast, the unusual times meant that they would be eating yesterday's hunt venison. Half of a haunch was roasting on a spit and the rest of it was being chopped, ground and seasoned fit for pies and pastries. The remainder was being wrapped for preservation.

'That won't last long,' said Tom to Lady Ellen as soon as he saw her, 'unless you're putting it out in the cold, like John.'

'It won't have to,' she answered brusquely. 'It's going up to Hermitage with Sir Thomas, when Lord Robert calls us to the hawking.'

'I've come about Father Little.'

'Ready to be laid out, is he? That may have to wait until morning, bless the man; though the weight of the guilt's on your soul not mine.'

'As you say, Lady Ellen. But I called upon you to wait for good reason, I promise; and a part of it shows in this at least: whoever prepares the body must take the most especial care. Even the water that washes him might pass on something dangerous.'

Lady Ellen's eyes were wide suddenly. 'Do you tell me it's a contagion? Like the plague?' A plague in an enclosed society such as this would be the worst thing imaginable – like a contagion spreading in a ship at sea.

'No. I do not mean it spreads through air and vapours like the plague, but that it is a clinging thing that might pass from hand to hand; so take care. And, again, Archie did not give vent to any waste before you finished cleaning him? Especially in the matter of foam on the lips.'

'He did; but we cleaned him with care and are cleaning his clothes, as you know. But the other . . . Are ye sure, Tom?'

' 'Tis my next task to find out. By what Gerard called *experiment.*'

Tom hesitated again on the way to his experiment. He hesitated, not because he was doubtful of the importance of his task, but because he felt himself surrounded by half-truths and tangled motives. He had arrived here believing that he knew these people; but now he found he had done so with the eyes and understanding of a child.

Now, like the remembered Barguest he had discussed with Eve, everything seemed very different to the man. There were new elements in the mix, new characters and complications. There were tensions that the child who had gone away to Carlisle and Glasgow could never have understood; and, of course, the young man had only just been beginning to comprehend the terrible goads of lust for power, money and sex – and that from books and study – when he had been called away by his fate. The demons of violence, self-delusion, lies and murder he had conned all too well; but he had grown to his painful knowledge only upon the battlefields, schools, stews and courts of Europe and the South. And even there, the desperations of privation, starvation and utter ruin were only just beginning to bite. In all the deadly tangle he saw stretching away around him now, he simply did not know whom to trust.

But he went to Hobbie anyway.

'Mice?' said Hobbie. 'If ye want mice, then ask a cat!'

'I need them alive.'

'Still . . . Och, come along with me.' They went deeper into the stables and Hobbie kicked a bale of hay that lay in the centre of the byre there. ' 'Tis half the size it was when we put it by,' he said, 'but it's still got the same number of creatures hiding in it. They come out at the calling much easier now. Watch out!' He kicked the bale again and, sure enough, half a dozen thin mice ran desperately out of it. The two men were nowhere near as quick as cats, but they captured one each. The cats got the rest.

They carried their squirming captives through into the tack

room, where there was a little table. They held the little creatures firmly by their tails as Tom got the tiny pots out of his pouch. As his fingers sought the stoppered vessels, they rubbed against the gold-coloured rock from the cave that Janet had hidden in and the golden pebble itself. More elements to be weighed carefully before they were added to the calculation, thought Tom; but it was the stuff he had scraped from Father Little and Archie Elliot that he wished to test now. Out came the pots; out came the stoppers. Tom placed the little clay containers beneath the noses of the starving mice. They would not touch a morsel.

As Tom and Hobbie sat, nonplussed, the summons to dinner rang through Bewcastle. Both men were as sharp-set as the mice and it required a good deal of Tom's self-control to hold the pair of them. He looked around a little desperately. There, on the far side of the little room hung a pair of panniers like his own. They were stout, leather-sided and strong enough to hold a mouse through dinner. In an instant they were on the table and a mouse with its pot was in each side.

'Wash you hands with care before you eat, Hobbie,' warned Tom.

At dinner they sat in the same places as they had at the festive meal that had greeted Tom's first arrival – except that Janet Kerr was elevated to the place left vacant by John. Thus Eve and she sat shoulder to shoulder, competing for Tom's attention. Eve did this because, still too ill to make much of the venison, she was keen to understand what Tom's investigation had discovered thus far – and, seemingly, to help its furtherance. Janet had other motives and, had Tom been inclined to succumb to youthful beauty beautifully, if modestly, presented in Lady Ellen's tartan plaid, he could hardly have resisted her; but his mind, of necessity, was on other things. Later he might console himself with the thought that it was the importance of his mission, and not any phlegmatic coldness after the fiery heat of love, that kept him aloof from her looks and deaf to her conversation. There was much, on the other hand, that Tom needed to discuss with Eve, no matter whether or not she was strong enough to bear it. With

158

his rough-cut slice of venison haunch upon his trencher, therefore, and its juices running thickly off the solid, black, near-
unleavened bread, he turned to her.

'They brought him down St Thomas's Morn,' he said. 'So he
died St Thomas's Eve. Where were you then?'

'I had returned home and sat by the smithy, minding the house
and waiting for him. There is always much to do in that season, for
Sir Thomas always calls us to the fort here in the Yule itself. The
whole of his festivity turns around the hunt on the feast of Stephen
and he likes the blacksmith to be there for that – in case his guests'
horses cast their shoes . . . you can see it well enough.'

'I see. And John would be at home himself?'

'Not usually. He was a proud man. He would never wish you
to know . . .'

'If he is watching us now,' prompted Tom, 'then he will not
be too proud to hear the truth.'

'He would be out on the good. St Thomas's is the day he'd go
agooding. There's little enough wheat or barley grown up here
these days, but folk have fallen into the way of sometimes
giving a little gift instead of it – if a man has worked hard for
them and well.'

'So,' said Tom, his voice constricted suddenly at the thought
of it. 'On St Thomas's Eve and St Thomas's Day, John went
begging round the men that he had worked for in the year –
gooding, as it's called. Instead of grain to be boiled with a little
sweet milk for Christmas creed or frummety – a kind of porage,
as I remember – they gave him other charity. They would give
him – what? – an egg here and a chicken there?' He leaned
towards her fiercely suddenly, as though the fault were hers.
'Were ye beggars after all, Eve? and ye never told me of it?'

'He was a proud man, Tom. He would never have come to you.
And, in any case, he said it was his right. He had earned it; he was
owed it. Therefore he took it, little enough though it was.'

'And his uncle here, the Lord of the Waste?'

'Sir Thomas was the soul of generosity whenever we came to
him; and we came, of course, every Yuletide – whether we were
needed or not.'

'As soon as the gooding was done.'

'As you say.'

And your secret dowry? The Black Lyne: the river and both sides of the valley? Was that not an item ready for the market when the hard times came?'

'He would have none of it, Tom. I would have sold it a thousand times, but he would have none of it.'

'As you say: a proud man, then. And this St Thomas's Eve?'

'I was at home, preparing. Yes.'

'Dear God, Eve, 'Tis like pulling teeth. I'm no barber-surgeon. Let me reason past your reticence. If you were at home, then John was not. Agooding all the day?'

'So I thought, yes.'

'But not in fact?'

'He had no clients up at Arthur's Seat, Tom. There was no good to be gotten there.'

'But that is the cunning of the Barguest, Eve. Making him seem to have died under its claws cuts us off from anything before that. Where he was and what he was doing on Thomas's Eve seems unimportant in the face of that. All that is important is that he was hunted and killed by this monster; but I tell you he was not – neither up the Black Lyne nor out over Arthur's Seat. John did not die there, Eve. He had not been there. He died somewhere else and his frozen corpse was taken there later.

'So now the question of St Thomas's Eve does become important after all. Where could he have been, scarce seven days since? Not *any* St Thomas's Eve, but *this* St Thomas's Eve? If not with you in the smithy, then where?'

Hobbie leaned round the frustrated Janet on hearing Tom's question – asked far louder than the inquisitor would have liked, had he been thinking clearly. 'Why, Tom, there's no mystery about that. You need only have asked me and I'd have said. 'Tis no secret and I thought you knew: the day before he died, the blacksmith went up to the Hermitage in Liddesdale, to see Lord Robert Douglas.'

CHAPTER TWENTY-ONE

Black Robert's Invitation

'Yes!' said Hobbie quite fiercely. 'Arthur's Seat is on the way back from Liddesdale; and Liddesdale's where he went, for I saw him myself that morning all dressed in his Sabbath best as we found him. So he went to the Seat on his way back down. Or mayhap even on his way there, though it's unlikely that the Barguest hunts on a sunny afternoon, even one as cold as that. Arthur's Seat's likely where I'd go myself if I was being hunted by the Barguest!'

'But he wasn't being hunted,' repeated Tom angrily, 'and he didn't go there. He was taken there when he was dead already.'

'Dead how? Taken by who?'

'That's what I'm hoping to test at the next stage, and perhaps offer some proof. After the supper.'

'Proof?' demanded Sir Thomas suddenly, turning from his factor Fenwick. 'Proof of what?'

'How they were all killed,' said Tom forthrightly.

Sir Thomas looked at him for an instant, his face haggard and set. The adventures on the Black Lyne yesterday seemed to have aged him, thought Tom. Certainly they had done nothing to improve his temper. 'Ye think ye're making good progress with that, do ye?' Sir Thomas continued.

'I believe so, yes,' answered Thomas gently, and a lot more guardedly, suddenly aware of how little he had shared with his uncle so far.

161

'Well ye'd best get your arguments clean and clear with all the despatch ye may,' grated Sir Thomas. 'This place has been attacked by Kerrs at the very least. I've not heard back from Hugh of Stob nor One-Hand Dand over the head of our visitor there; but I've had men killed, property burned, men of my family and my command threatened as they've gone about their legitimate business for me, and my reputation damaged. There's reparation to be made.

'I may have stayed my hand a little because of the season, and given your mission and your loss; but the Bishop will be up over Father Little's death and that will stir up both Church and Court alike. You may be on the quest over your brother's death, but you've no commission to stand crowner to the rest. We've our own law up here and that must take action. Time is running out. I'll be sending down to Carlisle for the garrison soon, whether I hear more or not; and we'll be scouring out bandits and Barguests from here to Annandale if needs be . . .'

No doubt he would have added more besides had a servant not come scuttling into the hall at that very moment. 'There's riders at the gate, Captain Musgrave,' he said.

Such was the coil that the last such announcement had brought with it that this one was a call to arms at once; but the watchman's nervousness had also overstretched his nerves. The riders at the gate turned out to be a leader and two followers.

'It is Sir Nicholas de Vaux,' called up the leader in a courtly, southern accent. 'Do I speak to the Lord of the Waste?'

'Ye do,' called down Sir Thomas.

'Then I bid you good even, My Lord. I beg to inform you that I bring the Laird of Hermitage's compliments, and an invitation to all here . . .'

Sir Nicholas de Vaux gave extra life and some badly needed gaiety to the dinner in the hall. In spite of the fact that he had ridden from Hermitage, he was dressed for court and powdered as white as the fashion demanded. The darkest suspicions must needs be put aside: he was a guest and an honoured one, welcomed by the Lord of the Waste himself. He must be treated well – treated well but watched like a hawk. He was invited to the high table at once and occupied the Lady Ellen's seat upon Sir Thomas's left while she went to ensure that the meat with which they would entertain their late guest was still of the finest quality – which he obligingly, effusively, said it was; and that compliment, of course, cheered Sir Thomas himself. Tom, suddenly aware of her absence, looked around for Eve, but she had gone to Geordie Burn; and that was apt enough, for in the face of the powdered interloper he suddenly discovered in his own bosom the same truculent mistrust as Geordie must have felt for him.

If de Vaux felt any embarrassment at separating the lord from his factor Fenwick, he did not show it, being content apparently to sit and radiate goodwill and cheerful bonhomie like the god of amity come to life. Unlike Tom, who had never really lost the plain blunt border roughness, de Vaux was a practised courtier whose manners were as burnished as his golden rings. It was hardly surprising that Tom's dislike and mistrust of him, founded on the knowledge that he was one of the Earl of Essex's faction, grew. For, no matter how flattering the man might be as a messenger and bearer of an invitation to go hunting at Hermitage on the morrow – a mysterious message in that they had been promised hawking – nevertheless, thought Tom, what an elegant spy he must make. What an effective engineer to come armed with a petard of deceit to undermine still further the defences of Bewcastle and those still left alive within it.

The practised courtier remained cheerfully evasive, however, easily able to shrug off Tom's most probing questions with courteous, inoffensive and impenetrable answers. Yes, he was of the Earl of Essex's faction. Indeed he had come north from one Lord Robert to another – from Essex to Douglas – with gifts and greetings, little more. And his silent companion the Spanish Don: a foreigner and a man impossible to know – of what interests and expertise he could not begin to fathom; nor of what interest to the Earl or the Laird, come to that.

With growing frustration, and finding himself in Geordie's position, feeling like a sulky child in the face of de Vaux's brittle cheerfulness, Tom almost unthinkingly resorted to Geordie's first tactic, if not his actual words.

'I see you favour the rapier, sir. Would you care to edify the Lord of the Waste and the Lady Ellen with a pass or two at play with me?'

'With you, Master Musgrave? With the famous Master of Defence? I fear I am not worthy, sir. I should show myself as little more than a figure of fun, like that foolish actor Kempe that frighted the Queen so terribly. Has Master Musgrave told you of the incident, Lady Ellen? Too modest, perhaps. Well, I was there and I can reveal how Master Musgrave and the Earl of Essex both together won the patent of standing with naked weapon in the royal presence by protecting Her Majesty . . . *from an ass!*'

Finding himself unexpectedly foolish in de Vaux's barbed but witty account, Tom had little choice but to sit and brood as Ellen and even Janet had their heads turned by their stylish, sparkling guest. Then, before he knew it, Tom found that he had been challenged in his turn.

'A Master of Defence must needs be fleet of foot,' gushed de Vaux. 'I stand certain Master Musgrave must be at the very point of fashion in the thing. I will assay the lady Janet and he must take the Lady Ellen. Will you not, sir?'

'In what? Take the Lady Ellen whither? Forgive me, I . . .'

'In the *volte* – it is still quite the rage. I saw Her Majesty herself perform it at Penshurst . . .'

Tom gaped like the veriest hayseed, scarcely able to credit de Vaux's stupidity – or daring. The volte was the most scandalous of dances, requiring the male to grasp his partner around the waist – or on any convenient hand-hold lower – as he threw her up into the air. De Vaux might look with pleasurable expectation on tickling young Janet's fancy in such a way – and she, all aglow, was lost in innocent anticipation too – but the thought of such an assault on Lady Ellen's modesty was beyond what Tom dared. As he would never have done in any other circumstances, he pleaded the wound in his side as an excuse and made an ignominious escape out of the hall.

'It must be poison,' he said to Hobbie, finding that he did indeed need someone with whom to share his suspicions. The

Master of Logic needed to see and hear his ideas being bandied by a confidant as surely as the Master of Defence could only practise to his utmost upon the blade of an opponent. 'I would judge it must be the same poison for Archie and Father Little. On the other hand, Father Little and John share other, subtly different signs. Let us say, however, that there was one poison, which killed John, Archie and Father Little and even touched myself, Eve and Captain Burn.'

Hobbie looked down at the stiff corpses of the mice. Distantly, from the hall, music was struck up. 'The same poison used at least twice, then, and at times and places far apart at that,' he said. Then he paused. 'Unless of course it is a poison tied to Eve herself.'

'Why do you say that?'

'Because Eve was at each of the places at both times, was she not? John went out agooding upon St Thomas's Eve, but was called to Hermitage by Lord Robert. Who's to say he did not come home and partake of the poison in the smithy? He went out agooding again and was taken by the poison and died.'

'Halfway up a clawed tree in the middle of nowhere,' inserted Tom.

'As maybe. And clean enough at that, for it was I who lowered him into the cart with my own hand. But then she washed him and laid him out, did she not? Why, then it could have passed to Eve exactly as we have passed it to these mice; and she, before the force of it took her, passed it to you, who sickened, and to those who died – as, no doubt, the cats would sicken or die if we fed these mice to them. Why could it not have gone like that? Apart from the conundrum of the tree.'

'If you mean that Eve passed the poison on like an infection, then I agree, it could be done, for so I have warned Lady Ellen; but if you do mean that, then we must ask, *Why now?* Why did she not pass it on to me in the coach – while she was tending my wound? Or in any of the taverns or ordinaries we frequented on the way, in London or New Castle?'

'She could never have passed it to you in the coach,' said Hobbie thoughtlessly. 'She was too busy filling your wound with unguents, potions and powders for that . . .' Then Hobbie stopped speaking, as though he realized of a sudden that he had broken an important confidence.

Tom paused, his mind racing. Then, in the face of Hobbie's continued silence, he answered his own question: 'She would have chosen to do it now only if she knew the truth of it . . . if she were passing it on apurpose. And even then, why wait?'

'Your head is as swelled as that courtier de Vaux,' answered Hobbie shortly. 'Does it never occur to you that, even if she did pass it on apurpose, she might not be aiming for you – that she might have plans and stratagems that do not concern you at all? You've been a soldier, man: have you never seen one man struck down by a shot aimed at another?'

'Then why was I poisoned? By accident?'

'Why were any – except the man she meant to kill? If it was she, and she meant to kill.'

'Why would Eve wish to kill Archie Elliot? Why would she wish to kill Father Little?'

'Or Geordie Burn, who she now nurses? Why would anyone?'

'Learn that, Hobbie, and I think there would be few questions left to ask and no more answers needed, like as not.'

'If you say so, master.'

'But this is all moonshine, is it not? For there are several things that make the whole hypothesis unlikely if not impossible. In the first place, John could not have died at the forge because Eve could never have cleared his person and raiment of the foulness of death, could never have washed his clothing, dried it, re-dressed him and carried him to the oak; never have swung him up into the branches and left him there for you to find, having left no trace but the Barguest's claw marks.'

'Not alone she couldn't,' said Hobbie; 'but then no one could have.'

'Secondly, what reason could she have? They were poor, but she says they were happy. He was proud and intractable, but she loved him. There may have been temptations, but she was proof against them. Why would she kill him and put up this charade, therefore?'

'Again, why would anyone? Singly or confederated, why?'

'Thirdly, why indeed? What good does the resurrection of the Barguest bring to whoever has brought the beast back from the midwinter tales our grandams told us to frighten us to sleep? It did not kill John. *Quod erat demonstrandum.*'

'What?'

'As has been demonstrated. What good can they pretend?'

'Well, however he did die, he *looked* as though he had died of fright,' observed Hobbie.

'Indeed,' said Tom, dropping the scholarly mode. 'And if you were suddenly saddled with a corpse that looked as though it had died of stark terror, upon what else might you blame the fear? What else is there on the border here that might stop a strong man's heart with terror?'

'Apart from Black Robert Douglas, the Laird of Hermitage, ye mean?'

'We'll talk to Lord Robert on the morrow. Let us leave him aside until then, and think, perhaps, a step further. For John's corpse and the fear on its face has been used, has it not? It could have been hidden. Dropped in a bog-hole up on the Waste and never seen again. What has the rebirth of the Barguest gained for somebody?'

'Well,' said Hobbie without further thought, 'it has stopped all visiting and wassailing. The season is more like Lent than Christmas since John's body was brought down. Even visiting church to hear mass has ceased after darkness. Apart from that mad southern gentleman who doubtless knows no better, only the Kerrs dare venture out after dark – and only then in large companies. Everyone else bolts their doors at sunset and shivers or prays in their bed all the night. 'Twill be the ruin of the kirk at Blackpool Gate that Father Little had such hopes for. No one will ever go there now.'

Tom fell silent then, thinking of his own visit to the kirk at Blackpool Gate, quite distracted from the matter at hand. The strains of music from the great hall echoed as they had done since soon after his departure – and the clapping and stamping told of energetic dancing too. He continued to disregard it all, so fearsome was his concentration on the dark matter in hand. He must find Janet later and take matters further with her; but in the meantime, there was the matter of the heavy golden pebble he had discovered in his boot there – and, indeed, of the golden-coloured rock he had pulled from the cave Janet had used to hide from the Barguest the night it had taken Selkie.

He opened his mouth to bring his discussion with Hobbie on to a new level, when they were interrupted. 'Ah, Tom, here you are,' said the Lady Ellen. She was flushed, breathless and aglow. She might even have been elevated in the volte, from the look of her. 'They said in the servants' hall you had come out here with Hobbie, but I could scarce . . .' She fanned herself with her hand, then continued. 'Nevertheless, I have come to tell you your sleeping quarters have been moved.' The pink in her cheeks deepened to denote embarrassment. 'I offer my apologies for the inconvenience, but there is no help for it. Sir Nicholas de Vaux is honoured guest and you, though honoured, are Musgrave, and family. Sir Thomas therefore says that Sir Nicholas must have the chamber you occupied so lately, and you may move down into my little herbal – the room you saw me treating Eve and Geordie Burn in. Apart from Geordie, it is private; and he's in the deepest of slumbers. We'd another bed in there to nurse Eve, but she is well enough to move in with me. You will be warm and dry.'

In the face of her obvious embarrassment Tom could not be anything other than magnanimous; and, as she said, he was family. ''Twill be my pleasure to obey the Lord of the Waste,' he said with a bow that might have graced de Vaux, 'and infinitely warmer and drier than my sleeping place of last night to boot. Doubly welcome, therefore.'

'That's strange,' said Lady Ellen, tartly; 'young Janet says ye were warm and snug enough, the pair of ye, last night.'

That was the end of any conversation Tom could sensibly have with Hobbie, whose eyes were suddenly wide and aglow with a dangerous combination of speculation and amusement.

Tom left the stables with no further thought except that he should cross the yard quickly, mount the stair silently and move his belongings from his late room before the music stopped; but the cat prevented him.

The cat was unremarkable – no different from any of the castle's cats except that it was stiff and dead. It lay at the foot of the little flight of steps that mounted to the main door. It lay with its face in a puddle of milky liquid that had obviously been cast down from a window in the hall immediately above. It lay in a puddle of torchlight also cast down from the window, so it was easy to see in spite of the fact that it was of one colour with the shadows. Tom knelt beside it and stirred it with his fingertips. It was warm and stiff, as though someone had contrived the experiment he had discussed with Hobbie just now and fed it with one of the poisoned mice.

Tom had reached thus far in his thought when the window above him opened again and someone's shadow fell on him. 'Gardy . . .' sang out a servant's voice.

'Hold!' cried Tom, and the man obeyed. Springing erect, Tom looked up a few feet into the eyes of a young servant who held a washing ewer. 'What is in that?' demanded Tom.

'Why, water, sir.'

'What water, man?'

'Water from where Lord Thomas's guest washed his face when he was hot with dancing.'

'As he did some moments since?'

'As he did indeed, sir. And I threw it down as I throw this now.'

'Very well,' said Tom, and stood well back. Then he crossed to the well, filled up the biggest bucket and washed the whole milky mess away – the corpse of the cat along with it – down into the mud of the Gully Hole. Lost in thought, he returned to the empty stables and there, under the light he rinsed out one of the dangerous pots and shook into it the contents of the glove finger he had found on the ground close by. A grain or two of fine white powder – which turned to seeming milk in the water. This too went down the Gully Hole, to the obvious suspicion of the soldier taking up his night-time guard there.

Much later than planned and deep in thought, therefore,

Tom skipped past the door into the hall and scurried silently up the stairs. He could have made much more noise than he did and still have passed unnoticed, for the consort of viols had been joined by a lute and a pipe. As he passed, 'Lang Flat Foot of Garioch' passed energetically if not very accurately into 'The Dead Days'. Distracted by the dark aptness of the music and by an unexpected mental vision of Janet hurled high in the volte by de Vaux, he ran on heedlessly. Round the final corner he sped and into the little passage outside his late room. Only to freeze.

All unaware, he had caught up with the man who had supplanted him. De Vaux swung the door wide and entered Tom's room unaware that Tom was behind him, deep in conversation with the man who had sat beside him at dinner. Over their shoulders, Tom could just see the tell-tale saddlebag lying across the bed in place of his own; and, on the settle beneath the window, a pewter bowl of fresh water where his precious letter pouch had lain.

He breathed a silent sigh of relief and would have turned away again – except that Fenwick stayed him with his first word: 'Janet,' said the factor. 'A pretty filly. Hot to the hand. With all the wildness ye'd expect in a Kerr, and something more.'

'Indeed,' laughed de Vaux. 'She dances as though she were all fire. I believe I've come near to burning my fingers. If a man had the mind to her, she'd answer well enough – in place of a hot brick to heat the sheets.'

'Well, time will tell, no doubt, sir. And I may risk my own fingers in that particular furnace, if time or opportunity should arise; but in the meantime, the Lord of the Waste bids me tell ye . . .'

The door closed.

Tom was against it in an instant, his ear pressed to the wood.

'. . . the girl . . .?' said de Vaux, a seeming snarl in his voice.

' 'Twas worth the risk . . . for Elliot, after Burn . . . with the club. 'Twould reveal all . . .' Fenwick's voice came and went, sounding low but forceful. 'And she'll be . . .'

'. . . not at the supper nor the dance . . .' insisted de Vaux.

'. . . Burn,' explained Fenwick.

'. . . take your word. But even so . . .'

'. . . be there on the morrow . . .' insisted Fenwick.

'And in the meantime, the smithy . . .' De Vaux's voice came suddenly straight towards the door. His foot trod down on the boards immediately within. The handle turned.

Tom, thinking at fever speed, took the handle on the outer side and turned it further, pushing the door apparently by accident into de Vaux himself. 'Oh,' he said, foolishly, as the pair of them came face to face. 'I thought you were dancing still.'

'Obviously not.'

'I came for my chattels.'

'Gone – to wheresoever you are destined to go.'

Fenwick came up behind de Vaux's shoulder, his bulldog face folded into a frown. 'Lady Ellen went to find you, sirrah,' he huffed.

Tom had been standing still, locked eye to eye with de Vaux, but his hands had been busy enough. Now he held up one black leather glove. 'I seek the pair to this,' he said. ' 'Twill have fallen by the bed, as like as not.' And in he stepped, avoiding de Vaux as though he had been a clumsy opponent on the piste.

'There,' he said at once and stooped, seeming to catch up a second glove from the floor. He held it for them both to see. 'Oh,' he said, seemingly foolish once again. For as he had stripped the thing so swiftly off his hand, so he had curled his finger and one finger of the glove itself now lay inside out within the palm, and the glove, seemingly, was lacking a finger altogether.

Tom looked up, and just for an instant he thought he saw something in Fenwick's bloodshot, baggy eyes.

'Now that you're in here, Master Musgrave,' said de Vaux, his voice like poisoned honey, 'I must tell you I bear a message for you as well. It is from my friend and master and it is this: *Interfere in any of my business again and I will see you die for it.*'

'That will be a message from Lord Robert, will it?' asked Tom at his most urbane. 'Douglas or Essex, 'tis all one; but I have an answer either way. I serve the Queen and Council. My business is theirs. And should either friend or master interfere, 'tis not my head will answer it.'

'The voice of the Queen and Council are but far faint echoes here, Musgrave, and you know it,' sneered de Vaux at that.

But Tom leaned forward until de Vaux stood back. 'Their tongue may seem to be distant,' he whispered, 'but their *teeth* are very near . . .'

The herbal room was dark and still the half of an hour later – silent, apart from the rustle of the settling fire, whose embers cast only the deepest dull red glow, as though this were some dungeon in the foundations of hell itself; but it was snug and warm and there were lamps available to taper ends that brought Tom a little light. A little physical light, at least; mentally things remained murky still, despite all he had reasoned, seen and heard tonight. His panniers, swords and clothes lay neatly arranged on the little table where Lady Ellen made her medicines, potions and possets. Remembering Eve's words, Tom thoughtlessly caught up the last of his washed and mended shirts. Under the bright lamplight he could see that the bloodstain was gone, and that the holes that the dagger had left were neatly darned. The cloth itself had a strong, warm smell where it had been dried over the kitchen fire, and he smiled to see a tiny slip in Lady Ellen's perfect housewifery: the shirt tail was just a little discoloured where it had been hung too near the fire.

There came a scratching at the door. 'Aye?' he answered quietly, folding the shirt with a soldier's easy expertise. As he turned from returning it to the pile on the table, there was Eve in the doorway.

'You've come to see Geordie,' said Tom, still whispering as though the man might awake. 'Come in, come in.'

She sat, perforce, on Tom's bed as she tended Geordie. Tom watched, silently to begin with, as she performed a simple routine to check on his vital signs and comfort the last thing at night. Her hands were brusque, almost impersonal, as though she wished every gesture to establish that the man she was tending was nothing more than a patient in her eyes.

'So,' said Tom, at last, able to contain the Master of Logic no longer; able to resist the chance to talk to her utterly alone no more. 'John went off agooding in his Sabbath best as he always did on St Thomas's Eve, and that was the last you saw of him 'till Hobbie brought him home.'

'That's the truth of it.'

'And the messenger from Hermitage who called him to Lord Robert – he came to you first?'

'No: he must have met John upon the way; but there's no great matter there. I was not at home through the whole day – I was called up here to help Lady Ellen; and there was nothing new there, for Lady Ellen often needs my help, especially at this season. You can see it, perhaps, as part of the price of our Yuletide entertainment, year on year; and John would have gone up to Hermitage in any case. Black Robert owed him a gooding the same as many nearby.'

'He'd worked for Lord Robert Douglas? In what regard?' Tom's voice remained lightly enquiring, though he was actually surprised. He had taken against Lord Robert, firstly through Father Little's words and then through the Black Douglas's own threats beneath the clawed oak, and finally through his messenger de Vaux and the message he had sent.

Eve shook her head as though angry – upset, perhaps, that she could not enthuse about some special skill, some unique ability that marked out her dead beloved. 'Smithing,' she spat. 'What else do blacksmiths do?'

A simple question, on the face of it, but one that echoed, resonated. What else did blacksmiths do?

'Is the smithy locked?' he asked suddenly.

'Locked?'

'I came upon a house left open in the wall, you'll remember – but only because the owner paid his blackmail to Jock o' the Side. I doubt either John or you would pay the blackmail. Or that you would need to, living this close to the Lord of the Waste's protection. So, is the smithy open? 'Tis well past the time I should have taken a look at it.'

CHAPTER TWENTY-TWO

The Black Smithy

As silently as they could, they saddled two ponies and led them to the Gully Hole. The sentry there let them through, and gave them a flaming flambard to boot. As Eve explained in a whisper while they trotted down the first of the hill below the castle, all the sentries knew her and John – and their comings and goings, even at night.

The sky was black, so the flambard was welcome. Right from the start, however, its rugged flames were under common assault from the brutal wind. Still in the north, and responsible for the blinding cloud cover, the gale was howling fit to burst and gusting icily, at the very edge of bringing snow. Too cold, opined Eve; snow would come when the frost eased. Then the chill would really close in.

The darkness was so total that only the sure feet of the ponies knew the way down from the castle. Had it not been for this, Tom would have had to walk at his pony's head, using the wildly guttering flambard to actually see the path. As far as Tom was concerned, they were riding with their tiny star of light at the black heart of the universe. The howling, sobbing of the wind could have come from amongst the icy, untuned spheres, straight from the frozen heart of hell. There was nothing at all to take the eye except the flambard in his hand, and that near blinded him with brightness every time he looked at it. Yet such was the fathomless ocean of dark upon whose bosom they were tossed, his eyes seemed sometimes to play tricks on him, bringing tiny glitters of brightness to the very corners of his eyes, there and gone like fireflies in southern climes, as beguiling as the wills o' the wisp that tempted benighted travellers to their doom in the bottomless bogs.

Concentration was difficult, clear thought out of the question – and conversation a rank impossibility. It seemed to Tom that they had little enough to say for the nonce in any case. Tom himself could not conceive what work John would have done for Lord Robert up at Hermitage, for Lord Robert must have a smith of his own. What could John do that the smith of Hermitage could not?

Tom wasted a few moments on speculation – and the speculation was not ill-founded after all, for he had been brought up in a smithy and he knew well enough the range of work that a blacksmith might be asked to undertake; but what for the Laird of Hermitage that he could not – dared not – ask his own smith to do? Another question for the morrow, perhaps, but in the meantime, Tom was confident that his brother's smithy would tell its own tale, had he the light and the eyes to see.

The door was locked and double-locked, a fact Tom had not noticed while passing the place with Father Little at his side so seeming-long ago in the final moments before Lord Robert, the Black Douglas, had entered the picture. He noticed now, however, as he held the flambard so that Eve could put her keys into each of the locks. 'That's new,' he said. ' 'Twas never so before I left.'

'You've been gone a long time,' she snapped and pushed the door wide.

He stepped in first with the flambard and was cast back into far memory in an instant. He had last seen this room at sixteen years, near half a life ago; but it seemed to him he knew every detail of eye, ear and nostril as though he had been here only yesterday. So overwhelming was the feeling that he forgot all his caveats to Eve and Hobbie about seeing childhood things with new eyes now that he was a man.

The place had been designed and built as a smithy and the

focal point was the fire. In this, the domestic section, the door at which they lingered led into a living area floored with hard earth and furnished with one rude table and a scattering of chairs. Beyond, against the rear wall, stood the open grate under the bell-shaped chimney. The back of the grate, he knew, rose only a little up beyond the skirt of the brickwork bell of the breast. Beyond it, on the other side of the wall, out in the smithy itself, the great fire, with its bellows and open grate, would whoosh like the flames of hell itself up into the same great chimney, day and night, year on year. He had never seen it dark, he realized – never in all his life. Above, and reached by a ladder in the corner, the sleeping room had space for the smith and his wife and their family; and, as was common here – and not just with smithies – the whole was roofed with slates that would not burn rather than thatch that would.

Around the walls stood chests and dressers exactly as he remembered; an ancient wooden sideboard with a great metal ewer and a pail for water up from the river hard by. Out at the back, beyond the smithy and up on the hillside were the sink and the usual offices.

As he stood and gawped like a hempseed looking for the first time at St Paul's or London Bridge, Eve brought a taper and used the flame of the flambard to ignite a couple of lamps. When that was done, she turned to him.

'Well?' she demanded. 'What is it that ye need to see? Be quick or we'll be taken for ghosts. Or lovers.'

'The smithy,' he answered at once, and walked past the dead fire to the door that led on through. Eve let him pass through; for, again, the door was locked.

The sight, the very smell, of the cavernous smithy carried him back through time like a sparrow lost in the blast of a gale. Yet he could not waste precious moments on distant years. Roughly he dragged himself back to the immediate past – and the prints that it might leave upon the present: to St Thomas's Eve, little more than a week since, in fact, and what John might have been doing here before he went agooding to collect his Christmas dues.

The smithy was as Tom remembered it, except that it was cold. The great fire gaped full of charcoal, wood and black sea-coal brought laboriously up from the coast. The bellows lay beside it, one pair on either hand, like dead birds awaiting stuffing. The anvil stood before it and the hammers, tongs and chisels hung serried on the wall to the right, for John, like his father before him, had always been a neat worker.

Along the wall on the left-hand side stood the work benches, cupboarded beneath, where the fine work might be done when the work of blacksmith and farrier began to overlap and John was called upon to do more than simply shoe the horses. There, indeed, above them hung the tack, the reins, harness and blinkers in various states of repair; and, beyond again, another area where John's expertise with metals overlapped with others. For here lay bits and pieces of weaponry: jacks only half-covered with metal plates; armour bent and battered; bonnets broken and bruised – to the terrible damage, Tom had no doubt, of the heads that once had worn them. Here stood the great grindstone, and swords in various sizes, styles and states of repair; Daggers, knives, axes – common axes for felling trees and Jedburgh axes for felling men.

At the end of all these workbench cupboards stood the big double doors, the equal of any in barn, byre or stable, where the horses were led in for shoeing, and various stock for marking or mending in various ways. These doors were locked, bolted and barred. The bolts in particular, fashioned no doubt by John himself, were new.

There, between the trailing tack, the battered armour, the half-sharpened weapons and the padlocked doors, was a little area of unexpected refinement. Tom's eyes narrowed and his brow creased, for this area, too, was new. Here the massive hammers, tongs and chisels were replaced by balances and crucibles. There were solid metal moulds, a range of fine equipment, all neatly packed away. In place of the anvil, a mortar and pestle, designed to grind down . . . what?

'What was John at work on here?' Tom asked at once.

Eve shrugged. 'The new passion for shooting – and with

177

crossbow as well as guns. There's a fletcher in Brackenhill, but he's old and works with longbows only. Not that his arrow-heads are up to much these days either. He'll not fashion good steel quarrels. So my John does. Did. Then, you brought an arquebus and a matched pair of pistols yourself, besides what-ever that monstrosity is in with Lord Henry's letters . . .'

Tom frowned at her, still not quite following.

'Carlisle is a good long way away, and that's the nearest gunsmith, down in Botchergate. John would mend, for he could not make. He was in a lively way of supplying quarrels for the crossbows and shot for those that will not make their own . . .'

'Hum,' said Tom. He knew a gunsmith well: Ugo Stell, his closest friend; and there was something on this bench that did not quite fit with what Tom remembered from Ugo's bench in Blackfriars. 'Hmm,' he said, as though satisfied. Perhaps the difference lay, as Eve suggested, in the fact that John was not a gunsmith, merely a mender of guns that others made; or that he fashioned quarrels as well as shot. Even so . . .

'Had he any particular customers?' Tom asked, crossing to the bench and lowering the flambard to bring the brightness closer.

'None,' answered Eve, again dismissively.

Tom touched the icy instruments as though they might tell his sensitive fingers what his mind could not yet frame or fathom; but it was his eyes not his fingers that gave the game away, and his memory, not of Ugo's workshop at all, but of Master Panne the Goldsmith's that he had visited on London Bridge six months before. Yes: that was it. These were not just the instruments of the gunsmith and the blacksmith – but of the metalsmith as well.

Above them, on the wall, stood a new cupboard Tom did not recognize. It opened under his absent-minded grasp and, sure enough, there stood several guns: an arquebus, clearly in need of a new matchlock; a new Dutch dunderbus, bell-mouthed and dangerous-looking, the screwheads holding its side-plates firm all gleaming and recently tightened; and a pistol, almost the match of his own beautiful pair, exquisitely chased in silver and gold. The gold chasing had clearly seen better days. It was dull, and the foil was beginning to peel off. One side was in far better repair: John had clearly been part-way through replacing that as well. Thoughtlessly, Tom brought the flambard lower. Eve hissed with fright.

'What?' he asked, without turning.

'He has black powder over there. He grinds it himself.'

Tom did not raise the flame. Instead he pushed his finger into the bottom of the mortar and stirred the powder there; and his frown deepened. For he knew black powder well. He had helped Ugo Stell prepare it. He knew its form and formulation at every stage of its composition from rocks of ore and blocks of charcoal to the finest, most explosive grains; and no black powder he had ever made or seen had tiny flecks of gleaming metal within it – metal like the gleaming grains that lay in the mortar here. Without thought or calculation, Tom unloosed the top of his purse and pulled out the two rocks it contained. Lowering the light still further, oblivious to Eve's strangled gasp, he put them down beside it and poured the glittering contents out. He saw at once that the gilded pebble fate had washed out of the Black Lyne into his boot was far too bright to bear comparison; but the other, on the other hand – the rock he had found in Janet's cave up beside the oak – that rock was identical in colouring. Indeed, he thought, still far removed, almost in a world of his own, if he was to grind up this very rock, he might well get dust of identical colour, indistinguishable from this . . .

'Where did you get that?' asked Eve again, hitting his shoulder and making the flambard flicker.

Tom jumped awake again and the howling, stormy night crashed in on him like the waters of the flooding river. He realized Eve had been almost screaming at him and she was doing so again: 'Where did you get that rock?'

'This?' he pointed to the bright pebble.

'No! Not that! The other . . .' But before he could answer, a massive crash came against the door beside them. Whatever had hit the wood struck with sufficient force to pull John's new bolts free of their sockets – pull sections free of their planks.

Tom passed the flambard to Eve at once and reached up into the cabinet full of his brother's latest work. A second great blow pulled hinges loose and ruined the seeming strength of the new bolts. So that at the third blow the door sagged, from floor to roof, and fell back, half-opened.

Tom pushed Eve back and stood before her as the brunt wind threatened to tear the flames of the flambard out and scatter the fire into the little house. Then the wind hesitated. The flame sprang up. Out of the darkness appeared a part of the darkness; a tall man on a tall horse, both as black as the night. A black-gauntleted hand pulled a black cloak back to reveal a pallid face framed with red hair at whose heart burned feverish eyes.

Eve gasped again – a very different sound from the one she had made when she was considering mere explosions. 'Ye know me, woman,' said the man, and Tom felt her nodding silently.

The wind came, stirring the black cloak so that Tom knew their visitor too, and his expression gave the game away. For though the horseman needed a gauntlet on his good right hand, he needed none for the bandaged stump of his left.

'And you know me, sirrah. And I know you, Master Musgrave,' hissed One-Hand Dand Kerr.

CHAPTER TWENTY-THREE

Liddesdale

Tom swung the dunderbus up until the wide bell of its deadly mouth pointed at One-Hand Dand. 'I know you, Dand Kerr,' he said easily, 'and I stand sure you have half of Stob and probably of Liddesdale at your back; but I warn you: if you make a move or say a word beyond my liking, your head at the very least of it will join your hand in hell.'

Dand eased himself in his saddle, the stirrups and girths creaking. 'And after me,' he answered, 'it'll be yourself sent hot to hell, Master Musgrave, and then the lady Eve, the Lord of the Waste and the rest; but I've a choice to offer ye before we fall to fighting here.' The shallow eyes wandered apparently thoughtlessly away, past Tom himself and on to Eve.

'And that is?' pursued Tom, well aware of how little time he had in hand.

'Come to Hermitage,' said another voice, a new voice, cold and strange from the darkness – strange and yet oddly familiar.

There was a second of silence.

'Hell or Hermitage,' said Tom. 'That's not much of a—'

The blow took him smack across the back of the head at ear-tip level. It felt as though he had been hit with a Jedburgh axe, so piercing was the pain; but the feeling lasted less than the flicker of lightning that seemed to outline Dand. Then all was darkness, into which he pitched as though falling.

'Don't kill him,' came an urgent, echoing voice that soared

away up into the air as he fell. 'It is he who keeps the Barguest alive.'

His forehead hit the hard earth floor and bounced. It seemed that the crown of his head must have broken off like the top of a roasted egg. The darkness was joined by a whirling, rushing roaring that sucked him down to its depths. All sensation vanished.

Except, from an almost infinite distance, a sudden and terrible pain in his hand. It was there and gone in the merest atomy of time, but it speared his unconsciousness for just long enough to release a terrible, fearful revelation. Dand and the Kerrs had taken Eve; and Geordie Burn was confederated with them, carrying her away to Black Robert's lair. For the second voice had been Geordie's – there was never any doubt of that.

The pain in his hand woke him first, though the pain in his head was likely to have done so soon. 'Agh!' he shouted. Then he whispered, '*Eve!*' Of course, there was no reply. His whirling, stunned and sickened senses informed him he was face down on the floor. He stirred, automatically, tensing to push himself up – and regretted it at once, such was the agony in his right hand. It felt as though he had plunged it in a crucible of boiling metal. He remained where he was for a while, bathed in icy sweat and gasping fit to burst. Then he opened his eyes. It was full day. Dull, wet light was streaming in through the wreck of the smithy door across the hard-earth floor. The dry-mud surface was broken slightly by the sharply indented crescents of hoof-prints; and so, saw Tom as he blinked owlishly, was the black leather stretched across the back of his throbbing right hand.

Ready for the stab of agony this time, teeth gritted and nostrils flared, he pushed himself up again. He made it on to all fours, then tore himself erect, lifting the agony of his broken hand off the ground as though the black Spanish glove had contained a great weight. He clutched it to his breast and cradled it in the crook of his left arm, forcing his mind to clear with almost superhuman swiftness. Only the circumstances gave him the strength; and the most potent element of the situation was the fact that they had taken Eve to Hermitage. Years as a soldier, student duellist, Master of Defence and courtier in some of the darker and more dangerous theatres of Europe had given him all too clear an idea of what Black Robert might be doing to her; and, the daylight told him, all too much time had been awasting since Dand and Geordie had carried her away.

He staggered to his feet, therefore, still moving as though his crushed hand were the same weight as the anvil that stood at the cold fire just behind him. He glared around the wreckage of the smithy, registering how the dunderbus and most of the guns were gone – how the mortar and pestle, with its powder – black or not – were gone; how any piece of weaponry, saddlery or equipment of even the faintest use was gone; except for his own guns and swords, which still hung miraculously safe about him. Mockingly left on the assumption that he could no longer use them, of course. Other than these it was all, like Eve, long gone. It was time to be gone himself.

Back through the wind-swinging doors that Eve had un-locked last night he stumbled, only to find that the light-fingered Kerrs could not resist hobbie horses any more than gold, guns, weapons and helpless women; but he knew from a wide range of sources, as well as from years of childhood experience, that Bewcastle fort was only half an hour's walk up the hill from here.

It was a hard walk, one of the most difficult of his entire life, but he shambled on regardless of the weighty agony in his hand and the stabbing pains in his head until he had achieved his object and the great gate of Bewcastle fort seemed to swim in the air before him.

Tom staggered under the portcullis into the open square of the fort, his teeth still so tightly gritted that he could not even call for help. So it was fortunate that the Lady Ellen saw him weaving across the yard amongst the stable grooms who were sweeping aside the straw left over from the departure of the Lord of the Waste's party as they answered the Laird of Hermitage's invitation to a hunt that day.

'Dear goodness,' she said, rushing up to him. 'What's amiss? The whole of the fort is abuzz with speculation about whither you spirited Eve away to last night. Young Janet is almost out of her mind with rage and frustration. And now you return alone and like this.'

' 'Tis a lengthy story,' he warned. Then he asked, 'How long ago did Sir Thomas and the others depart?'

'Not long. Let me see to your hand while you tell me what's transpired.'

'I will, but we must be quick. It is imperative I overtake them before they get to Liddesdale. When did Geordie Burn leave?'

'He woke a little stronger this morning and so he left with them; but he'd fain have come after the pair of you if the Lord of the Waste had allowed.'

'That he would never do: the honour of the Waste stands on the shoulders of the lord's command; but I must after them as swiftly as I can, and now I bethink me, I had best take along the lady Janet into the bargain . . .'

'You may take her and welcome, for she is certainly no lady, not after the way she danced the volte last night! But I fear you will have to consult her at the least, for she will doubtless have her own mind in the matter and you are in no condition to enforce your will upon her should she prove intractable.'

Tom sent for her nevertheless, and as the Lady Ellen had worked upon him, so he worked upon her.

'To Hermitage!' exclaimed Janet, her tone more calculating than horrified.

'You must come. You know you have unfinished business there,' he tempted, like the devil in the old plays.

'Perhaps. But what do you know of that?' she countered.

'More than you suppose. I will protect you,' he promised manfully.

She gave a bark of laughter at that. 'From the look of you, you will stand in need of *my* protection when Black Robert gets his hands on you.'

'In that assumption also you are deceived, Janet,' he countered with quiet confidence. 'But let us both own Black Robert

184

our enemy for the moment, and let us stand confederated against him and each of us help the other as we beard him in his den. Was it rape, such as your mother warned you of when we talked in the Blackpool kirk?'

'Rape as ever was. A pretty lass among the Kerrs taken by force on an afternoon's hunting near twenty years since. I'm the result. The vessel of my mother's rage and sorrow and of all my family's shame. I am bad blood and bad cess and Black Robert's bastard. And I doubt he even knows I exist for all he's seen me often enough of late.'

The Lady Ellen's eyebrows rose irresistibly towards her hairline as she worked and pretended, unconvincingly, to be too preoccupied to listen to this sad bitterness.

'And we seek the lady Eve,' continued Janet with a jealous frown; but it was a short-lived expression: Tom had already won her.

'We seek so much more than that, Janet,' he concluded.

Janet sighed and nodded. She was his. So he sent her to change back into the clothes of the seeming boy he had almost killed at Housesteads. Lady Ellen finished her work while she did so, and the pair of them moved on.

Tom took the first pony he could find. He reserved for Janet the little steed that had carried him through the hunt, and was glad to do so. It was a beast he knew well and respected. He soon found that his own was the match of it, however. He could rely on both of them to run their hearts out catching up with the others. He believed that, no matter in what state his wounds or Lady Ellen's tending had left him, he could rely on his own plucky little animal to carry him up with the procession of guests as they headed for Hermitage. He could rely on Janet's to do the same, though he could only guide his mount clumsily enough with the reins in his left hand.

As Janet had changed her clothing and found a light jack to match his own as well as a stout travelling cloak, Lady Ellen had completed her ministrations. His right hand was wrapped in bandages thick enough to make his arm seem almost like a club. Like the wounds to the back and front of his head it had been rinsed and spread with unguents. Unlike them it had also been bandaged, but as lightly as Lady Ellen would allow – too heavily for Tom to resume his glove or grip his sword, but lightly enough for him to move the fingers a little still, as long as he could stand the pain. It should have been in a sling, but his vanity forbade that it should be so and he rode with it at his hip, resting on the pommel of the sword it could no longer hold. Janet rode at his right hand; if he drew a sword, it would be with his left.

Tom and Janet set their ponies' heads a little north of west and they cantered easily over hill and dale, south of Blackpool Gate, crossing the River Lyne at Oakshaw ford and following the steep little valley straight on up past Sleetbeck on to the saddle between Chamot Hill and Wakey. The pair of them came a little south past Beyond the Moss and caught up with Sir Thomas's party on the border itself at Penton as they prepared to cross Liddel Water and swing north into Liddesdale and Scotland. While they rode, they talked: of Janet's birth and background; of her upbringing amongst the Kerrs, by Hugh of Stob himself, and his wife, and Janet's mother, while she was still alive.

They caught up with Hobbie and the huntsmen as they splashed across the ford, tight-packed and laden with the hindquarter of the hart. There was no way past them and up along the festive column towards Sir Thomas and de Vaux at its head; and, were there no way pass the column now, no more would there be for a good few miles still. For on the west side of the valley, over the river, which grew wider and shallower as it prepared to join the River Esk, the steep hillsides gathered swiftly into cliffs. The roadway all too soon became a pathway, and that narrow thoroughfare swooped off up the valley side into a steep and precipitous little ledge just wide enough for a sure-footed hobbie horse to follow.

With the wild rock reaching upwards on the left hand and the bewildering cliffs falling downwards on the right into a roaring wilderness of russet foam, there was no place to hurry, let alone to overtake. Tom and Janet perforce remained with the quiz-

186

zical Hobbie, therefore, as Sir Thomas, unreachable, the merest bowshot up ahead, pierced the Laird of Hermitage's stronghold of Liddesdale all unaware of the situation into which he was riding.

'Tom!' called Hobbie. 'Where ye been? And why in God's name have ye brought the lass with ye?'

' 'Tis a long story. Is Geordie Burn with Sir Thomas?'

'Aye: at his left hand up ahead, with Fenwick the Factor and Sir Nicholas de Vaux. Or more likely in line behind him now, for they're up on the narrow path already, I see. The Lady Ellen's cures have strengthened Geordie beyond measure. He's none too hearty, mind, but hale enough for this. Now 'tis your turn to answer me.'

'If I can. What?'

'Where's Eve that ye stole off with like some thief in the night?'

'Eve's up ahead, and I pray she's awaiting us.'

'Up ahead? *Where* up ahead?'

'At Hermitage. One-Hand Dand carried her off last night and the last I heard they were headed thither.'

'Carried her off? And ye're alive to tell of it? Tom, ye're not the man I thought ye!'

'I was near enough dead when they left with her. When you've leisure, you can feel the blood that's set my hair like marble and marvel at the colours – and shape – of my hand.'

'Aye, now I have the leisure to look, I see ye've a great bruise like the eye of a Cyclops right in the midst of your forehead; and that explains young Janet here: a bargaining counter. She'll not be worth much put up against Eve herself, mind.'

'The bruise is least of my hurts, I assure you; and Janet may be worth more than she seems, for she's Black Robert's only daughter.'

Hobbie mulled that over for a while before he asked, 'Who hit ye? Dand?'

'The only one of them I am sure did *not* hit me was Dand; but 'twas he who walked his horse across my hand as I lay fainting on the floor.'

'Ye should have let me kill him – aye, and her, while we had the chance.'

'I know. It is always our good deeds that come back to do us most harm.' His laughing words were called out loudly, to cover Janet's angry retort.

Hobbie grunted with a half-laugh himself and had the grace to look shamed under the girl's indignant gaze. 'True enough; but Dand was for taking Eve to Hermitage, ye say?'

'If not Dand, then one that rode with him – rode with him and stood above him, for Dand answered to his commands.'

'And who was this that gave orders to the Kerrs?'

'I'd have said it was Geordie Burn.'

'But he was ill in bed all night, with many an eye to swear to it.'

'Then it was Tam himself, that fell out with Geordie for love of her all those years ago. Tam has got her at last – but not for himself, of course: he's taken her to Black Robert.'

Their conversation had to end there because the ground beneath their ponies' hooves rose up abruptly and they were suddenly on the narrow path. It was many years since Tom had ridden this route. Then he had been an able, scrawny horseman in full control of his large and steady steed. Now the position was very different. He was a large and heavy body on a little pony, his left hand only clumsily in control of the reins, the pair of them in the grip of a wild north wind that bounced off the wall beside them like the old king's tennis balls, and threatened to topple them into the abyss.

Tom was the rearmost of the procession. The position gave him a little blessed relief from the dangerous wind and pricked his pride into the bargain. All the others – Hobbie laden with a quarter of a deer, Janet with her plaid cloak flapping in the wind – seemed to be trotting forward without a second thought. So he settled himself in the saddle, gripped his right-hand sword pommel until the pain in his hand became too much to bear, and followed the Lord of the Waste into the dangerous valley of Liddesdale and the lair of the laird himself.

CHAPTER TWENTY-FOUR

Hermitage

The valley side circled round below Hermitage. As they approached the dark old castle, the pathway widened and faded into the slope, becoming a pathway, then a rough roadway, leading up towards the forbidding place; but as soon as it did so, the roadway became contained within defensive walls, so that even now Tom could find no way past the riders ahead to get his message to Sir Thomas.

Tom had no choice, therefore, but to use his eyes instead of his heels and scour the castle itself for further clues that he might use in the coming confrontation with its dark and dangerous captain. To Tom's eyes, Hermitage seemed to have an evil and sinister aspect, fit indeed to be the lair of Black Robert Douglas. The walls were absolute, reaching nigh on fifty feet sheer, grey stone standing on the frost-grey crag outlined against the winter-grey sky without any softening or decoration. Even the smoke that rose from its invisible chimneys was thick and grey and at one with the place and its setting. It was what it was designed for: a perfect blending of form and function, thought Tom – a place of impenetrable defence, a source of absolute leadership, a threat of unrelenting terror. For terror alone would keep the Armstrongs, whose bothies filled the valley below, from the throat of the men who garrisoned Hermitage Castle. A previous captain had been boiled alive in the castle yard before the keep, and the current captain was not about to share his fate.

On the other hand, the man who had built the castle in the first place had been in league with the devil, and that was a dark part of its history that Robert Douglas was, apparently, happier to share. If any man had raised the Barguest from its kennel in the deeps of hell through the exercise of black, forbidden arts, then it was he.

'Witchcraft?' said Hobbie in answer to Tom's enquiry. 'Oh aye. That's what they say. But what grounds they have I cannot tell ye . . .'

'It is the lights,' said Janet, suddenly, 'and the sounds in the night. Deep sounds that make the whole head of the valley shake. They do not come from the castle, but they spread out down the dale . . .'

'You had this from Dand, I assume?'

'And Hugh. When the Kerrs do business with Black Robert, they keep their longest pikes to hand.'

' "Who sups with the Devil needs a long spoon," ' confirmed Tom, his eyes looking upwards towards the great gateway that stood astride the road immediately in front of them.

There were two Kerrs hanging at the main gate to Hermitage as Black Robert had promised. If they disturbed Janet, then she showed no sign of it as she rode between and below their swinging feet. Everyone, in fact, trotted into the castle without hesitation or, apparently, any second thought at all – except, that is, for Tom.

Tom reigned up below the slowly revolving corpses and stood in his stirrups, looking up and frowning with thought. They were hung too high for anyone to see their faces clearly, but it seemed to him that their bulging eyes and gaping mouths bespoke terror as eloquently as did John's or Father Little's; and that put him in mind of executions he had seen in his new home of London, where there was a gallows on every major crossroad, with a whipping post, a cage and a set of stocks to match them. For now he thought of it, the faces of all the dead men he had seen of late might well have shared with many a felon in the South that terrible look of someone slowly choking to death, aswing and kicking helplessly in a hempen noose.

Except, of course, for the facts that there had been no reddening of bulging, bloodshot eyes and no thick, bloody tears; no tearing of tongue and lips by wildly gasping jaws; no emptying of bodily wastes. Most especially, there had been no thick black cicatrice around the neck, such as marked an official execution done according to the law. Just how many of these tell-tale signs adorned the corpses hanging at Black Robert's gates Tom could not quite make out. He would have given much to look more closely at that pair of Kerrs who hung like a brace of pheasants ripening for the table.

'As I promised, Master Musgrave,' came Lord Robert's icy voice, as gentle as a devil's sliding through the wind.

'Give ye good den, Lord Robert,' said Tom, swinging a little clumsily down off his horse and recovering into a courtly bow. 'Did the lady Eve arrive safely last night?'

Lord Robert had turned away, however, and was taking his place at the head of his reception line, every bit as formal as the Lord of the Waste had been before his Christmas Hunt. Now at last Tom found himself beside Sir Thomas. He had precedence as honoured guest, as Queen's messenger – or the Lord of the North's at any rate – and as the old man's nearest living relative; but the position at his uncle's side was of no use now, for the man against whom he wanted to warn Sir Thomas was at his other hand, unctuously introducing him to the garrison and their guests in turn – men whom he knew already; but with more detail in the description.

As Lord Robert introduced his uncle, Tom had time for a glance over his shoulder to see Janet indistinguishably join the mass of the Bewcastle garrison at Hobbie Noble's shoulder. Then he allowed himself a swift look around the sparse, functional interior of Hermitage Castle. They stood assembled in a flag-floored yard with what looked like a well at its heart. Here, as in Bewcastle, there were stables and smithies and storehouses leaning against the inner side of the outer wall; but over all loomed the keep. Huge and threatening it loomed on them, rising without any feature at all for three sheer storeys before a balcony thrust out with a great door behind it – a main door fit to welcome kings – three storeys too high for them to reach without wings. Everything below that was impenetrable and unassailable, a killing ground for any unwary invaders caught within the portcullis with nowhere else to go.

Suddenly the dark keep's black captain was talking to Tom himself: 'Of course you must know Sir Nicholas de Vaux, the noted courtier and friend of the Earls of Essex and Southampton. You are aware, I am sure, of his great houses, Camborne House, London, and St Erth under Redruth . . .'

'Sir Nicholas.' Tom bowed just enough for courtesy: a duellist at the piste.

'Sir Thomas. Master Musgrave . . .' De Vaux nodded.

'And Senor Juan Placido Flores de Sagres, lately returned from his most Pacific Majesty Philip's dominions in New Spain.'

'I'm surprised that Drake and Raleigh let you through,' said Tom pleasantly, bowing and smiling. Then he continued after a moment of silence in which even Lord Robert was shocked speechless by his crass incivility. 'Ah, a thousand pardons, señor. I see you do not speak English . . .' The latter words were spoken in his inelegant, if serviceable, Spanish.

'There seems to be no end to Master Musgrave's accomplishments,' Lord Robert inserted smoothly in Latin. 'Let us hope we do not come against an end to them today; but we speak in English here, sir, as Señor Sagres understands, in notion if not the words themselves. There are too many ignorant ears that grow dangerously suspicious of anything they do not understand.' He stepped sideways again, taking Sir Thomas and Tom with him almost irresistibly. 'And this is my factor, Mr Beattie,' he continued in English, as though the foreign syllables, living and dead, had never tripped so smoothly off his tongue.

There was no Hunt Mass. Instead, they were all remounted at once when the introductions had been done. In their saddles, as in Bewcastle, they partook of a brief hunt breakfast – mostly of baked and roasted birds.

'Our hawking went well yesterday,' said Lord Robert, 'and you reap the benefit of it doubly. Not only does it furnish breakfasts now, it also presents us with vital intelligence as to our quarry for today . . .'

With every eye upon him, Lord Robert rose in his saddle, easily commanding the moment, so that even the restless, excited horses fell quiet under his spell. 'For weeks we had been hearing rumours that something big and dangerous had come avisiting into the darkest of our thickets down the dale; but rumour was all we had and Armstrongs, though brave and resourceful, are not always absolutely reliable in matters such as telling the truth. In any case, for some time since the whole of the Borders has been alive with whispers of the Barguest – which is what the Armstrongs seem convinced our mysterious visitor must be – and the Barguest, as we all here know, is a thing of fable, a toy for a winter's tale – a thing for women to frighten children with; nothing such as would invade the wise credulity of men such as ourselves.

'But yesterday at hawking, down by the mouth of the dale itself, my guests and I found unmistakable signs of the beast. It is there; and I have invited us all here, the best of the Borders, north and south, the flower of Scotland and England, to hunt it.'

A whisper, a rustle, a stirring of breath, of movement of hoof and tack, went round the place as the storm wind battered across the battlements high above. Lord Robert held up his hand and even the wind was silent.

'And, to make the hunting worth more than mere glory, we have a prize into the bargain.' He held up his hand higher in a signal and the great upper door of the keep slammed open. Out on to the balcony three storeys above stepped a pale, fair woman, all alone and apparently moving at her own will under no duress at all.

'To the man who kills the Barguest will go the hand of the woman it widowed. Eve Graham Musgrave has sworn that she will marry the man who avenges her against the beast that killed her husband, and I have sworn to protect her. Under my protection and in my own poor keep at her own request she stays, therefore, until one brave man can prove he has won the quest and may take her and all that is hers at her word.'

As his wild words echoed around the grim old keep, Lord Robert tore the head of his hunter to the right and galloped straight out of the gate. Tom saw at once that the Heritage garrison, also all astride, had prepared for the moment by positioning themselves in a circle around their all-unsuspecting guests. When Lord Robert led, and they followed, so did the Bewcastle contingent, perforce, driven out on to the valley side by the friendly cavalry charge behind them.

To be fair, thought Tom, as he went out with the rest of them, many of the Bewcastle men were following without a second thought. It was only Sir Thomas, Tom and mayhap Geordie Burn who saw something terribly amiss here. For the rest, the case seemed clear and perfectly understandable – perhaps even reasonable. For the laws of the Borders were strict and un-varying, as they needed to be in that constant war zone. Otherwise life in this morass of constantly changing allegiances and ever-shifting family bonds would have been simply im-possible. When a man gave his word, he upheld it – thus Sir Thomas and his guests rode under the safe protection of men that would kill them unhesitatingly under different circum-stances; and when a woman was widowed violently, she might be expected to go to any lengths avenging the man she had lost. Many a border widow had promised herself, her house and home to the man that avenged her husband, and this was different only in that Eve Musgrave wished to be avenged upon a monster. So she needed a monstrous bargain to fulfil her plans. She certainly had a monstrous friend in Lord Robert to hold the square for her, a friend who apparently had every intention of taking the prize for himself, if he could, so swiftly was he leading the wild hunt down into the valley-foot.

Here the thickest brakes of the most timeless woodland might be found, stands of oak and yew as massive and ancient as the heart of Inglewood, dense enough and dark enough to hide monsters without number over centuries beyond counting. And yet, ran on Tom's busy thoughts as he pounded with the rest of them down the dangerous slope, it was a wilderness under threat, as Hobbie had said. For all along the edges of the forest he was approaching in his scarcely controlled gallop were tall, banked fires issuing slow, thick smoke, burning in steady series, not to give heat – even in this frost-bound season – but to give charcoal. As they turned south on the last clear slopes above the thickest of the trees that stood along the river plain itself, he saw great avenues reaching inwards and downwards, dense with working men. It was as Hobbie had sadly said, he thought. The whole of the dale was like the forests further south, like the circles of Dante's Inferno, where helpless men toiled, lost and hopeless; where the shipmasters and the metalmasters, steel-masters and all the rest, were tearing the heart out of forests that had stood untouched since the dawning of time.

Hobbie was riding on one side of him and Janet on the other. 'Did you know it was like this here?' he demanded of them both, bellowing over the thunder of their gallop.

'Harvests have been bad,' yelled Hobbie. 'They're starving here as well as elsewhere. There's been murrain in the flocks. The raiding took most of the cattle last year. They're starving, so they'll turn their hands to anything.'

'And when the men are starving, the master goes hungry,' added Janet. 'Black Robert'll be suffering lean times. You must know others at court . . .'

Truth to tell, Tom knew almost no one at court who wasn't desperate for money. Essex would do almost anything to add to the one steady income he got from his monopoly over the sweet wine trade. Why else was Raleigh off searching the Indies? Why else did Drake constantly attack the armadas from New Spain? Only men whose income did not rely upon farming their lands stood firm – men like young Lord Outremer, whose life he had saved six months since, whose massive fortune was earned from the spice trades; men like his friend and landlord Robert Aske the Haberdasher, building his fortune on feathers, lace and silk, buckles, buttons and ribbons shipped in from far abroad; like Ugo, earning his gold through making and selling guns. Only men like these and Nicholas de Vaux were assured, which was why de Vaux stood so close to both Essex and Southampton, whose positions and pastimes consumed gold like furnaces consumed fuel, thought Tom grimly; only men like de Vaux, who could get their riches not from the land itself, but from beneath it, where riches themselves seemed to grow.

CHAPTER TWENTY-FIVE

The Grave

'The Grave,' called Tom quietly, into the almost impenetrable undergrowth through which he was silently insin-
uating himself.

'The Waste,' came Hobbie's voice in reply, distantly on his
right.

'We need to go over towards him,' said Janet nervously. The
gloom of the place, the increasing sense of isolation and the
burgeoning fear of what they were just about to meet were
combining to shred her nerves at last.

'Perhaps,' said Tom. 'But there are more games afoot here
than the one he is playing. '*Hola!*' he called, more softly than he
had called to Hobbie.

'*Hola!*' came a nervous reply on his left. The Spaniard was
still close at hand, he thought; and that was to the good.

Lord Robert had brought their wild charge down the valley
and over the shallows of the lowest ford on the Liddel to a halt
at the edge of the deepest woodland on the eastern bank, on the
very borders of the debatable land itself. Here a circle of silent,
suspicious Armstrongs had stood like ill-controlled animals
waiting to take their horses. All through this excursion, Tom
had been watching Señor Sagres. The man was plainly out of
place here – indeed, had seemed out of place in all the companies he had shared with Tom so far. He was no courtier –
even in the Spanish Court, with whose forms and manners Tom

had a nodding acquaintance, he would have been out of place. He was a solid, sinewy man. His arms and legs were muscular, but his shoulders and hands were massive, almost the match of John the Blacksmith's. Tom had observed those hands through the Master of Logic's eyes. They were broad, spread like the feet of a shoeless peasant. They were callused. The nails were almost as thick as John's had been, and as ingrained with dirt, as were the knuckles. The hands alone told Tom the man's likely occupation; but he was keen to make assurance double-sure.

Sagres was silent but watchful – clearly no buffoon, in spite of his lack of manners and English. His Latin was as work-manlike as the rest of him – conned because he needed to use it rather than enjoyed as a thing of beauty, a proof of his decorated mind. His clothes were no cleaner than his hands – cleaner than those of the Kerrs, of course (except for Janet's), and cleaner by far than the Armstrongs', but lacking that fastidiousness which had allowed Sir Thomas to skin a deer without soiling the lace of his cuffs; failing to meet even the slightly less perfect expectations Tom remembered in the Al-hambra, where heat and dust made English Court perfection out of the question. Sagres was no courtier, and that was plain enough.

Nor was he a soldier. He seemed never to wear even a sword other than at the dictates of fashion. He was slow to accept weapons and seemed uneasy in the handling of them. The only men similar to Sagres who habitually moved in circles shared by Lord Robert Douglas and the Earl of Essex were spies, sor-cerers or poisoners – or all three dangerous professionals distilled into one; but even this elegant train of logic failed to satisfy the Master of Logic who drew it out. Closer inspec-tion was required, therefore, and testing of his one alternative theory.

Amongst the hunting weapons on offer were Jedburgh axes and crossbows – even the odd arquebus had been pressed on them; but in the face of it all, Tom had preferred the only weapon he could control to his own satisfaction with a left hand

198

and the club of his bandaged right: a huge, long-shafted spear. It had a great iron blade shaped like a sycamore leaf a yard in length, bedded on a vicious cross-piece, all atop an ash shaft as thick as a quarterstaff, more than a fathom long.

Janet, unremarkable still in her lad's clothing and light jack, took a crossbow without raising an eyebrow and followed at Tom's heels like an apprentice with her master.

Sagres had taken the one dunderbus on offer, seemingly unaware in his increasingly nervous state, that this was the least practical, least reliable and least handy weapon here – or, in fact, that Tom was watching him with more and more lively interest. Tom had seen, though the Spaniard had not, the looks exchanged by the others – even his companions in the Hermitage garrison – and knew that everyone would be giving the señor the widest possible berth. Which, as far as Tom was concerned, was all to the good – particularly as it seemed to support the elegance of his reasoning so far. Why bring a Spanish spy or sorcerer here and then avoid him? Either the one or the other was likely to impart information about the situation, or the future, of crucial importance; and even were the man a poisoner, it might well behove someone amongst his employers to keep a careful watch upon him. But no: simple terror of the massive dunderbus seemed to have spread almost as wide as its shot would scatter – if Sagres could get the matchlock to fire in the first place.

'Do we need to follow so close upon his Spanish heels?' hissed Janet, sharing the general – and by no means unreasonable – nervousness.

'I do; you do not,' answered Tom shortly, and so saying, he eased himself through a tight-packed spiny brake into a little clearing where Señor Sagres stood, looking lost and very worried indeed.

'Hola, Señor Sagres,' said Tom easily in rough, slangy Spanish. 'Is all OK?'

'Hola,' answered Sagres guardedly. 'Is OK.' He wrestled for a moment with himself, and Tom took leisure to observe the man's natural reticence and vivid awareness that he was talking to his employer's foe here both wrestling with the simple desire to speak his mother tongue once more – even with an enemy. Wisely, Tom held his peace, paced silently across the little clearing and began to ease himself into the thickening undergrowth on the other side. Distantly, Hobbie called, 'The Grave? The Grave . . .'

Blessedly, Janet also had the sense to stay in the undergrowth.

'Señor . . .' The word grated out of Sagres as though got by a torturer.

'*Si?*' answered Tom airily, apparently innocently.

'This creature that we hunt . . . what manner of creature is it?'

'It is a huge hound of legendary size and power. It kills with a look. It carries away horses. It can reach up for twelve feet. It is the Barguest.'

'But surely you jest! Lord Robert cannot believe such a thing exists. None of you can. It is a thing of childhood stories. Like the Seven Cities of Gold and the Fountain of Eternal Youth.'

'Indeed it may be,' said Tom equably; 'but I am here because it killed my brother and I have sworn to kill it in my turn.' Sagres went silent at that, so Tom continued smoothly, 'Had not Lord Robert already told me that you are lately returned from New Spain, then I would have known it from your mention of the Cities of Gold and the Fountain of Youth. Are you, perhaps, some bold adventurer who has sailed in search of such wonders?'

Sagres gave a rough bark of coarse laughter. 'No. I am a plain, honest working man. Much good has it done me!'

'But sir! Surely in the golden glories of New Spain there is work only for soldiers and priests – and accountants, of course, to tally the tuns of gold for the King of Spain's armadas?'

'Not I, sir! You have listed almost all professions except for my own. Where do you suppose all the gold comes from? Does it grow upon trees? Does it flow in the rivers? Does it fall from the sky?'

Thus, for Tom, almost all of it fell into place at last.

Before he could spring into action, however, there came the most awful cacophony of sound. Lord Robert was clearly using the Armstrongs as beaters to scare the dangerous game they sought out of its lair towards them, he reasoned. Judging by the noise, the Armstrongs were close in front of them indeed. If their quarry was between Sagres and the beaters, then they had better prepare for action immediately. He glanced away from Sagres and discovered that Janet had materialized at his side like a ghost – pale enough to be one, indeed, her linen cheeks made even whiter in contrast with her raven locks. What a figure she would cut at court, he thought, irrelevantly, with her cheeks powdered dead white after the current fashion and her black hair bound up in ringlets.

When Tom looked back at the nervous Spaniard, he found that quietly determined individual was taking action where Tom, as yet, had not. He was pushing determinedly through the undergrowth on his left, where the valley side was beginning to gather into a considerable slope, eastern echo of the high-tracked precipice along which they had entered the place. With a speaking glance at Janet, Tom followed the frightened man.

The sounds made by the nearby beaters abruptly changed their timbre. The fearsome shouting suddenly contained more than a note of panic – a whole chorus of panic indeed. Manly bass bellows became boyish treble screams and even counter-tenor shrieks; and below them, like the ground in a raucous song, came a basso profundo snarling. They had stirred the beast they sought, and something huge was crashing invisibly but all too audibly through the undergrowth near at hand.

Sagres broke through into a clearing and took to his heels across it, with Tom and Janet hard behind him, Tom at least only just in control of the fearsome weapon he was carrying. Across the clearing they went, and into a pathway that opened unexpectedly in the press of saplings opposite. Tom realized at once that Sagres was not simply running – he knew where he was going and was racing thither, certain that it would offer refuge against whatever monster the Armstrongs had started in the timeless woods. The path they were following led up the steepening valley side where the woods began to thin. The higher it rose, the more marked it became as other little tracks joined it at unexpected moments, like streams adding to the might of a river, until it became obvious to Tom that here was a road that lay at the heart of lively industry – lively and recent, for the tracks over which they were careering at full tilt had crushed away the frost so that they were running over black mud.

As they came up out of the trees, Sagres seemed to regain his courage and his reason. He began to slow, obviously aware that he was leading the one man destined to remain ignorant – in Lord Robert's plans at least – towards some kind of answer. As the Spaniard turned, bringing up the dunderbus, so Tom, just behind him, brought down the great spear he carried; and he felt the stirring as Janet brought up her deadly crossbow. But, before they could come to blows, events overtook them.

Events overtook them, not in the shape of the Barguest after all, but in the shape of a huge black boar. Its massive back and Herculean shoulders were bristling. Its face was all covered in blood from broad, flesh-pink snout to burning, heart-red eyes – a thick rouge of redness that was smeared across its teeth and huge, curling tusks and was clearly not its own. It charged out of the undergrowth at them, screaming like an Irish banshee.

Sagres swung the dunderbus away from Tom and pulled the trigger. The smouldering match snapped down into the pan, but the pan was empty, the charge of powder long since scattered to the winds. Nothing further happened, and Sagres shook it as though it were a recalcitrant child. Janet's crossbow cracked and whipped. A black iron quarrel slammed into the huge boar's black shoulder and turned it so that it did not trample them after all; but having run past them, it turned and came screaming back again.

The three of them were long gone by the time the monster slowed and turned on the slippery, frost-slick slope. With Sagres in the lead they were at full tilt up the path towards a fold in the valley side a hundred yards or so ahead. The Spaniard had cast his dunderbus away, but Tom still kept his spear in case it came to close work and Janet, cool as a man in this strange sort of battle, was fighting to load her crossbow as she ran, hoping to prevent matters coming to so close a conclusion. Sure of his way, Sagres looked back, his face as white as salt, and gave a gasp of fear. 'It comes,' he shouted. This was no news to Tom, whose ears had told him so much already.

The vertical fold in the rock was just ahead of them, becoming clearly visible only because they were coming so close to it. Like the other cave mouth, a few miles south of here at the head of the Black Lyne, it had once been covered with undergrowth and, but for the pathway that spoke of so much bustling activity, would have been invisible altogether.

As Sagres dived right round a tall, rocky pillar, Tom followed and turned at once, levelling the spear, even as Janet stood at his shoulder, crossbow raised. The boar came charging heedlessly round the little corner, its head lowered, showing all of its terrible armoury and revealing no real weaknesses at all. Another black quarrel joined the first in the solid meat of its shoulder and Tom's spear blade glanced off its solid forehead, opening a terrible wound the boar simply disregarded as the stout shaft shattered.

Had they not been able to tumble backwards on Sagres's heels through a narrow, rock-lipped opening above a high stone sill immediately behind their dancing heels, they would both have died at once; but they could and they did, and so they did not die yet. Instead, they found themselves lying, shaken and winded, on the wide rock floor of a cavern much larger than its little cousin on the Black Lyne, and heard the boar doing its best to tear away the skin of the mountainside, which was all that lay between them.

'This way,' called Sagres, clearly all too certain that the boar was more than equal to the task and would soon be in here after them. He ran deeper into the hillside, down a tunnel – a tunnel which, Tom saw as he picked himself up, was filled with dim, uncertain torchlight. It was exactly as the Master of Logic in his mind had reasoned.

And if the Master of Logic had been correct about this, then he might well be right about the rest of it. 'Take the utmost care,' he said to Janet as she sprang erect at his side. 'There is deadly danger here.'

The mad boar's iron-hard forehead hit the sill outside and the whole cavern mouth shook and rained rubble. Tom and Janet were off down the tunnel after Sagres, so swiftly, in spite of Tom's wise warning, that they left their weapons lying on the floor. The sides of the passage were high, wide and square-cut. Every few yards there stood a three-sided frame of wood designed to strengthen the walls and support the roof. The light gathered, coming from dead ahead, revealing more details of the construction of the mine and also of its reason: the walls glittered with bands of gilded brightness just like the rock Tom had picked up in Janet's cave.

The passage was carefully dug, well constructed and long. Although the floor seemed to be sloping downwards only slightly, there was a gathering sensation of great weight pressing down upon them as though they were in some infinitely deep place and rushing deeper still. It took Tom only an instant to realize that this was because, although the shaft was only slightly angled, the hillsides above it were reaching up into the high, wild fells over which they had ridden to get here this morning.

The pace of their wild retreat began to slow, for the air in here was still and none too fragrant. It brought a savour of sweat and bodily waste to Tom's nose and the most unexpected, disconcerting odour of garlic that took him straight back to his student days at the academy of fencing run by Maestro Capo Ferro in Siena. To the back of his throat, however, it brought a disconcertingly metallic savour. To his lungs it brought little nourishment.

Out of the tunnel mouth the three of them staggered, into a larger chamber where a dazzling array of torches hissed and crackled. Here stood several men whose faces were at first impossible to distinguish, not least because they all had their backs to them, looking down into some kind of pit; but even when they turned, things became little better, for they all wore kerchiefs over their mouths and noses. The pit into which they were looking was edged with a little rail, and as they turned, one of them leaned back nonchalantly against this, the black sweep of his eyebrows rising. Beside him, a smaller man started forward, his bulldog's forehead frowning. Another little piece of the puzzle fell into place for Tom.

'Give ye good den once more, Lord Robert,' he said. 'Tam, de Vaux; Master Fenwick . . .'

'I expected you sooner, Master Musgrave,' said Lord Robert smoothly.

'Your daughter slowed me,' countered Tom, 'and I was waiting for Hobbie in any case. It must have taken him longer than planned to kill the pig and come after us. Though I believe you were expecting the pig as little as I was to suspect Hobbie's treachery.'

Black Robert Douglas gave a bark of laughter, but his eyes registered shock, even in the flickering shadows of the place. Shocked and glowing, they lifted to Janet's face. 'Well I'll be damned,' he said. 'You're right, and I never even realized. You supposed she was confederated with me? You are mistaken in that at least. A youthful indiscretion with one of the Kerr girls, I assume; come back to haunt me now. But not for long. Señor Sagres, I am sorry to see that you have been unwise enough to lead my enemy into the very heart of my secret plans. You will have to join them, I'm afraid.'

As Lord Robert was speaking English, Sagres stood gaping slightly, clearly having no idea what was going on. Tom helpfully translated into Spanish: 'They're going to kill us all. You too.'

Sagres started with shock and opened his mouth to expostulate, but the quarrel of a crossbow was shoved unceremoniously into his back and Hobbie Noble, to whom Lord Robert's words had been addressed, stepped down into the room, pushing all three of them forward.

'Hobbie was right,' said Lord Robert, his sangfroid well recovered. 'Your acuity is close to witchcraft, Master of Logic.

It is even as the Earl of Essex warned me. I salute you, though only as a parting gesture. Bring them here.'

'There's no need for the rest of you to stay covered either,' said Tom as he walked slowly towards the wooden barrier. 'Factor Fenwick, I assume you were seduced away from your master Sir Thomas by the promise of wealth from this mine. You are a man ruled by money; the riches promised here must have made that almost inevitable.'

Sir Thomas's factor Fenwick tore the mask off his face at that. 'He knows!' he snarled. 'Lord Robert, he must be made to tell us all he knows, or I may be taken when I return, and then our plans may go for nothing! And remember, the lady Eve is by no means a certain way. Better by far that I continue with Sir Thomas's ruination that you may inherit the Waste through me.'

Black Robert smiled. 'His only hope,' he said, 'is that he calculates that if he throws us such scraps as he has discovered, we will hold off killing him while we wait for the rest of the matter; and that while we wait, we might let slip more of our plans – as you have just done, Master Fenwick – then we will somehow mistake, and he may manage to escape. Do you expect to talk to us, Master Musgrave?'

'No, Lord Robert, I expect to die,' said Tom.

'In this also, you reason soundly, then. Behold your death.'

Black Robert reached back and upward, taking a torch from the wall. As he did so, Tom said, 'I have seen it, Lord Robert – in the faces of my brother, of my friend Father Little, and of the Kerrs hanging at your gate. You have the Barguest in that pit.'

Fenwick laughed an ugly laugh at that and Black Robert stood with the torch held high. 'If you believe that, then you are not the man I have taken you for! But I think that, even now, you fence with me, using wit and words instead of swords.'

'What killed my brother John lies in that pit and you have called it the Barguest – you and the Kerrs your confederates, Hobbie, Fenwick and the turncoats that work with you. What lies in there makes men die seemingly of fear and you have done the rest by rumour and secret strategy!'

'Close on witchcraft indeed. We should burn you, Master Musgrave. But as you see, we cannot.'

They were by the low fence now with the dark pit at their feet and as he spoke, Black Robert dropped his torch. Down it tumbled, flaring, end over end, into a circular well some twenty feet deep, about the same measure across. The sides of the place were lined with one wooden gallery halfway down. There were rough steps leading up here and down to the floor where the torch lay guttering. The gallery was lined with half a dozen men, all looking upwards, all screaming silently, with their eyes and mouths stretched wide, all frozen in place, apparently dead of sheer, naked fear – men, calculated Tom, such as the brace that hung at Hermitage Gate.

The three on the edge of that terrible grave had only an instant to see what awaited them before the torch choked into darkness and Lord Robert said, 'Throw them in.'

CHAPTER TWENTY-SIX

The Waste

'*NO!*' screamed Sagres, and needed no translation, the word being the same in both Spanish and English. He threw himself to one side, as though to run away, though the act was clearly futile, as Hobbie was surrounded by half a dozen Armstrongs whose arms indeed lived up to their name. He careered into Tom and Janet. 'You must not breathe down there,' he said in rapid Spanish, his lips against Tom's ear, as he did so. 'It is death to breathe down there!'

Tom, of course, had worked that out for himself long since, and was at least one step further on. For everyone here had died erect, like Father Little, clutching the rails and fighting for breath, freezing solid where they stood, apparently stricken by terror; but John had died on his hands and knees, and Tom could not imagine his brother crouching like that because he was beaten, broken and going down to death without a struggle.

A melee began at once with everyone except Black Robert and Fenwick getting involved in the scuffle. Tam Burn joined Hobbie and his men in subduing the three condemned to die.

Then, most unexpectedly, coming near to confounding even the Master of Logic, another voice, made rough and breathless by the struggle – tantalizingly impossible to identify – whispered in an undertone almost impossible to hear, 'Don't breathe!' and the words were in English this time.

The minute the rough hands closed on his arms and it was clear they were all bound downwards, Tom squeezed his eyes tight shut. He did not need eyes as he was dragged with Sagres and Janet, grimly struggling along the wooden fencing, to the gateway of the pit, but he would need them clear in the darkness at the foot of the pit all too soon. Bearing in mind the advice offered twice, he was trying to control his breathing, all his concentration on sucking the dank but life-giving air into his lungs until his chest was straining full, like a swimmer preparing to dive deep.

At the last, he opened his eyes for an instant so that he could see what lay below him, then the rough hands pushed him and he jumped.

He landed on the balcony halfway down, where Father Little had died and where all the dead Kerrs stood. He let his legs give and he rolled, careful to keep his lungs as full of air as possible. As he paused there for an instant, all of his being focused downwards, he heard Black Robert call the almost inevitable order, 'Not the girl. We'll take her back to Hermitage.' Then he leaped on down again on to the floor of the pit, falling into John's dying stance, down on his hands and knees, looking around with his dark-adjusted eyes to see what John might have been looking for if this was indeed the place his brother had died. Vaguely, he heard Sagres come tumbling down behind him. Then everything except immediate experience was blanked out of his mind.

For Tom saw what his brother John must have seen.

The torch Black Robert had thrown down before them lay on its side, its flames choked to death as surely as any Kerr up on the scaffold – except that, on the side nearest Tom, there was an ember glowing red, still alive, just. As he put his hand towards the spark of hope and fire, Tom felt a little breeze blowing steadily across the back of his fingers. Somewhere, over there behind him, was a tunnel where the air was clean enough to keep the fire alight – cleaner than here, at least; perhaps even clean enough to breathe.

He grabbed the torch and moved it gently around, his eyes on that faint red spark. As soon as it gathered a little more brightness in the breath of that hopeful draught, he began to crawl across the floor, following it. As soon as he moved he could feel Sagres at his side, silently following his lead and crawling for dear life.

The ember guided them like the star that led the three wise men to the crib of the infant Christ – across the floor of that hellish place, to the southernmost wall. Here the sheer and seemingly solid rock face was pocked by a low tunnel mouth, all but impossible to see in the Stygian gloom of the place. His hand made unerring by the guiding light, Tom pushed the torch forward and the ember started into life – just enough to show the low lintel of the rock above. As he pushed it in and followed it, Tom felt his lungs give their first warning twist of pain as they demanded that he breathe, even though it still meant death to do so.

In that moment he heard a distant voice, echoing mockingly from an ironically heavenly height: 'Like brother, like brother. That is the last I saw of the blacksmith before we dragged his frozen corpse out onto the Waste, as we shall drag you out on the morrow and put you all up in the tree where they found him. Then even the Kerrs will be too scared of the terrible Barguest to venture out in the night!'

The last distant phrase dripped with distracting irony, but it was as nothing compared with Lord Robert's mention of the Waste. Even that, however, sat unconsidered at the back of Tom's mind. For all of his conscious concentration remained upon the point of light at the tip of the torch. He held the thing perforce in his left hand, for his right hand would have dropped it, bruised and swathed as it was; but on the other hand (a distractingly amusing figure in Tom's increasingly whirling mind) he was forced to put his weight on the broken hand instead. Only the fact that he must at all costs contain his breath stopped him from shouting aloud with pain each time he did so. Such was his iron self-control that he remained breathless and silent for minute after minute as he scrabbled forwards through the massive, constricting, freezing, labyrinthine darkness fathoms deep below the Waste. The only other thing that gave him the hope and desperate strength to carry on was the speed with which the little tunnel he was following began to slope back up towards the surface.

After the first couple of minutes, the darkness of the twisting tunnel sides became irrelevant in any case, for the edges of his vision began to flicker and close down. The slope of the ground beneath him also became irrelevant, for he lost all sense of position and direction – as drowning men are sometimes said to swim downwards towards their final end, lost even to the conflicting attractions of earth and sky.

Only the unreal glimmer of the one spark still alive in the near-dead torch broke the narrowing beam of blackness along which Tom was twisting like an arthritic serpent; and, as his sight was beginning to dim, so his hearing was beginning to fail as well. The desperate scrabbling of the man who followed at his heels soon was swallowed in a pulsing, thunderous roar as his starved heart demanded sustenance from his lungs that they stoutly still refused to give. The heart began to overheat, robbed of the cooling draughts of air the throat habitually provided. The hot humours began to swirl in his brain, making him light-headed and bringing curtains of pulsing red over the glowing tip of the torch, while the heavy phlegm of earthy, liquid melancholy sank sadly to his legs and feet, making them almost impossible to move, so heavy did they become.

The red curtains of uncontrolled fiery humour swirling before his eyes became so thick that he almost missed the moment that the spark sprang from ember into flame; but when that one flicker began to spread, as yellow as a field of daffodils in spring, across the wintry stubble of the blackened torch, he realized that the faithful flambard at least had found air enough to breathe. Yet still, almost dead of suffocation, still he did not dare to let his pent breath out. Onward in a kind of frenzy he pushed his shaking body, watching the yellow flames spread like wildfire, yet still refusing to breathe as the fourth minute began to pass and the passageway began, unnoticed, to widen and lighten around him.

In the end, a blast of icy air came battering into Tom's fixed and frozen face. The torch, just below his left shoulder, exploded into volcanic life, singeing his cheek, near singeing his moustache and shocking him into a gasp of surprise. And so it was he found that he could breathe.

'Breathe!' he shouted over his shoulder, in English, so far was he from controlling his thoughts and actions – only to be surprised by utter silence. Not even a croak issued from his frozen throat. His voice, like his breath over the last four minutes and more, was stopped. Twisting on his side and pressing his back against the wall, he thrust the torch back past his feet to bring the message home to the man behind him; but when he looked back into its brightness, to his horror he found himself alone. The tunnel was just wide enough now to allow him to turn, and so he did as fast as he was able, shuffling back down into the deadly darkness, pushing his torch ahead of him, following the cheery brightness of its flame back into the gathering horror below. Sagres had been hard on his heels when his hearing went and he found him first, just at the point where the torch began to gutter, twenty long and agonizing seconds later. He lay face down and apparently dead where the narrow tunnel began to open out. He half-turned and put his beard at risk of singeing like the King of Spain's as he threw the torch away into the good air further on. Then he laced his good left hand into the solid leather of the Spaniard's doublet and heaved.

'Are we alive, then?' asked Sagres in Spanish some time later. They lay side by side immediately outside an utterly unremarkable hole on a frozen hill-slope, gasping like a couple of fish thrown up by a high tide.

'I can hardly tell,' said Tom in the same language, squinting up into the dazzling daylight, 'but we are breathing, and that seems to be a start. Perhaps full life will return if we wait.'

'The air upon this mountainside is already performing that miracle for me,' said the Spaniard dreamily. 'After a childhood in the heat of La Carihuela and a manhood in the deserts and jungles of New Spain, to think that I should thank Our Lady on bended knee for the icy air of this accursed, frozen place!'

'Is it gold they are mining, then?' Tom demanded after a moment. 'Or copper? Or tin?'

Sagres sat up and gaped at him.

'You are an expert in gold mining from New Spain,' Tom persisted, also pulling himself up off the frosted grass. 'De Vaux owns half the tin in Cornwall and most of the mines north of Redruth; but all I have ever heard tell of in these parts is copper, and it must be a metal of some kind or the Armstrongs would never need all that charcoal for smelting what they and the Kerrs bring out of the mine.'

Sagres crossed himself – and not just because his prayer to the Virgin was done. 'Witchcraft,' he muttered.

'Logic,' countered Tom.

'Lord Robert thought at first he must have discovered copper, as you say,' agreed Sagres reluctantly; 'but then indeed he hoped for gold. In the end he got neither, as things transpired; but they have discovered something that might be worth more than both, so they hope.'

'And what is that, pray tell?'

'It is arsenic.'

'Arsenic!'

'Yellow arsenic. It looks like copper – like gold, indeed, in some lights; but if you put it in a furnace carefully, you may reduce it to the purest of white powders, and that is what they have done. There is a fashion, Señor de Vaux and Lord Robert the devil tell me, to wear such powder upon their faces at court. It is popular but fabulously expensive, for most of it must be imported, I believe, from the north of Germany. They find it in the silver mines there.'

'And whoever owns a monopoly on an English supply might find his fortune well and truly made,' whispered Tom, in English.

'That's the answer. The answer to almost all of it, as I knew it simply had to be!' Tom said, after a moment of thoughtful silence, reverting to Spanish as he sprang erect. 'Sagres, d'ye not see where we are?'

He turned the Spaniard round and they stood shoulder to shoulder, looking away south across the gathering slope that folded down into the valley of the Black Lyne.

'I see,' said the Spaniard slowly. 'I know the shafts run northward to Hermitage Castle itself, but there is nothing of worth within them. All the good ore is down here.' He paused, looking across at the vibrant Englishman, then asked a little nervously, 'What is it that you mean to do, Maestro Musgrave?'

'I mean, señor, to avenge my brother, rescue my sister and perhaps young Janet too. Then I shall put paid to a nest of turncoats and traitors; and, finally, I shall bury the Barguest into the bargain,' he said.

'But how?' whispered Sagres, simply awed by the scale of the prospect. 'How under God can you hope to do so much?'

'Why, señor,' he answered with grim exultation, 'I can do it because I am dead. I can do it because the pair of us, like my brave brother John, have been taken by the Barguest already and lie dead and buried beneath the Waste! Or, lest ye think me mad when I need you to help me, let me be more plain and square with you: I can do it because Black Robert and his murderous confederates *believe* we are dead and buried. He believes there is no one now living who can interfere with his plans, but he is terribly wrong in that. For I, the Master of Logic, know every detail of what he has done, is doing, and plans to do, so that when I begin to act against him, he will fall helpless into my hands – and mayhap even bring his friend the Earl of Essex with him.'

CHAPTER TWENTY-SEVEN

The Dark Designs

The pair of them were waiting in Sir Thomas's study when he returned from the hunt that night, with Geordie Burn pale but determined at his side. He gaped to see them together at all, let alone so footsore and filthy. He frowned to see that his ledgers and private papers lay open on the table, some pages marked with rude and muddy fingerprints; but such was his surprise that he forbore to comment and heard his nephew out. Then his astonishment simply grew and grew as Tom tersely briefed him on what he had discovered and the actions they all must now take as a matter of the extremest urgency.

He began with the spy. 'Sir Thomas, can you confirm to me that Hobbie is your spy in Lord Robert's camp, though he pretends to be a traitor to you and yours?'

Sir Thomas hesitated, then he turned to Geordie. 'See to your command, Captain Burn. We will be back in Liddesdale before moonrise, if I am any judge – and ye can continue your quest for the Barguest and your lady's hand then.'

As Geordie left, the Lord of the Waste turned, looking elderly and weary. 'A good man and a good soldier, but there's little place for bravery and honour in this black coil. 'Tis better he remains in ignorance and dreams that Eve might ever come to him, as he has done for half his life.

'Now, as to Hobbie Noble: it is a dreadful, ungodly thing to demand of any man, but on the Borders there is little choice. I

215

am astounded that you have seen so much so quickly in the matter – you are every bit as uncanny as the Lord Hunsdon inferred in his letters, and as well versed in the black arts of espionage. I see I must be open with you and pray that you are correct and that Lord Robert's Spaniard there speaks no English.

'I began to place Hobbie Noble so that he could move in dangerous circles when I helped him release Jock o' the Side Armstrong from gaol a few years since. I have used him sparingly but he has reported fully. Only now have I been forced to risk him in the very heart of the lion's den, for as ye see from my ledgers, my income is shrinking daily, and ruin stares me in the face despite the best efforts of my factor – or I supposed I was getting Master Fenwick's best efforts until Hobbie suggested the man had been seduced away by Black Robert as he seeks my ruin; but 'tis all moon-shadow and will-o'-the-wisp, nothing a man can lay a hand to. Even now, Hobbie seeks truth enough to go to law; but the case must needs be unanswerable and the groundwork set in sure foundation or Fenwick and his true masters will stand across the Scottish border and laugh at our English courts. On the other hand, my other true servant, your brother the blacksmith had come to me with ores he had been sent – from Hermitage no less – to see if he could tell what they might be; but nothing came of that, for he was dead soon after we talked.'

'And ye saw no coincidence in that? I see from your face you did; and I suspect you were not alone in that. A wise move to risk Hobbie, therefore, for there is everything to play for here; but he in turn has risked all his careful placing to whisper a warning to me and I am fearful Lord Robert would not let such a slip pass without notice – and, I doubt not, some action. Has Hobbie returned with you?'

'I have not seen him since the boar broke loose this afternoon.'

'Let us pre-empt them all and counter their dark designs with immediate action. I will explain what I have discovered to you as we proceed. You should know that I have not been sitting idly awaiting your return, but have usurped your seal and authority to summon reinforcements from Carlisle, for we must return to Liddesdale and Hermitage tonight if Eve, and mayhap Janet, are to survive.'

'Well, well,' said Sir Thomas grimly. 'We will fill the interim with your explanation and then I will judge who's bound for Carlisle gaol.'

'Let us begin with John's death and the lady Eve,' said Tom decisively. 'Whatever she told you at your inquest into the matter, the facts are these: Eve knew John believed in the Barguest – and that he shared his superstition with half the Borders – though he believed he had seen it and the rest of them had not. Eve did not believe the Barguest killed John, however, in spite of the apparent evidence furnished by his terrified face and his discovery in the clawed tree at Arthur's Seat. Her reasoning was simple and based on her own experience, shared with the Lady Ellen: John was clean. Women who have laid men out for burial know that such a thing could not be. Death is a dirty business. Dying of fear releases all the body's foulness in a flood.'

Tom was not sitting idly as he talked. His hands were busy loading guns and sorting weapons on the little table in Sir Thomas's study. Sagres, silent and understanding nothing of what was being said, nevertheless followed suit, so that they would all be ready to leave the very instant reinforcements arrived from Carlisle.

'John was not foul,' continued Tom grimly. 'In fact, his clothes were recently washed and fire-dried; but that had been done in haste, for his shirt tail had been singed, as was my own when Lady Ellen caused a blood-fouled shirt to be cleaned and dried. More than one man must have been involved in the doing of it, for not even Eve herself could remove the clothes from John's frozen body after Hobbie had brought him down to her.

'No simple death of terror in the face of a fearsome monster, therefore. Instead, in Eve's eyes and my own, a complex and sinister conspiracy of murder and concealment of murder by many men over several hours at the least – a terrible, calculated and brutal act, compounded and completed with the raising of John's washed, dressed, still-frozen corpse into the branches of the tree. It was done as you yourself raised up the stag for skinning on St Stephen's Day; I am certain of that, for the faintest of rope marks were left on his back and at his armpits, and the clawing of the trunk beneath completed their fearsome act. And it was an act: an illusion. Like the ass's head in my friend Shakespeare's new play of the midsummer dream.

'Father Little's clothing also had been cleaned and dried before he was returned to the scaffold in the church tower at Blackpool Gate – for the same dark reason and with the same desired effect.'

'But why? If, as you say, it aroused suspicion instead of allaying it, then why?' Sir Thomas now was restless, pacing the study and looking down into the castle yard. Clearly, thought Tom, his uncle was beginning to see what he had seen, and understand a little of Black Robert's dark design – keen, he hoped, for the men to arrive from Carlisle so that they could go off up Liddesdale and into the dangerous dungeons of Hermitage again.

'Because Lord Robert, who lies behind the twisted heart of this whole murderous matter, was willing to run a small risk in order to cover a huge truth,' Tom explained. Then he demanded, 'What was it that was washed off the dead men's clothing?'

'The foulness of their terrible deaths,' hazarded Sir Thomas.

'No.' Tom paused for a minim beat, as though this were a duel with swords and in form. Then he began to explain slowly, for this was near the very marrow of the matter: 'What had at all costs to be cleaned away was the mud from Lord Robert's mine. That is the secret heart of the business here – Lord Robert's mine, which I will describe in more detail later; but in the meantime, Sagres and I have been there and are lucky indeed to have returned alive. Look at us; we are filthy, soiled with mud and stained with the tell-tale green of the ore. So were John and Father Little. Above everything else, Lord Robert wishes to conceal the fact that he is mining. That is why

everyone he cannot trust to keep his secret has to die. That is
why he must have decided to rid himself of John even though
my brother could not tell him what his strange gold-coloured
ore could be. That is why he brought the Barguest back to life in
the first place.'

'To hide a mine?'

'Indeed. To hide his mine and conceal the fact that he had the
Kerrs scouring the countryside looking for other ways into it.
Gangs of Kerrs come and go nightly through the Busy Gap past
the bastle farm at Housesteads, where we first met Janet and
Dand – and came close to killing the both of them. They range
abroad every night, scouring the Waste, while the weather
holds icy but snowless. They leave no tracks on the frozen
ground, but will do so when the snow comes and so will
perforce leave off their murderous excursions if the matter
has not been settled by then. Scores of Kerrs come and go,
armed with clubs that have steel hooks driven into them –
clawed clubs that can scratch a tree to the heartwood like the
claws of a giant dog, up to twelve feet from the earth, if they
stand in their stirrups and reach up to the fullest stretch. For
while they scour the Waste, so they perpetuate the story that the
Barguest is abroad.

'I had thought, at first, that it was all like my friend Will
Shakespeare's play of the midsummer dream, where men dress
up as monsters and bushes may be mistaken for bears; but there
is more to the matter than that – much more – and all of it
bloodiest and most devilish evil.'

'You have seen these clubs?' Sir Thomas's eyes were narrow,
his face pale with horror at the lies Lord Robert was per-
petuating. He was almost ready, thought Tom – almost ready
to ride.

'I have seen what they can do,' Tom continued smoothly.
'For one of the Kerrs used just such a club on Archie Elliot's
back on Christmas night – the night I thought Geordie Burn
had tried to kill me, when really it was his brother Tam, Lord
Robert's captain from Hermitage, riding in secret with Hugh of
Stob. The claw-club left three lines parallel in Archie's flesh and

the razor mark of a fourth in the hair beside them. Word of that terrible error was carried up to Hermitage, I would judge by your factor Fenwick; but whoever passed the warning, Archie was murdered the next day by the poison I have just mentioned, and which came close to killing several others of us too.'

'What poison? How?'

'By this, I would judge, and in this.' Tom pulled out of his pouch the apple-sized piece of earth he had found in Janet's cave, which he had seen ground up in John's smithy, and which he now knew to be yellow arsenic ore. Beside it he laid the severed glove finger he had found. 'It was done at the Hunt Mass, and by Fenwick again. I am certain of that this time, for I tested the man last night and saw the guilt within his eyes. And I tested the poison, too, on two dead mice, while de Vaux unknowingly further tested it on a cat.

'He filled the glove finger with the poison powder and slipped it into his mouth. It is of Spanish leather, like my own, and waterproof, but polished only on the outside and not watertight enough to contain a liquid safely. He used powdered arsenic, therefore – this white powder that Señor Sagres assures me is derived from the other here, and with which all at court powder their faces according to the fashion. He stood beside Archie at communion, and when he seemingly sipped from the holy cup, he emptied the poison in. Archie took the largest dose and died. Eve, Geordie and myself were poisoned too and Father Little, who emptied the cup himself, was poisoned last of all. We were none of us his target – only Archie.

'But, as Hobbie said in our discussion of the matter, we were hurt incidentally to the main object of the crime. When word got out to Hermitage that Eve was amongst the poisoned, de Vaux himself was despatched to contact and castigate the blundering Fenwick and find out the truth of her health.'

It was at this point in Tom's explanation that the men from Carlisle arrived; and Sir Thomas, seeing this, was in no mood at all to linger further. The Governor had sent thirty, and the Bewcastle contingent made the number up to fifty. They were all well armed and armoured in their jacks, plates and steel bonnets – sharp but steady, and ready for bloody work. Within moments they were all formed up and cantering purposefully out of the gate again, Geordie at the shoulder of the captain from Carlisle, but Tom, Sir Thomas and Sagres at the head.

'Unlike us,' continued Tom as they rode up towards the Waste with Sir Thomas leaning over dangerously, the better to hear him over the muted thunder of the troop behind, 'Father Little must have suspected something when the poison began to grip him. He was certain that Lord Robert was up to evil, as he told me on the day Lord Robert and I first met, and must have ridden not to Blackpool Gate but right up to Hermitage to confront him, sick as he was; but the end of all his bravery simply served to put him, like John, in the pit of death that stands at the heart of Black Robert's mine. Like John, he died there, and I can only pray his death was swift and painless, for he was already half-dead with Fenwick's poison from the desecrated chalice.

'Then, like John's had been, Father Little's frozen corpse was removed, cleaned and put on show as another victim of the Barguest – and that gently and secretly, for it was done while Janet and I slept in the kirk below.'

'I had shared some of my suspicions with the good father,' admitted Sir Thomas grimly. 'Unlike you, I am old enough to remember how the confessional can lighten the heaviest-charged of souls. But if they saw you alone in the kirk as they brought the father's body there, why did they not take you or kill you?'

'By this time, my own investigations were the cause of an unexpected effect. They were spreading word of the Barguest ever wider – and convincing even hard-headed men that the beast must actually be real. Suddenly and unexpectedly – and temporarily – therefore, I became useful to Lord Robert, which is why I am alive to tell this black tale now.'

Tom stopped talking for a while as they thundered up over the Waste, sending the frost-mist swirling away under the last of the light to where the will-o'-the-wisps glimmered over the frozen bog-holes there.

'But what in heaven's name is the motivation for all this madness and death? A mine full of poison somewhere up ahead in Liddesdale?' Sir Thomas demanded, his voice aquiver with outrage.

'Not just in Liddesdale, no. That is the nub of the problem, you see,' answered Tom, with a broad gesture of his broken hand comprehending all the dangerous beauty around them. 'The Waste and all the fells between here and Hermitage are a honeycomb of caverns and tunnels, into which Lord Robert is driving his shafts to mine out his arsenic; but his main shaft starts on the east side of the Liddel valley far to the south of Hermitage. It runs east and south from there, reaching right down to the head of the Black Lyne itself, only a mile or so ahead of where we are riding now. Do you not see what this must mean?'

Sir Thomas folded his forehead into a thoughtful frown, but his nephew had not the patience to allow considered rumination. 'It means that all Black Robert Douglas's new-found wealth lies under English soil! If you cannot reach north across the border to catch at him for plotting dark ruin against you, no more can he reach south across it to mend his own fast-breaking fortunes. The arsenic that will mend the fortunes of Lord Robert and the Essex faction in the Court cannot belong to a Scottish laird, for it all lies south of the border – in our good Queen's realm! It belongs to whoever holds title to the Waste at English law; whoever owns the Black Lyne.

'Lord Robert created the Barguest to frighten all of you off the Waste, and, with John's body in the great oak, out of the Lyne valley as well, while the Kerrs found out the extent of the problem and he worked out his solution – as he has done now.'

'What solution?'

'He knows that the entrances he seeks on English soil are in the valley of the Lyne. He holds the woman that owns the land he covets. He will not let her go. He will keep her and hold the title to the Black Lyne. He sees himself victorious and unopposed now, for he believes that I am dead and he supposes I am the only man outside his control who has begun to suspect the truth. He has only to force Eve into a form of marriage, then he can swiftly widow himself into untold riches. It is his easiest, most certain way.

CHAPTER TWENTY-EIGHT

Liddesdale Ablaze

As Tom reached that point in his reasoning, so the war band left English soil to enter Liddesdale and Scotland. As they did so, like a blessing from on high, a steady, strengthening south-westerly wind sprang up behind to blow them on their way. Over the ford at the valley mouth they went, then up on to the path that led across the precipice itself, in through the sheer-sided throat of the place. Here reason must perforce give place to further preparation. As they followed the track up across the curves of the undulating valley side, so Tom and his uncle agreed their plans for action and passed their orders back. When there was no more to be done, Tom returned to his tale of horror and double-dealing.

Tom and Sir Thomas crushed side by side on the narrow way so that the Master of Logic could continue with his explanation to the Lord of the Waste. 'Let us return to the beginning. Eve was nearly certain that John was murdered, then, and likely murdered for the land they owned, because there seemed no other cause great enough to create such a terrible consequence; but in her heart also she feared the work that he was doing – in secret I should judge – on the strange ores that had been brought down from Hermitage to him. Eve is a woman who will not trust what she does not understand. Tom no doubt felt lowered by this grubbing with metallic, smelly dirt and would not discuss the matter with her. She brought enough of her fear to you, however, on the night after his death so that you held swift inquest and then despatched her with Hobbie to the Council, to the Lord of the North and, ultimately, to me.

'In the meantime, however, she had sufficient leisure to turn to the method of John's murder, leaving aside the reason for it. She reasoned thus: if he was not killed with terror by the Barguest, then she must at once consider poison. Knowing nothing of secret mines and deathly airs, she thought of herbal lore. Mayhap she consulted Lady Ellen, but she had no real need to do so, for she heals with the same mastery as Ellen and that bespeaks equal knowledge.

'There are poisons – poisons close to hand – that might have killed anyone in the way John seemed to have been killed – certainly with much the same effect. Even Fenwick's white arsenic left a corpse in Archie Elliot bewilderingly similar to that of both John and Father Little: the rictus, the straining muscles, the look of tortured agony that might be mistaken for terror. She had a wide variety of possibilities but only limited time for investigation, however, for no sooner were the inquest and the funeral done than you warned her to prepare for the journey south with Hobbie; but the possibility was ever in her mind.

'Then the fear arose that whoever had poisoned John would be as quick to poison the man looking into his death. The elder brother being murdered, therefore, the younger brother might well stand in mortal danger in his turn. The younger brother: to wit, myself. But poisons have antidotes. Indeed, it is a common proof that if a man is to taste the antidote before he takes the poison, then the poison may not touch him at all. So it was that Eve herself stabbed a dagger into my side at Ware.'

'What are you saying?' Sir Thomas came near to steering his hunter off the cliff edge in surprise. 'It was Eve herself that wounded you?'

'Aye. Then, as she tended to my hurt,' shouted Tom to reassure him, suddenly aware of how the wind was strengthening at their backs, 'so she put into the wound, and my medicines, all the antidotes to the poisons she feared might be used on me. The treatment gave me a fevered, dream-filled night as we sped northward in the coach; but it was all to good effect, for I have been poisoned and I have survived!'

At this moment they rode out on to an outward curve of the path where the whole thin road seemed to hang in very air. Here they came across the first of the great horrors of the night. It was a gallows, recently built into the jutting cliff under which they rode, which reached across their narrow track so that the body hanging from it must needs obstruct their way. A hooded man dangled from it, faceless, but with a body that twitched and writhed in faint but lively agony, aswinging in the wind. The hanging man had been hooded with a bag then bound on to the gallows in such a manner that he could hardly breathe, for there was a rope tight across his throat. Yet there was another rope that held his arms behind him and ran upward as well, taking just enough of his weight so that he should choke but never faint and not quite die until thirst or famine clung him; and, given the quantity of rain of late, it was likely to be a lingering wait before he gained his peace.

Tom and Sir Thomas came up against this unfortunate creature first, for they were in the lead. Had Sir Thomas been alone, he would likely have pushed past with his men. The Master of Logic was given pause and slowed them both, however. At the very least, thought Tom, his enemy's enemy, here displayed, might make a lively friend, as Sagres had done. So he looked up at the jerking body and tried to figure what the face would look like behind the hood; but the form itself was swift to tell its own story.

'HOBBIE!' called Tom, urging his horse forward until Hobbie's pendant feet could rest upon the withers and Tom could reach up in an unconscious echo of the men that had clawed the oak beneath the corpse of his murdered brother. Standing in his stirrups on a steady, patient horse, he reached up with the longest of his sharp-sided daggers and cut his old friend free. Sir Thomas had ridden onward. The rest of the command perforce remained behind.

Hobbie slid down on to Tom's horse, swung wildly out over

226

the sheer drop, then swung in again to bang his hooded head against the sheer wall beside him. 'That you, Tom?' he whispered.

'Aye,' affirmed Tom. 'It is.'

'Should never have warned ye to hold your breath. That devil Lord Robert heard me . . .'

'But then I wouldn't have been here to cut you down; and he would have found you out sometime.'

'True enough,' croaked Hobbie.

A little more dagger work released Hobbie's hands and allowed the removal of the bag and all the ropes.

'Who did this to you?'

'Need ye ask?'

'Not Lord Robert himself? No. Fenwick, more likely, as proof of loyalty after the flapping of his big, loose mouth . . .'

'Ye're in the right. And Tam Burn joined in for the pleasure while that whoreson de Vaux looked on and laughed. 'Twas de Vaux suggested the running knots and the slow strangulation – bad cess to him.'

'Is he strong enough to come with us?' bellowed Sir Thomas over the gusty roaring of the wind, rendered impatient rather than sympathetic by this new proof of Black Robert's devilish perfidy.

'Needs must', sang back Tom. 'There's no one here to take him home.'

'Besides,' choked Hobbie painfully, 'there's the matter of revenge now. So I'll come along with you until we meet the several men I've to settle with.'

For the next few minutes, as they shared Tom's horse, Hobbie and he brought each other up to date with their thoughts and plans. Then Sir Thomas's patience ran out and he demanded the explanations include him.

'Tom's right,' said Hobbie: 'Eve stabbed him then swore me to silence as she tended him with all her cunning. Her object was to make the treatment of a slight hurt at Ware into an armour of fitness against any other poisons that might be fed to him.'

'On the way north she tested my belief in the Barguest too,'

227

continued Tom, 'and found I believed in it as little as she did herself; but she would not confide all of her fears to me – or, perhaps, it was not so much a reluctance to tell me what she feared as a wariness to do so in front of Hobbie, whom she has good reason not to trust.'

'Has she?' demanded Hobbie and Sir Thomas in unison. 'What good reason is that?' completed Sir Thomas, while Hobbie choked on a cough.

Tom answered his uncle directly: 'The fact that you have not told her that Hobbie is your spy in Lord Robert's ranks. Or *was*, rather. She sees only the double game he was playing, not the single purpose behind it.'

'A fair point,' allowed Sir Thomas, and Hobbie nodded too – once, painfully.

'But in any case, she had good reason not to share all her doubts and suspicions with me, for I was here expressly to find out the truth of the matter, and that truth, she feared, might reveal some ignoble dealing between John and Lord Robert to echo what she feared of Hobbie. For had not John secret contacts with Hermitage over the matter of the ores? Was he not on his way there for his gooding when he disappeared and died? Better by far to watch what I uncovered and to see then how well it fitted with what she believed.

'But that is all irrelevant now, for Black Robert has taken her.' He held up his hand at Sir Thomas's expostulation. 'I know, you believe what Lord Robert said this morning: that she has gone to Hermitage so that he will bring her the Barguest; that she has given her word and he has given his. But he took her by force, and I believe she has demanded the Barguest as a last, desperate ploy – not out of a desire for revenge for John's death, but as a way to slow events. She does not believe the thing exists, therefore she does not believe anyone can bring it to her. Therefore she is safe until we can work out a way to rescue her; but Lord Robert holds one final ace, and if ever a man was born to play it, that man is himself.

'Black Robert knows that the Barguest is real. Janet certainly knows this, because it took her horse, poor Selkie. News of that will have come to him recently, but I am certain Black Robert already had some knowledge of the thing. Perhaps he has even seen it in the wild woods of Liddesdale, as John and I saw it a little further south, when we were young. So if the monster is real and he knows where it lives, Lord Robert can now have Eve and the Black Lyne whenever he wants, all legal and in the full light of day, after all. For Eve has trapped herself: he has only to bring her the Barguest and she must bow to him as she has sworn; and he will take her, body and soul, with all she stands possessed of. Then he will kill her when he tires of her, and all his fortune will be made.

'That was designed to be today's business: to rid himself of all his problems at a stroke; to kill me, in the same way as he killed Father Little and brother John; to keep my body back for display tomorrow; to hang up Hobbie as a suspected spy and leave him as a warning to anyone approaching Hermitage; to kill the Barguest, which he is certain haunts the wild woods of Liddesdale; to win Eve and to lay legal hold of the Black Lyne.

'Things have not worked out that way, however. For the first time since John discovered what was afoot in Liddesdale when he went agooding unannounced on St Thomas's Day and met his end and began all this, Lord Robert's plans have gone awry. He will have them back on their destined road by the morrow, I have no doubt; but tonight belongs to us, and we have the chance, now and only now, to upset these evil schemes of his and bring this all to a happy ending.'

The light was almost gone now and they had not brought torches with them that would only advertise their presence further to the Armstrongs and their master. Torches would never have survived the wind, in any case.

As he spoke, however, so something buzzed between himself and Sir Thomas to spatter and spark off the rock beside his head, and a shot echoed through the gusty shadows. The first shot was followed at once by a second, and the man behind Geordie Burn was hurled off his horse, his bonnet shattered. 'Sir Thomas, we must go down!' bellowed Tom, and the good old soldier swung his horse towards the edge of the slope at once. Even as the rest turned to follow suit, Hobbie leaped off Tom's horse and ran to the suddenly vacated spare mount. Then, fifty-four of them, abreast, set their horses straight down the slope and went sliding into the depths of Liddesdale.

This was what Tom and Sir Thomas had planned and, except for the acquisition of an extra companion, they had covered every eventuality. Sir Thomas took the fifty riders and went straight into the attack. It was a feature of the place that it was deep, dark and thickly forested, full of *ambuscadoes* where Armstrongs could hide and snipe, particularly at this time of day. The main attack was designed to use the terrain and their own activities most effectively against them, however. Sir Thomas's men went at once for the charcoal fires. Each of these stood ten feet high, a palisade of inward-leaning logs at whose heart was a slow fire, choked of air where the wood was rendered not to ash but to charcoal; but the fires, when toppled with line and long spear and scattered across the ground, exploded into great balls of flame like the fire invented by Archimedes for the Greeks. So intense was the burning of the charcoal when the air of the strong southerly gale breathed new life into it, that it set even the frozen trees of the forest around it alight. There were scores of charcoal fires ranged at the outskirts of the forest between this and Black Robert's haunted lair. The southerly gale funnelled up the valley and blew the wildfire northwards before it, straight towards Hermitage itself. Thus Tom and his uncle's bold plans at once robbed the Armstrongs of shadow and shelter and Lord Robert of his means to roast his arsenic – as well putting his woods and his stronghold at risk. The attack was unexpected, fearsome and effective beyond measure. In seeming minutes Liddesdale was ablaze, a river of fire running true to its element and surging uphill along the valley where the River Liddle ran ever down.

CHAPTER TWENTY-NINE

The Barguest

Down, indeed, went Tom and his companions, but down and away from Sir Thomas. Led by Sagres, they ran into an upper cave mouth leading into the older sections of the mine. Far to the north of the present workings and the pit of death, they followed the glimmer of the torch Sagres had brought from Bewcastle along old, deserted passages that led across the head of Liddesdale and through the slopes immediately below Hermitage itself. Tom had known these tunnels must be here, for had not Janet talked of the haunted sounds issuing from the fort's foundations and echoing through the hillsides? Sagres had suspected them and indeed had explored the castle end of some that led out of the dungeons. As well as that, he had noted every tunnel entrance along the valley – those of the old mines as well as those of the new. He was a useful guide, therefore, though Tom was glad he had thought to instruct him to add torch and tinder box to his weaponry.

The four of them ran out into a dungeon under Hermitage hardly realizing they had done so. The chamber they so suddenly stood in was little more than a cavern chopped out of the hillside whose ice-bound walls were supplemented with roughly dressed stone sections higher up. There was a mess of boulders and scaffolding on the floor, little better tidied than the foot of the church tower at Blackpool Gate. Rough steps were carved in the far wall, visible only as glitters of icy light in the flicker of Sagres's torch, and they led up to a little open-sided balcony, where a rotting door gaped.

'This explains why Black Robert's so desperate for gold,' said Tom as his long sword hissed out into the steady grip of his good left hand. Then, with Sagres still holding the torch aloft, they were off. The door took them to a higher level of dungeons, slightly better walled but no warmer and in little better repair. They were, blessedly, deserted, for no one secured within them would ever have lasted long. Chains and fetters hung from the walls, rust-red and rotting in the torchlight. Only in the torture chamber was there evidence of anything recently used and new.

Through the silence of the deserted place the little band ran on. Tom was not alone in finding the mouldering, icy silence disturbing, he observed, though he alone had been expecting something of the kind. The other faces in the torchlight wore the same expression of half-fearful bemusement that he knew was expressed on his own as he tested his logic once again. He thought back to the band of guests that Lord Robert had brought to his uncle's hunt. It had been that band that had caused this plan, for they had all been men – hardly a social group, though Lord Robert had meant it to be, as a cover for his darker plans at the very least. Had there been women worthy of note in the place, he would have brought them too. Therefore there were none: servants and captives; otherwise men – a front-line command on a war footing. Like Bewcastle on Christmas night – except that the Douglas was prepared for battle, so he had emptied his rotting shell of a castle of everyone except his warriors and the least number of servants needed to see to them. Most of the servants, indeed, were likely to be Armstrongs and able to double as footsoldiers too.

Now Liddesdale was under attack – down in the valley, currently, with no obvious danger to Hermitage, as had been planned as well. Therefore it was hardly surprising that the garrison was up and out. So logic dictated that the place would be near-deserted – which was why he had been prepared to come with Sagres alone to find Eve and Janet, but was glad to have Hobbie, if not the sickly Geordie.

Sagres led them up to a closed door and then, at Tom's order, he fell back again lest the light of his torch should show through the grille to which Tom pressed his eager face. He found himself looking across the castle's little courtyard towards the keep. They were in the lower sections of the gatehouse, therefore, and there must be men here if nowhere else. The portcullis was either up or down – whichever one, it would needs be moved when Lord Robert rode back again. 'Silently,' he breathed, and they tiptoed away from the door across the tiny chamber towards a second, narrow, inner portal. Tom put his ear to this and heard beyond it the quiet conversation of two guards tensely on watch. He looked speakingly at Hobbie, the door handle and his swathed right hand. Hobbie nodded stiffly and replaced him with his shoulder to the wood. A beat of time and the reiver kicked the door wide. All four of them boiled into the little guard chamber. The work was swift, silent and bloody.

Their weapons thus supplemented and their expedition still secure, the four returned to the door that looked out into the castle yard. They had to compromise their secrecy now, for they could only go out or back. Out they went, therefore, at Tom's back, across the broad way behind the closed portcullis and into the guardroom at the other side, which doubled as the winch room. The inner door that only opened into the safety of the castle yard was unlocked, of course, and the three guards sitting watching the fast-approaching fires were never prepared for danger so close behind. Two minutes later, Tom came back out, thoughtlessly wiping his blade on his bandage. 'Black Robert may knock until hell freezes over,' he said, 'but he's not coming in here again unless I let him.'

Even as the smoke-tainted wind whipped in through the bars of the portcullis and stole the words from his lips, so a scream came echoing out of the keep. The voice belonged to Janet, and Tom could think of only one thing other than the Barguest that could have wrung such a sound from her. At full tilt he ran towards the keep, only to find his steps faltering. There seemed no way into the place other than across that strange balcony three storeys above their heads, where Eve had stood to promise herself to the man that killed the Barguest; but once again Sagres proved his worth, for he led them across to an apparently unimportant little doorway that seemed to pierce the outer wall. This led to a short passage and a long flight of stairs. Up these they rushed, led by Janet's screams that flowed like Ariadne's thread through the compact labyrinth of the place. The keep was massive in construction but small enough in space. This was a border fort, not a great castle like Carlisle. It was not long before they burst into an upper chamber and found the girl tied tightly to a bed, screaming fouler and fouler invective at the man who had stripped her clothes to near rags and was preparing to ravish her. With his breeches round his ankles and his shirt tail up, there was only one part of the man's rear clearly on view. So when Hobbie croaked, 'I'd know that face anywhere,' Fenwick the Factor rounded on him in understandable rage.

When he saw who stood in the doorway, however, his rage was swift to wilt. 'He's yours, Hobbie,' said Tom.

'Up with yer breeks first,' said Hobbie broadly, his broken voice trembling with rage. 'Then oot wi' yer sword. Then on wi' ma revenge!'

Tom brushed past the gobbling man and reached down to restore some dignity to Janet; but as he did so, she tore her right hand free of its binding and snatched one of his new-primed pistols from his belt. In spite of the rough handling, there was still enough powder in the pan for a shot; and, although she was badly positioned and partially unsighted, the shot went true enough.

Tom reeled back, his face full of powder smoke, his eyes dazzled by the muzzle flash and his ears near deafened by the sound. 'Janet,' he cried. 'Ye're mad!'

'She is that,' mourned Hobbie. 'She'll have roused anyone left in the castle with that. And she's robbed me of ma revenge.'

'I had call for some revenges of my own,' snarled Janet.

'True enough, but mine took precedence. He only came close to raping you, but the little bastard did hang me . . .'

'Well, hang him too,' spat Janet.

'I can't. Ye blew his bloody head off.'

Tom's eyes cleared enough to see the truth of this, and to see that Sagres had put down his torch to restore some decency to the outraged girl. He had priorities of his own, however. As he untied Janet's left hand, unhandily with his own left hand, he in turn spat, 'Geordie, keep close lookout. Janet, where's Black Robert hidden Eve?'

'He took her with him,' answered Janet, slapping Sagres's hands away.

'What?' demanded Tom, simply stunned by the turn of events.

'The Master of Logic did not foresee this?' asked Geordie dryly, glancing over from his post by the door. Then he glanced back and fired a shot himself. 'Kitchen wenches,' he said tersely over some fading screams.

'No,' said Tom shortly in answer to his question, 'I did not guess Black Robert would take Eve out with him. We must out and after them. Quickly!' And, once again they were off at a run, with Janet half-dressed behind, more worried about getting Fenwick's sword than with restoring her decency.

Sagres led them through the empty castle to the stables where the horses belonging to the dead gatekeepers stood. By good fortune, they also found a couple of spare jacks, a bonnet and a breastplate there. Janet was thus rendered safe and secure – above the waist at least – needfully so, for there was never any doubt that she was going to ride with them. Hobbie and Geordie opened the portcullis just enough for them to lead the horses out. Tom regretted leaving it like that – he had enjoyed the thought of Black Robert locked out of his own fort – but there was really no alternative, if they were all going to stay together.

Tom led them down the slope towards the valley head. What had begun as a wild charge began to moderate at once, for Tom was suddenly much struck by the way in which the fires in the forest were gathering into an inferno that seemed to be rushing up to meet them. The whole of the southward slope and the horizon behind it seemed to be walled with fire. Clouds of smoke came and went, apparently illumined from within – monstrous cousins to the will-o'-the-wisps on the Waste. Outlined against the fearsome and gathering brightness, small squadrons of riders sped across the slope in the distance, the sound of their battling and passage utterly lost in the stormy rumble of the fire in the forest. The flashes of clear sight of these rushing knots of men would have bewildered all but the coolest mind; but the Master of Logic knew well enough what he would see when he had found his goal: a tall figure on a tall horse leading a slighter one on a hobbie. Other than Black Robert and Sir Thomas, they all rode hobbie horses; those two alone had hunters. Sir Thomas would not be leading anyone, but Black Robert would have Eve in tow. To whom else dare he surrender her? Wherever dare he leave her? As he had brought her, he must hold her. She was all that was left of his hope. She was also likely to prove his doom.

'There!' bellowed Tom as he saw the tell-tale pair. Gesturing towards the sharp black figures with the pale club of his bandaged hand, he was off at the gallop again. The others fell in behind and followed – which was as well: Lord Robert and Eve were by no means riding alone. Amongst the half-dozen figures following behind them, Tom reasoned, Tam Burn and Nicholas de Vaux would be close by their leader, but he knew none of the others until one of them turned in the saddle, raising an arm, and Tom saw that it ended in a stump instead of a hand. 'On!' he shouted, leaning forward and kicking his hobbie horse's sides.

Such were the vagaries of perspective brought about by the flickering light that the chase – like the need for it – came close to surprising Tom. The figures came and went as his little band pursued them, passing through weird clouds of smoke. They were there for instants and then gone, leaving only their ghosts to linger strangely in his eyes. There was no sense of them going or coming – just of them being where he saw them, outlined black against the yellow fire. Had he been granted the liberty of guessing how things were proceeding, he would likely have said

Lord Robert was fleeing and he was giving chase; but he would have been wrong.

Lord Robert's men came thundering out of the smoke running flat out for Hermitage and Tom's little command ran straight into them, as Geordie's charge had crashed against the Kerrs on Christmas night. There was no warning at all to either troop and their horses simply smashed into one another, head to head, like two fleets of ships colliding under full sail. Lord Robert jerked his hunter's head aside and Tom's horse crashed straight into its solid shoulder. He was hurled forward and near unseated. He had a glimpse of Lord Robert's face made devilish with surprise and rage, then Eve's horse hit the far side of the hunter and she, her hands tied, was thrown to the ground at once. Tom followed the impetus of the collision and swung himself down even as Lord Robert did the same. The air filled with such crashing and shouting that even the gathering bellow of the fire seemed drowned for an instant. Tom tore out his sword, careless of where the rest of the Hermitage men might be, relying on his Bewcastle command to take care of them and watch his back as he went after Eve.

As it had been with the Queen at the start of this, so was it now at the end. A moment more of reasoning would have warned him to be wary of coming between Eve and Geordie at the last, but he had no moment to spare. If he had an enemy more than he had reckoned behind him, he had a better friend there too. 'Tom!' screamed Janet in a voice even more fearful than that which had greeted Fenwick's rapine. He swung round, daring to take his eyes off Lord Robert because the laird was busy pulling Eve on to her feet. He swung round and leaped back as Geordie came charging wildly past him, claymore swinging wildly not a hair's breadth from his head. Beyond the wild figure he saw de Vaux wrenching his horse's head round, screaming something at the four men riding with him – and Tom was certain the word was not 'Attack!' Hobbie and Sagres were close behind him, both spurring wildly.

Janet's cry also made her father turn and Lord Robert saw both his nemesis and his attacker in an instant. He let go of Eve and turned, his hand striking down to his belt and up again with snake-like speed. Thus Geordie ran full-tilt into the point-blank range of Lord Robert's Dutch dag. The powerful little handgun exploded with all the reliability and accuracy for which the weapons were famed. The claymore hurtled forward, end over end, missing Eve as nearly as it had missed Tom. Geordie flew backwards and crashed on to the ground, as still as death already. Tom wrenched out his rapier and continued the charge that had hardly paused during the despatching of Geordie Burn.

The shoulder of a horse hit him and spun him sideways across the slippery grass. In the confusion of the melee he thought that Janet must have ridden him down. But no: it was Tam Burn, Geordie's twin. He leaped out of the saddle, brandishing a claymore, indistinguishable from the dead man on the ground, save that he was up and screaming. 'My blood,' he screamed, 'my brother and my blood.'

'Ye should have done the work for yourself, then,' yelled back Black Robert, his visage simply satanic with rage. He hurled the empty dag into Tam's screaming face and ripped out his own long rapier, but had no immediate use for it. One-Hand Dand burst out of the smoke at his master's shoulder, the last of the troop to stay faithful and still astride. His claymore was the weight of Tam's and it came down from ten feet high with all the Kerr's fearsome power behind it. The blade took Tam on the top of his bonnet and did not stop falling until it had severed the chin strap far below. Dand wrenched it free at once and immediately turned on Tom. He steered his mount on to its new course with his knees, raising his smoking sword once more. Then he hurtled sideways as Janet calmly shot him through the one part of the jack that had no armour, slamming through his breast from one armpit to the other and killing him so swiftly he never knew who had done the deed.

Black Robert had Eve on her feet again, and was reaching for the reins of his hunter, made unhandy by the sword he still held, when suddenly Tom was there. He ducked under the stallion's rearing chin and rested the point of his rapier on Lord Robert's heart. 'It was you who invented the Barguest, Lord Robert,' he said coolly, in a clear, carrying voice. 'Perhaps the lady will accept your corpse in its place – especially as it was you who killed our John and put his body up in the tree.'

The Laird of Hermitage's eyes flicked around the immediate battlefield, but with the senses of an old soldier Tom knew well enough that there was no help for him there. The Burn twins were dead – and burning indeed, he guessed, or there was no hellfire. De Vaux was gone, with the rest of the four mounted Armstrongs to guard him and Hobbie with Sagres in pursuit. Hobbie, robbed of two revenges, would not be happy to lose a third. Janet was up and Dand was down; and that left just the pair of them to fight it out over Eve.

The rapier, Tom knew too well, was often of limited use on the battlefield, and the rules of defence – let alone its niceties – even more dangerously out of place; but this situation was unique. Narrow-eyed and silent, he fell into his guard, therefore, and mutely invited Lord Robert to answer in the form. Perhaps because of Lord Robert's speed and character, Tom assumed the guard called *serpentio* with his hilt hand – the left – close in and his long blade pointing steadily forward.

Lord Robert still held Eve in his left hand and his reins were wrapped around his own hilt in his right. Ever with an eye to the main chance, he began the fight by jerking the horse's head hard down so that its solid jaw – and the metal buckles and rings of the tack – all slammed into the crown of Tom's own head, setting his bonnet to ringing.

Tom lunged in answer, but Lord Robert was spinning away, and knocked Tom's blade aside inelegantly but effectively. Eve fell back, but calculatingly, her eyes flicking like the flames from the forest from Lord Robert to Tom to Janet and back. Both the women were as busy watching each other as the men and the fight; and it was a fight not a duel, as this was a battlefield not a *piste*. Tom assumed the 'serpent' guard again, his eyes flicking from Lord Robert's point to his person and back, readying his defence but planning his attack: to the face beneath the bonnet or the throat above the jack, if he could get past the iron gorget there; to the laces of the jack where the leather was not so well protected by the metal plates, or lower, to the groin or thigh where the great blood vessels lay carrying hot life – and quick death.

Lord Robert struck from the 'falcon', swooping down. The attack was not well conceived, for Tom's bonnet had a peak that protected his face from such assaults. He accepted the blade, however, and at once got the measure of his foe as an unexpected dagger swung in, aimed at the very weakness in his jack where Janet had shot Dand dead; but, as with the sword stroke, he stabbed down from on high, and that gave Tom his strategy – the pattern of moves that his Master Capo Ferro had said would come at moments like these, falling into place like complete sections of a chess match, seemingly governed by their own inevitabilities.

Tom stepped forward with his left foot, driving his sword up along Lord Robert's as he angled his body from his solid, steady right heel, and letting the dagger slam down on to the metal plates on his breast. They were designed to stop such blows. They had stopped an arquebus shot; they would turn a dagger point, he thought. They did.

Only the desperate strength in Lord Robert's own right wrist saved his eye – but at the price of a cheek laid open to the bone. He stepped back, but Tom followed relentlessly, leading still with his left – an ability that seemed to disconcert his foe. This time he assumed the lowest of guards and saw Lord Robert frown for the instant he had available as he realized how open was his body to an attack from down there. His bonnet peak would direct an upthrust into his head. All the iron plates on his jack, hanging down like fish scales, would direct an upthrust under and into his chest. Even the metal gorget that protected his throat would simply guide a blade up through his jowls and into his brain. He mimicked Tom, trying for an even lower guard, crouching with his dagger near his knees, almost attaining the 'iron door'.

Tom stepped forward once again and feinted the fearful upward thrust. Up went Black Robert just that instant too quickly, defending instead of attacking, using both sword and dagger to protect his vulnerable body from his belly upwards. Grunting with the effort of turning the feint back into a real attack, Tom completed his low lunge and sent his point through the inner side of Lord Robert's right knee. He felt the blade slide past Lord Robert's kneecap and into the joint itself. He felt the great tendons that held the joint together behind the leg and he twisted his wrist with all his strength at the very instant his feet slipped and he tumbled forward, overreached.

Lord Robert Douglas screamed. Tom hit the ice-hard ground, and shouted aloud himself. His left wrist twisted until it cracked and popped, brought near to breaking, for the hand remained enmeshed in his rapier's hilt. His right hand slammed down jarringly and felt as though Dand had stepped his horse upon it once again. The sounds made by the two men frightened the high-strung hunter. It was already deeply offended by having its aristocratic chin used, like the ass's jawbone in the Bible, as a weapon. It jerked away from its erstwhile master and galloped up over the hillside above, gone out of the firelight in a twinkling, like a shadow. The hobbie horses followed for a little, then stopped. Only Janet's remained.

Black Robert turned, just maintaining his balance on his left leg as he looked down at the utter ruin of his right. All the tendons across the back of his leg were cut. He was hamstrung – a cripple doomed to halt and limp for the rest of his life. Tom hauled back his left fist with all his might and the blade slid out. The sword was useless, for his hand flopped like dead fish tail, almost as powerless as his right. Lord Robert howled, far beyond reason, quite bedlam-mad with rage and, no doubt, the agony of every muscle from right hip to right knee tearing loose of its moorings and twisting into balls of cramp. Such was the simple horror of the expression on his face that neither Tom nor the women watching could move for an instant; and in that instant Lord Robert pulled out his second dag. He was as far beyond speech as he was beyond sanity, but he continued to snarl and whimper as he took the fearsome little weapon in both his hands and levelled it at Tom. Tom jerked up his right hand, pointing it at his towering enemy as though it would somehow protect him, and the moment seemed to freeze.

And into that frozen moment, out of the billowing hellfire of smoke, galloped the Barguest.

To Tom, who saw it from his prone position, the hound seemed monstrously huge, bigger by far than it had looked to the child in Inglewood – bigger even than it had become in his fevered dream aboard the coach. It stood taller than Janet's startled hobbie horse and was more than two fathoms long before its tail came near to adding a third. Its head was the size of a pony's but broader, squarer – red-eyed and fearsome; and that head reached above Lord Robert's shoulder to look him straight in the face as the great brute bounded towards him.

The hound, like Lord Robert, was screaming – using much the same sort of sounds. Its eyes were blood-red and running with the smoke that belched from its choking mouth and nose. Its jowls dripped red, drooling between its palisade of knife-sharp fangs with fire-sparks reflecting the flames themselves, and its coat was all aglitter with red and yellow sparks, terribly asmoulder, horribly near to catching fire. As it bounded towards them, so it left a ghostly, ghastly trail of smoke behind it. The pain and the terror had clearly sent it mad, so that it attacked the first creature that seemed to stand in the way of its wild and fearful flight.

When the Barguest reared up over Lord Robert, it topped him by almost a yard, it seemed to Tom. So huge was its chest that he seemed to shrink against it as the beast crashed down on him. The Laird of Hermitage flew backwards, like Geordie had done, propelled by the terrible impact. He skidded across the icy moss as the monster slid down on him to savage him. It ripped through the upflung arm, rendering it as useless as his spastically kicking leg, and snapped its gigantic fangs across his throat. Only his metal gorget kept the huge teeth from his flesh for a moment – just long enough for him to fire his trusty dag. But the shot that slammed through the monster's chest and exploded out of its back only seemed to enrage it more. The great jaws closed in a snarling scream of fury. The huge head

242

jerked up and back. Lord Robert seemed to take flight as though his soul was ripped in the moment straight up out of his chest. His iron gorget came crushed and twisted in the dripping fangs. Lord Robert's throat came with it. His soulless frame crashed back on to the frozen ground, and in place of his breath, his life's blood smoked briefly on the air around the monster's head.

Then the Barguest turned, drooling Lord Robert's blood, and leaped at Eve. Tom closed the tortured agony of his right hand into a fist then and the entire end of the bandage blew off in a massive cloud of smoke and flame. The little four-barrelled bastard pistol that Kate had stolen from Ugo Stell a seeming lifetime ago, and that Tom himself had wound in the bandages two hours since, did the work for which it had been designed – by Tom and Kate, if not by its maker. The monstrous Barguest slammed sideways, thrown right over Lord Robert's body by the impact of the four close-clustered shots. It rolled over and let out a great, rumbling sigh. Then it died beside the man who had brought it to a kind of life and whom it had killed in return.

It seemed to Tom that he lay on the freezing grass for a great length of time, with Eve on one hand and Janet on the other; and neither of the hands in question would work. Sir Thomas came and looked down on him. On Lord Robert and the Barguest. 'Well, I'll be damned,' he said.

'As will we all,' said Tom dreamily, 'some sooner than others.'

'Boy's run mad,' said Sir Thomas, but there was an ocean of awed respect and no little affection in the gruff words.

'He'll be fine,' said Eve. 'We must get a litter and bring him back to Bewcastle. I have medicines there.'

'I know,' said Sir Thomas shortly. 'I'll see to it. And I'd best be quick about it. The warm wind has brought the snow at last . . .'

Some time later, as he was bumping uncomfortably down Liddesdale towards the high, narrow path that led out above the smoking ruins of the Barguest's lair, it seemed to Tom that someone rode beside the wagon he was lying in and spoke to him in Spanish. 'I lost them up on the Waste,' said Sagres. 'The Armstrongs left de Vaux and ran for the Busy Gap. He rode away alone with Hobbie hard on his heels. He'll be fortunate indeed to get through a blizzard such as this alive whether Hobbie catches him or not. How my bones ache for *La Carihuela!*'

After Sagres was gone, Eve returned and Tom felt in his purse, having one last mission to fulfil. He pulled out the heavy, sensuous, golden pebble he had carried in secret since that morning at Blackpool Gate while he wondered what to do with it. He pressed it into Eve's cool fingers now, and felt them seem to take fire from the golden warmth of the thing itself. 'Forget the mines of copper and arsenic,' he whispered. 'Forget what lies buried beneath the Waste. There is gold in the River Lyne . . .' Then his soul, as light as one of the snowflakes, went drifting silently away.

As Tom drifted off to sleep, the silent snow began to fall in earnest. It softened the bleak, stark lines of the empty, master-less fort of Hermitage, tenanted only by the headless corpse of a factor in a bedchamber and five dead men in the gatehouses. It fell over the twisted corpse of Lord Robert and over the huge hound by his side. It fell, hissing, on to the smouldering ruins of the timeless Forest of Liddesdale, which had been the monster's final home. It fell with gathering force across the empty gapes of the deserted mineshafts along the hillsides by the border where frozen Kerrs stood unremarked in the black pit of death. It fell across the reiving, riding and raiding gaps that led from Scotland to England and back again, closing them tight and safe till the spring, down to the Wall and beyond. It fell across Blackpool Gate, drifting down the open tower of the kirk. It fell over Bewcastle fort. And it fell like silent feather-down across the Waste itself, covering sill, crag, moss and moor, filling up all the deadly bog-holes; and covering, beside the largest and most dangerous of these, the shoulders of Hobbie Noble himself, who lingered, leaning on his great long spear, looking down into the heart of a will-o'-the-wisp at his feet.

244

After a while, the reiver stirred and shook himself. ' 'Tis time I retired,' said he. 'Perhaps I should get Sir Thomas to arrange for me to be hanged before all the world at Carlisle castle, much as I was hanged in Liddesdale, able to walk away in secret afterwards.' He lifted his head to look at the patient horse that stood nearby awaiting him – the horse after which he was named. 'What a ballad that would make, eh?' he said. "The Ballad of Hobbie Noble". Why, they'll be singing it for years!'

So saying, he turned and whistled for his steed and it trotted down to him from the road. In the moment that he waited, he wiped the thick-crusted mud from the handle of his spear until the wood shone pale and clean; and behind him as he moved, beneath the black swirl of his cloak tail, the will-o'-the-wisp seemed to gutter and die. The mist lifted and the deadly pit of quick mire was, for an instant, revealed beneath – as was, at its heart and just for that moment, the dead hand of Sir Nicholas de Vaux, thumb and four ringed fingers reaching up helplessly, hopelessly; frozen to a claw already, just above the surface of the bottomless mire; an arm's length exactly above where the rest of his body was held, and likely to be held for ever, in the icy, iron grip of Hobbie's final vengeance.

Author's Note

Yes, Hobbie got his ballads, though neither was the one about the Barguest. In fact, he is the only character in Sir Walter Scott's *Minstrelsy of the Scottish Border* with two ballads to himself.

To be fair, the book did not begin with Hobbie at all. *The Hound of the Borders* began with *The Hound of the Baskervilles.* With my English set 9.3 (thanks, guys) I was researching how Conan Doyle came to write his masterpiece when I discovered that the Hound itself was based on historical legends of several spectral monster dogs told to Doyle by his friend Fletcher Robinson. Amongst the most terrifying of these genuine folk tales was that of the Barguest, said to haunt the Borders, where Tom was born and raised. The coincidence was too good to be ignored; but I wanted to introduce the beast itself and make it real. I turned, therefore, to Brian Vesey-Fitzgerald's *The Domestic Dog*. This recounts Tacitus's report that when Romans first invaded Britain, using large mastiffs as war dogs, they were shocked to discover that the British already had a native breed of gigantic mastiffs that stood nearly four feet to the shoulder. These have since died out, of course, but when did they do so, and where might the last of them have lingered?

The book was actually written on the coast below Exmoor (many thanks to Joanna, Belinda and James for use of the computer and the games room at ridiculous hours, day and night) and more than one early reader has detected more than a whiff of *Lorna Doone*. Its Borders setting was carefully re-searched, however, as well as being based upon personal memory. Thanks to the librarians at Combe Martin and Barnstaple for all their help with books about the far end of the country, as well as to those in Tunbridge Wells for all the rest. I lived in Carlisle for several years when I was younger, coincidentally in a house in Norfolk Road, reputedly exactly opposite George MacDonald Fraser's, of whom more in a moment. My memories of the town and neighbouring country-side up to the (new) Kielder Forest and Water remain vivid – not least from the hours my father and I spent fishing up there.

For the physical detail I augmented memory with the Ordnance Survey's Landranger series of maps, using most of those num-bered between 79 and 89. For everything else I turned to several of my favourite writers. Melvyn Bragg and Arthur Mee gave fas-cinating details of Lakeland's northern reaches and history – as did the National Trust of their property at Housesteads, which included Hugh Nixon's bastle farmhouse that overlooks the Busy Gap. John Lyly and Daniel Defoe gave much earlier records of their travels there just before and after my period. Sir Walter Scott, reputedly the first man to take a wheeled vehicle through the jaws of Liddesdale some 200 years after the events recounted here, supplied the ballads in his collection as well as unstinting inspiration since I first began to read.

But most of all, George MacDonald Fraser supplied a wealth of inspirational historical detail in his wonderful and definitive book on the border reivers *The Steel Bonnets*. He supplied some of the names – but fewer than it appears. I grew up in Ulster amongst these very people, transplanted from the Borders into Ulster by James I, hoping to solve two problems at once. I grew up, therefore, surrounded by Hursts, Littles, Bells and John-stons (my mother's family and relatives, whose crest is a winged spur, for they were famous horse thieves and proud of it!), Armstrongs, Kerrs and all the rest. No Grahams, though – the name was proscribed by James, and Ulster is consequently sprinkled with Mahargs instead.

A range of more domestic details was supplied by Alison Sim's *The Tudor Housewife*, Antonia Fraser's *The Weaker Vessel*, Mildred Taylor's *The English Yeoman in the Tudor and Stuart Age* and Ralph Whitelock's *A Calendar of Country Customs*.

The herbal lore was culled from Gerard himself and from Culpeper, both now in print. The facts about arsenic and its potential as a poison (as well as as an ore and an early component of bronze) from *Comprehensive Inorganic Chemistry*, ed. Sneed & Brastead (Sisler and Pray), vol. 5. The details of arsenical poisoning came also from the Internet (various locations) and the effects of various inert and poisonous gases associated with mining (including carbon monoxide and arsenic gas) came from a range of histories of mining, the most useful of which was by Time Life books.

The Internet also supplied a disturbing wealth of detail about the post-mortem behaviour of bodies – particularly those suffering from rigor mortis; how this could be affected by cause of death (reactions to various poisons) and temperature (especially freezing). But to those with Internet access I would far rather recommend the fascinating pages on the Borders, the clans and the ballads; and I leave you with just the slightest taste of one of them:

> From 'The Ballad of Hobbie Noble'
>
> Now Hobbie was an English man
> And born into Bewcastle dale;
> But his misdeeds they were so great
> They banished him to Liddesdale . . .

The rest, as they say, is history – or, rather, *minstrelsy* . . .

Peter Tonkin
Combe Martin and Tunbridge Wells

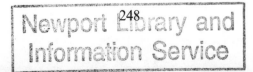